ALSO BY KATHERINE SHONK

The Red Passport

HAPPY NOW?

HAPPY NOW?

KATHERINE SHONK

FARRAR, STRAUS AND GIROUX

NEW YORK

Farrar, Straus and Giroux
18 West 18th Street, New York 10011

Distributed in Canada by D&M Publishers, Inc.
Printed in the United States of America
First edition, 2010

Library of Congress Cataloging-in-Publication Data
Shonk, Katherine.
    Happy now? / Katherine Shonk. — 1st ed.
    p. cm.
    ISBN 978-0-374-28143-4
    1. Widows—Fiction.   I. Title.
   PS3619.H65H37 2010
   813'.6—dc22
                           2009029509

Designed by Abby Kagan

www.fsgbooks.com

1   3   5   7   9   10   8   6   4   2

FOR VICTOR

HAPPY NOW?

1

When the front door of the coach house swung open, Claire saw her dead husband's cat trotting toward her.

"Oh," she said as she entered, chilled to the bone. "Fang is here."

The cat passed Claire, sat on the doorframe, and looked out at the yard, tail swishing. A tightness gripped Claire's throat. Fang was looking for Jay.

Claire's sister, Nomie, and Harry, Nomie's husband, brushed by her and the cat and disappeared down the long hall. Claire lingered, scanning the small yard along with Fang. It was February in Chicago, unless it was March already, and beneath the path they had made through the snow, moldering leaves were pasted to the patio brick. The young, spindly trees at the edges of the patio looked as brittle and delicate as the wrought-iron tables and chairs set askew. Across the yard, the glass doors of Nomie and Harry's renovated farmhouse faced Claire blankly. Her father's rusting red station wagon was parked on the other side of the picket fence. He had followed them home from their mother's house, like a private investigator or a mourner behind a hearse. He was still sitting there, his profile in silhouette.

Look at me, Claire thought.

He did not turn to face her, but the cat did, tufts of fur stirring in the breeze, green-marble eyes beseeching.

Not you, Claire thought. Not you, you fucking cat.

Fang and the ground seemed too far away. Wobbling, Claire pressed a palm against the wall and closed her eyes. When she opened them, her father still stared straight out the car window.

The cat backed inside as Claire slowly closed the door. Together, they moved down the hall, Fang's tail snaking around Claire's legs. For two weeks Claire had been at her mother and stepfather's house in Glencoe, where she was given drugs. It was as if Fang had vanished along with her owner—curled next to Jay in the closed casket, maybe, like an ancient Egyptian's treasured pet, just as Fang used to curl against him in the bed each morning before the alarm clock rang.

In the main room, Nomie and Harry were making a tremendous display of commotion: throwing down bags, snapping on lights, pulling curtains open, and tossing their jackets and scarves onto the canvas sectional. The coach house, where it had been decided that Claire should stay for the time being, was one large, high-ceilinged room with a hayloft that had been converted into a sleeping loft. When they bought the property a few years earlier, Nomie had decorated the coach house like a beach house, in seafoam green and tangerine, but the walls were scarcely visible now. Furniture had been pushed aside to make way for the metal racks flanking one wall, loaded with bags of diapers and shopping bags from

Baby Gap, Target, and Old Navy. Nomie, five months pregnant, had been in a quiet panic.

A line of enormous bouquets of flowers, many of them wilting, stood on the kitchen counter. Roses. Lilies. Chrysanthemums. Flowers Claire could not name, blurring into the same peachy, pinky hues she had chosen for their wedding almost two years earlier. After the wake, Jay's mother had come rushing across the parking lot with funeral bouquets and pushed them through the car window at Claire. But those flowers had been in bold, masculine colors—red, yellow, and purple—and they would have rotted by now.

"People have been sending them," Nomie said, catching Claire's eye. "I didn't know if you'd want them here or not." She and Harry were hunkered on the couch, he shuffling papers, she sorting through a pile of linens.

Claire understood that she was supposed to feel grateful. She should thank her sister and her brother-in-law for bringing her here, for allowing her to be a guest in their guesthouse. She should tell them that she was touched by the flowers people had been sending to—what? Show their sympathy, show that they did not blame her, although surely they could not help but wonder what she had done or failed to do.

Instead Claire said, "I didn't realize I'd be taking care of Fang."

A smile bloomed and froze on Nomie's face, reminding Claire of a paperweight she had gotten for her First Communion: a rosebud encased in glass. "She's been staying here," Nomie said. "We come over and feed her. I think I told you?"

"Maybe," Claire said. She would have to go off the pills. This was what they had made her dream: that the cat was living in the coach house, and she, Claire, was trying to nurse Fang back from an illness that had made her white fur turn black.

"Would you like us to take her for now?" Nomie asked.

"The thing is," Harry interrupted, coughing into his fist, "we'd rather Nomie wasn't around the litter box right now."

"Right," Claire said. "I forgot." The unborn trumped the dead, not to mention the spouse of the dead. *The Spouse of the Dead: Coming to a theater near you.* Tears welled in her eyes, threatening to spatter the hardwood.

"Oh!" Nomie cried. The stack of sheets she had been folding tumbled to the floor as she rushed toward Claire.

Her sister smelled like fabric softener. Claire tried to relax, but the belly pushed against her impertinently. Nomie had shown her an ultrasound of the baby when it was still in the amphibian stage, a ghostly sea monkey suspended in fluid, gender unknown. Since then the baby had staked a wide swath of real estate, just like her mother, who bounced over the cobbled streets of her Old Town neighborhood, decaf Starbucks sloshing in the cup holder of her Subaru Outback.

"We can take Fang for now," Nomie said. "Harry can manage the litter box."

Of course he could. He was a manager by trade, a senior manager in an accounting firm, to be exact.

"Or I could come over and do it," Claire said. So new to widowhood, she had already discovered its power—unless she was just doing what eldest children always did, bulldozing over her sibling's needs.

"I thought you would want her here," persisted Harry, who was the oldest of three.

"We should have asked you." Nomie backed away from Claire, who felt wobbly again. Without her sister—and admittedly, that damned baby—as ballast, she thought she might topple.

As if he'd read her mind, Harry took his wife's place, grabbing Claire in a bear hug. "I just thought, you know," Harry muttered into her ear, "that maybe old Fang would . . . not make you feel better, exactly, but . . ." She heard him sniffle, and when he pulled away, his eyes and nose were wet.

Claire patted his shoulder. Harry was her favorite Republican, the closest thing she had to a brother. She imagined him at her and Jay's house, lying on their bedroom floor, slowly dragging the cat from under the bed as her claws tore the varnish off the hardwood, thinking he was doing a good deed, saving Fang from starvation and reuniting the two creatures most bewildered and disrupted by Jay's sudden disappearance.

"Disappearance"—not the right word. There was a word Claire had been using as a placeholder until she thought of a better one, but now she couldn't remember it. It started with an *i*. Some people (Jay's mother, most notably) had been saying "accident," but that wasn't right. At the wake Claire had heard someone say "tragedy," but that sounded melodramatic. Not "event," which made her think of a boxing match. She needed a thesaurus. There were no books in the coach house and very few in the main house: John Grisham, Stephen King, and books that taught people who didn't mind being called dummies how to throw a wedding, buy a house, and give birth.

She remembered the binder then, and sensed it lurking somewhere in the coach house, like the cat. It had been found in Jay's office at the university. Not a suicide note, but an entire binder. The police had examined it, Jay's family had seen it, Claire's family had seen it, everyone had seen it but Claire, and she could see it whenever she was ready, Harry had told her, Nomie had told her, their mother had told her.

She didn't want to see it, though she wanted to have seen it: a dilemma.

"Incident." That was the word.

"Claire?" Nomie said.

Suddenly she wanted them *out*. "I'm sorry," she said. "Fang can stay. That's fine. Do you mind if I lie down?"

"Of course not!" Nomie cried.

Claire and Nomie followed behind as Harry trudged up the spiral staircase to the sleeping loft with a suitcase full of the clothes her mother had bought her. Claire had allowed Harry and Nomie to fetch odds and ends from her and Jay's house— her favorite lotion, the mail, the cat—but she had forbidden anyone to touch her or Jay's clothes and, most important, to do their laundry. She had had a terror of his scent being gone for- ever from the world. She needed to know that the bedsheets, the pillowcase, and the last T-shirt he had slept in would be there for her when she wanted them. So, after tucking Claire into bed in the guest room the morning after the incident, her mother had gone shopping and stocked the bureau drawers with a new wardrobe: pants, jeans, sweaters, shirts, and under- wear, all of which fit well and more or less matched Claire's taste, including the bras, which was disconcerting. Claire had found blouses and skirts hanging in the closet, as well as a black wool coat with a scarf strung around the lapels and attached with a hammered silver brooch, and two different black dresses from Ann Taylor. "Why are there *two* black dresses?" Claire had asked her mother, trying to sound casual, though her heart had begun knocking at the sight of the second one. Was there a second funeral she didn't know about? "In case the wake and the funeral are on different days," her mother said. "So you can wear a fresh one." Nancy had been right: the funeral was the day after the wake. Claire had carefully rehung each dress in the closet after wearing it. When she went to pack for the coach house, both had mysteriously disappeared.

Harry let the suitcase land with a thud on the far side of

the double bed. "If there's anything you need . . ." He threw up his arms in a helpless gesture.

"Oh, there is," Claire said. "I just thought of something."

"Name it."

"Can you tell me what day it is?"

"It's Friday."

"I mean, what date it is." She wanted to know if it was still February. If the world had moved on to a new month, well, that would be a stunning development.

"Um . . . ," he said. "It's February twenty-ninth."

"The twenty-ninth?" That sounded odd, though at first she wasn't sure why.

"Yeah, it's a leap year."

"Leap year?" Claire grunted. "Leap month, more like it."

Nomie immediately turned scarlet, her face as red as it used to get at the beach when they were kids, in the days before parents bothered with sunscreen.

Awkwardly, Harry approached Claire and kissed the top of her head. "Good night, Claire."

"I'll be right back," Nomie said to her.

Nomie and Harry bobbed down the staircase, out of view, presumably to talk about her. She started taking off her jeans, new ones her mother had purchased, a brand Claire had never heard of, with shooting stars stitched on the back pockets. They fit better than any jeans she had ever bought for herself and probably cost twice as much.

Nomie came back up to the loft and looked out the little round window—the porthole, the two of them had called it when they were up here painting the room sky blue a few years back. "Dad's still out there," she said. "In his car."

"Is he looking at you?" said Claire.

"No. He's looking out the windshield. He looks like a statue. Or like a . . . like a dummy."

"Don't call Dad a dummy," Claire said.

Nomie jerked around, her face again flushing scarlet. "I meant—"

"I know, Nomie." Apparently new widows weren't supposed to make jokes, even lame ones. Claire fell back on the bed. "He won't stay there all night, will he?"

"I don't know."

At Sally and Bart's Valentine's Day party, after the police had shown up at the door and the crowd grew hushed, Sally had taken Claire into the master bedroom, away from the other party guests, Jay's colleagues and their significant others. "You stay here," Sally said. "Don't move. I'll be right back." Claire had waited there in an armchair in the dark room for a long time, hearing murmuring voices beyond the bedroom door and sirens twenty-three stories below. The longer I stay here, she thought, the better. She *had* been in there a long time, a half hour or more, but in the end, it hadn't made a difference. Her father had been the next person to burst into the bedroom, followed closely by her mother. "I have to tell you something," her father said, crouching in front of Claire and taking her hands, holding them so tight it hurt, while her mother stood above them, her hand trembling in front of her mouth, her eyes wide with horror.

So it had been her father who told Claire, but since then he hadn't said much. He had come to her mother and step-father's house twice a day, once in the morning and once in the evening. In the morning he brought coffee and muffins, and he and Claire did the crossword puzzle together in the breakfast nook. At night he brought dessert—bakery brownies or cupcakes. Claire's mother had set up a thousand-piece jigsaw puzzle of the pyramids on the table in the family room, nothing but sand and stone, enough to drive a sane person mad, but for Claire and her father the perfect diversion from the long silences between them. They had never said much to each other, she and her father, and when they tried now, their efforts felt strained and pointless. He asked her haltingly about Jay's "troubles," and she told him what he might have guessed, that Jay went through spells of depression and he could be impulsive, but she had not known things were so bad. Then, distracted by the drone of her own voice, Claire simply trailed off. There was not much else to talk about, as the others had divided up the tasks of running her new life: Nomie returned calls from Claire's friends, Harry dealt with the finances and the police, and her mother shopped, cooked, and talked to Jay's family. And so, after about a week, Claire and her father had stopped talking to each other altogether.

"Do you want me to unpack?" Nomie said.

"Nah," Claire said.

"The cat's coming up," Harry called from below. "And I'm going out."

"Okay," Claire called out. "Thank you."

"We can block off the stairs if you want," Nomie said. "To keep the cat out."

"Bye," Harry shouted.

"It's fine," Claire said. "Bye!"

The cat appeared at the top of the stairs, blinked at them, and slunk under the bed. Claire tucked herself in.

"Do you want to keep taking these?" Nomie rattled a bottle of sleeping pills, or maybe sedatives, that a doctor at the hospital had given her that first night. Claire hadn't recognized the name of the drug on the label.

It hadn't occurred to her that she had a choice. "Maybe not. I feel so fuzzy. I'm having weird dreams."

"Okay. Can we not tell Mom, though? That you're not taking them?"

"Sure."

"Claire?" Nomie perched on the periwinkle bedspread. She was a swan: plump and soft above the waterline, neck impossibly long, lips swelling like a beak, green eyes gray in the dusky light. "I was wondering, did you want me to stay here tonight?"

"You mean, in the bed?" Claire asked.

Nomie shrugged shyly. "I just thought . . ."

"Sure. If Harry doesn't mind, I mean."

"It's okay with him. I checked already." Nomie took off her jeans, got into bed, and turned off the light.

They were a strange family, Claire thought, incident or no incident. "I'll be right back," she said. "I forgot something."

"Okay," said Nomie.

Downstairs, Claire fetched her cell phone from her purse and went into the bathroom. She dialed into her voice mail and called up the message she had saved over and over again throughout the past two weeks. Leaning against the door, she closed her eyes and listened.

The sound was a high-pitched swish, rising and falling: *SHWEE-ohh, SHWEE-ohh, SHWEE-ohh!* On and on it went, like windshield wipers on high speed in a rainstorm. An octave lower and it might have been a woman gasping hysterically.

She had listened to it for the first time during the party, in Sally and Bart's bathroom, where she had gone when she couldn't find Jay and was trying to convince herself that nothing was wrong. Fifteen or twenty minutes before, she had seen him go onto the balcony. In the bathroom, she took out her phone and saw she had a message. She called her voice mail and, for several minutes, listened to the frantic, steady sound. Then there was a blur of clicks, and the message ended abruptly.

The call was from Jay's phone, she saw when she looked at

the log, but he had left the message an hour before she met up with him at the party. She hadn't heard the phone ring, and he hadn't mentioned anything about trying to call her.

Since that night, she had been listening to the message whenever she was alone, a dozen or more times a day. She hadn't told anyone about it—not Sally or Bart, not the police, not her family, and not Jay's family. It was private, Claire told herself.

It was the sound of a heartbeat, powerfully magnified.

It was the sound of Jay's heart.

She knew this because she had heard his heart before. A few months after they were married, he had developed a murmur, a resonant thud that she couldn't hear even when she pressed her ear to his chest. Jay said it felt as if a little man were trying to pound his way out of his heart with a tiny timpani mallet—"Halfheartedly," he added, and nudged her. "Get it?"

He had asked Claire to come to the cardiologist appointment with him, and she had been pleased by the simplicity of the request; for once, she could help. The waiting room had been full of old people, which confirmed for her that they had nothing to fear: God would take these people first. In the examining room, Jay had lain on his side, his bare chest pale and vulnerable in the dim light as the technician massaged it with a jelly-coated wand. A rhythmic whirring filled the room, the sound of Jay's heart wheezing and swishing. Watching the monitor, Claire was filled with tenderness for the gray blur on the black background, struggling like a kitten in a sack.

Nothing serious had been wrong. The doctor told Jay to cut back on caffeine. He switched to decaf, ever the good student, and the murmur went away.

"Maybe I should ask him to take a look at my brain," Jay had joked to Claire.

"Nothing wrong with your brain," she chided.

"It murmurs, too," he said.

"Hush," she said.

Now here was his heart on her phone, a final memento. She imagined him sitting in his car before the party. He had called her and, when she didn't answer (what would have happened if she had?), impulsively pressed the phone to his chest so that she could hear how hard he had struggled just before giving up. That was her theory, which might also explain why he had chosen Valentine's Day—for the heart symbolism, and nothing more. It was an improvement on the more obvious interpretation: that their marriage was a calamity from which he saw no other means of escape.

When the message ended, Claire resaved it and joined Nomie in bed.

"Everything okay?" Nomie said. They were turned away from each other.

"Yeah." Claire turned the question over in her mind, practicing. "I was wondering . . . I heard about the binder. That Jay left. Is it here?"

"It's downstairs."

"Did you look at it?"

"Yeah."

"Was there something in there for me?"

"Well . . . I guess it was *all* for you, really." Nomie sounded apologetic.

"What do you mean?"

"There was a lot of information for you. There was a section about your house. There was a section about Fang."

"There was a section about the cat?"

"Yeah."

"And there was a note," Claire prompted. Their mother had already told her this. *Nothing of consequence,* she had said.

Nothing for you to worry about. Claire wasn't sure what that meant—how could a suicide note be inconsequential, and what, exactly, did her mother think Claire had to worry about?—but she hadn't asked.

"Yeah." Nomie shifted, her voice turning toward Claire. "There was a note for you."

"So I guess everybody's read it but me."

"Yeah. I'm sorry. I'm not really sure how that happened."

"Was it . . . embarrassing?"

"Embarrassing?"

"Yeah. Like . . . you know, did it say things about me, or me and Jay, or . . . whatever."

"Oh. Well, I'm not sure, exactly. I only skimmed it. You should look at it yourself, when you're ready."

"You *skimmed* it?" Her sister had never been a reader, but really, this was a bit much.

Nomie stroked Claire's hair, and the cup of her hand made the sound of the ocean. "I didn't want to read it too closely. I didn't want to invade your privacy. I only looked at it because I thought maybe . . . it would help me figure out how to take care of you."

"Oh. That's sweet," Claire said grudgingly. She shifted as gently as she could until her sister's hand slid away. "G'night, Nomie. And thanks for . . . everything."

"It's no problem. G'night, Claire."

Outside—just on the other side of the picket fence, Claire was sure—a car engine turned.

It was a long time before Nomie's breathing slowed. Birdsong came before the light.

2

"Why is your father outside?" Nancy called out in greeting, heels tapping down the front hall of the coach house the Tuesday morning after Claire moved in. Sprawled on the couch with the lattes and muffins their father had dropped off twenty minutes earlier, Claire and Nomie turned from the *Today* show to flash each other panicked looks. As usual, their mother was early. Once, when Claire was running late for school, her mother had accused her of being "passive-aggressively tardy"—a phrase Claire had needed her to explain, since she was eight or nine at the time.

"Hi, Mom," they said in unison as Nancy strode toward them, ignoring the cat lacing around her legs. Nomie grabbed the remote and snapped off the TV. Their mother believed it was uncivilized to watch television before 7:00 p.m., and even then only barely tolerable. Claire balled up used paper napkins and sugar packets while Nomie stacked dirty plates from yesterday's meals and took off for the kitchen area, returning with a damp sponge.

Nancy stooped for kisses, smelling of olives—her Estée Lauder lipstick—and her morning cigarette. The first day Claire woke up at her mother and stepfather's house, she had found Nancy smoking in the backyard in her bathrobe. "I am going to smoke three cigarettes a day for the next three months, and then I'm going to quit again," Nancy had said before tossing the butt into the snow and beginning to cry. Hugging her, Claire said, "Three months seems fair." Her mother had quit cold turkey many years earlier, after Claire, driven to panic by her fourth-grade health class, led Nomie in an antismoking campaign. For weeks they had left pamphlets with pictures of diseased lungs on their mother's pillow and, when she lit up, ambushed her with their battle cry: "Stop! You're paralyzing my cilia!"

"He brought us coffee," Nomie said in response to their mother's question about their father, which was true, though not the whole truth.

"When?" Nancy took off her camel-hair coat and tossed it onto the couch next to Claire, revealing a pink-plaid scarf with horizontal fringe draped loosely over a creamy cashmere turtleneck. There was no reason to look particularly nice for the errand they were running—Nancy had found a therapist for Claire, and they were driving downtown en masse for the first appointment—but their mother always looked particularly nice. The cat, who had been sitting at Nancy's feet, staring up at her—*Are you my daddy?*—skulked away.

"Just a little while ago," said Nomie as she scrubbed the coffee table, which they had been using as a dining table.

"Then why is he still outside?"

"He kind of hangs out there," Nomie said.

"For how long?" Nancy said.

"All day, I guess," Nomie said in a singsong voice as she

headed back to the sink. "He says he may as well be here as anywhere else," she said over the rush of the faucet.

Nancy looked at Claire. "What's going on?"

"I don't know," Claire said. "I haven't talked to him."

"Is there some reason your father thinks you need to be guarded?" she said, worry lines darkening her face.

"No," Claire said. "I mean, I don't think so. You'd have to ask him."

"I think he's just, you know . . . *concerned*," said Nomie as she dried her hands on a towel, which she absently let rest on her protruding belly for a moment before weaving it through the refrigerator door handle.

"Hmm. I'll have to talk to him." Nancy dipped her nose like a hummingbird into one of the wilting bouquets on the kitchen counter. "Have you been changing the water in these?"

Nomie looked at Claire, who shrugged. Claire had not left the coach house since arriving four days before. She had come to think of it as an ecosystem, albeit a slightly fetid one, sustained by offerings from the outside world: baked goods, casseroles, gift baskets, and decaying bouquets. The binder was here, too—on her first morning, she had spotted a thin navy blue spine at the bottom of a stack of her and Jay's mail on the coffee table—but she hadn't touched it.

"We should go," their mother said. "Robin's waiting. Though, if you had told me your father was going to be here, I would have asked him to drive us. Nomie, you're still coming?"

"She's coming," Claire said. She could not imagine leaving the coach house without her sister, let alone driving downtown to visit a shrink with only their mother and stepfather as company.

Things were moving a little fast. It had been only yesterday that Claire's mother called to ask if she was ready to see a therapist. After Claire agreed, her mother asked whether she wanted to see a man or a woman.

"Aren't they usually women?" Claire said.

"What? I don't think so."

"What are we talking about?"

In her mother's pause, Claire could hear her thinking, *My daughter is losing it.* "Psychologists."

"Oh. I thought you were asking me if I wanted to get a massage."

"A massage?"

"We talked about massages. When I was at your house. How relaxing they are." Maybe she had dreamed that, too.

"Oh. Well, I guess we did. But we also talked about you possibly seeing a *psycho*therapist."

"Oh. Uh-huh."

"So, do you want to?"

"Um . . . okay." It seemed like the right answer.

"And the gender?"

"I don't know," Claire said. She had never wanted to go to a male gynecologist, but she wasn't sure whether she was as modest about sharing her thoughts with strange men as she was about exposing her genitals.

"Well, in my experience," Nancy said, "the women are the supportive ones, but if you really want to deal with the heavy stuff, you need a man."

"Okay." Claire wasn't at all sure she wanted to deal with the heavy stuff, but she chose the answer most likely to satisfy her mother. "I'll take a man."

Half an hour later her mother had called back to tell her she had made an appointment for the following day with someone downtown. "A man," she said. "I got a referral from someone Robin and I used to see."

Robin and her mother had been in couples therapy? From the outside, their marriage had always looked like a placid, shallow pool.

"He used to be very jealous of your father, you know," Nancy added.

"The therapist was jealous of Dad?"

"*Robin.*"

"Oh. Huh." Her mother, private to the point of seeming superficial, had a habit of revealing intimacies at the most unexpected moments, catching Claire off guard.

"But he learned to let go of all that, once he understood your father would always be part of my life."

"Well, that's good." What was she supposed to say?

"Yes." Nancy had sounded vaguely disappointed. "Well, anyway."

It was time to go. The cat followed Claire, Nomie, and their mother to the door and gazed up stoically at Claire as she closed it. They crunched across the yard. Overnight, an inch of snow had fallen, refreshing the sooty underlayer. Douglas—Claire and Nomie's father—nodded grimly as they passed his car. Claire nodded back.

Just ahead, Robin was waiting in the driver's seat of their mother's cream-colored PT Cruiser. "Hey, kids," he said as Claire and Nomie climbed into the backseat of the warm car. Robin was about fifteen years older than Claire, but he still seemed to feel self-conscious about being nine years younger than their mother.

"Hi, Robin," the girls chimed, playing along.

As he turned the engine, another motor echoed behind them.

"Your father's following us," their mother said, her eyes on the rearview mirror.

"I'm sure he's concerned about Claire," Robin said.

Another of Robin's endearing qualities was his tendency to stick up for Claire and Nomie's father. Nancy's remark about couples therapy aside, the two men had always gotten along fine, whether because of their similar temperaments (quiet, well mannered), or because Robin had entered the picture when the girls were almost grown, too late for a stepfather to cause much drama. Once, Claire's father had told her that he thought Nancy and Robin were a good match: "You get the sense that he likes having other people make decisions for him." Robin apparently had wanted to become a weatherman when he was young, but by the time Nancy met him (the same way she met everyone, by representing him in a real estate deal), he was working as a model, mostly for Marshall Field's print ads, which turned out to be his life's work. When Claire was a teenager, she had been embarrassed to have a stepfather who posed in briefs and undershirts in the Sunday inserts in the *Tribune* (the undershirts always pressed and neatly tucked into the briefs, with their smooth yet alarming bulge). Recently, after Macy's bought Marshall Field's, Robin informally retired, saying he was tired of having to stay in shape and dye his sideburns. He had indeed gone a little soft and gray in the past year, changes that Claire thought gave him character: the lost look in his brown eyes now seemed soulful rather than vacant.

The southbound traffic on Wells Street moved steadily, sedately, as if orchestrated by a film crew. Inside the car, no one spoke.

Claire took out her cell phone, dialed into her voice mail, and listened to the message. No one asked her what she was doing, and she turned the volume down so they couldn't hear. *SHWEE-ohh, SHWEE-ohh, SHWEE-ohh.* She felt her pulse slowing to the beat. She could probably hire someone to make a CD of the message, an endless loop that she could play when she went to bed. Just as other people needed waves, flutes, or crickets to fall asleep, she would doze off to the sound of her husband's heart.

When the message was over, she hung up and checked her watch. In twenty minutes a strange man would be encouraging her to talk about the incident, about Jay, about her marriage, about everything she hadn't been talking about with the people who were supposed to be closest to her. The stranger would probably want to talk about that, too.

Claire hadn't seen a therapist since childhood. During and after the divorce, her mother took her to a string of child psychologists, but Claire never said much. The idea of talking about her family with strangers seemed disloyal. Her mother kept switching her from one doctor to another, blaming them, not Claire, for her refusal to share her thoughts and feelings.

The last therapist had been Claire's favorite—rather, the woman's office had been her favorite. The first time she entered it, Claire was drawn to the beautiful handmade dollhouse that sat on the floor in a corner. During their first session together, after asking permission, Claire sat down in front of it and quietly began rearranging the furniture. The therapist, a thin older woman with straight white hair and alarmingly thick black eyebrows, scooted her chair close and asked in a creaky, nasal voice, "Why did you take the people out and dump them in the yard, Claire?"

Claire didn't understand the question. It hadn't occurred to her to play with the ugly family of rubbery dolls, not when she could be rearranging the rooms full of lovely wooden hand-painted furniture, only slightly chipped and sticky from the grubby hands of other (more troubled, Claire assumed) children—and to refer to the gray carpet as a yard was silly. But she realized that she would have to cooperate for her mother to continue sending her to this doctor, who was probably expensive if she could afford such a nice dollhouse. So Claire made up stories that she thought would please the woman: the rubber parents were getting divorced, and the rubber dad, in his short-sleeved yellow shirt and red tie, moved to a small apartment while the rubber mom, with her cap of painted-on red hair, redecorated the house to her heart's content and the two rubber children (a girl Claire named Cammy and her younger brother, Nathan) played in their rooms. In retrospect Claire realized that the therapist must have been stuck trying to divine clues to her psyche from her decorating choices—viewing Claire's decision to move Cammy's room into the attic as sinister, maybe, when in fact Claire had been trying to re-create the garret that Sara Crewe from *A Little Princess* lived in at the boarding school after her father died.

Then Claire got a dollhouse for her birthday, and though it was not as large as the therapist's, there was no longer a need to keep the woman entertained, so Claire went back to rearranging the furniture and not talking.

Soon after, Claire's mother had said, "I think we're done with psychologists, don't you?"

Claire agreed.

What story would she tell today? The night before, while Nomie slept beside her, Claire had stared at the low ceiling in the loft of the coach house, worrying about what she would talk about with her new shrink. He would expect her to be distraught. She tried to imagine herself breaking down, as she had when her father told her what happened, so blind with anguish she could barely remember the hours that followed. If that didn't happen naturally today, maybe she could fake it. *That bastard! How could he do this to me?* she would wail, and then, *I feel so guilty. It's all my fault.*

But Claire had never been much of an actor. She would simply tell the therapist the truth: that she was reserved, not comfortable with strangers. (Not comfortable with emotions, either, according to Jay—there was a tidbit the doctor would like to hear.) If he was willing to be patient, she would answer his questions honestly, and maybe one day she would get upset and break down and start to heal.

Jay had been in therapy. His therapist had come to the wake, actually—that had been a shocker. At first Claire thought that the attractive, fortyish blonde in the receiving line might have been a cousin of Jay's, someone she had met briefly at the wedding or not at all. Claire felt the woman looking at her in a disconcerting way, as if trying to place her—as if it weren't obvious who she was, standing front and center before the closed coffin. Taking her turn in front of Claire, the woman introduced herself—Hannah something, that was all Claire remembered in the second after she said it—and then added, "Jay's doctor."

Claire had nodded, trying to understand: *Jay's doctor? Did Jay even have a doctor?*

"His therapist," the woman clarified, picking up on Claire's confusion.

"Oh, of course," said Claire, and added the filler line she had been giving everyone else, even as she felt herself shrinking back against the coffin: "Thank you for coming."

"I'm so sorry for your loss," said the woman, whom Claire started thinking of as Dr. Hannah. "Jay was a special person."

"Yes." Claire realized that she and Dr. Hannah were gripping each other's hands tightly. The woman was wearing emerald green contacts—no way did she come by that color naturally—but the whites of her eyes were bloodshot. Her stare was penetrating. What did this woman know about Claire?

"I gave my card to your brother-in-law," Dr. Hannah said. "In case you'd like to talk to me at any point."

"Okay," Claire said. Talk about what, she wondered—which one of them was more responsible for Jay's death? "I'll think about it."

"Whenever you like," the woman said before giving Claire's hands a quick, final squeeze and moving on to her mother.

"She seems pushy," Nancy murmured to Claire after Dr. Hannah had moved farther down the line.

"Pushy?"

"I'm not sure I'd have come if I were her."

"Jay liked her," Claire admitted. It was true. Though at times he had been frustrated that therapy wasn't solving his problems, he usually spoke of Dr. Hannah with respect and even pride—that he had an expert on his side, validating his choices. "My therapist," he called her, never by name, as if he needed to protect the doctor's privacy rather than his own. He rarely shared the details of what they talked about in his sessions.

"A lot of good she did him," her mother said.

"She seemed nice, anyway." Claire didn't know why she was defending the one person, aside from herself, who might have been most qualified to save Jay's life, except that the woman had been kind to her.

Carsick now, Claire lowered her window a crack and aimed her nose at the knife of frigid air like a dog. The tires hissed through the slush as Robin turned onto Chicago Avenue.

"That's it," Nancy said a few blocks later, pointing at a building on the right.

Robin pulled into a valet zone, and their father slid in behind them. Claire piled out after Nomie, joining their mother on the sidewalk.

The sun had sneaked out from the clouds, and Claire

squinted against the brilliant light bouncing off the plate glass of the office building. Young mothers and daughters with fist-fuls of red shopping bags came at them from all directions; the building was on the same block as the American Girl Place. She looked back. Robin had pulled into traffic, planning to drive around for an hour to save money on parking. Douglas hadn't moved yet.

Through the revolving doors and into the lobby they went. Claire let her mother forge through the lunchtime crowd pouring out of the bank of elevators.

The night of the party, Claire had surprised Jay by show-ing up at Sally and Bart's apartment.

At the start of the night, I went up in the elevator alone.

At the end of the night, I thought I would come down with Jay, but instead I came down with my father.

"Mom," Claire said as her mother strode ahead. Nancy didn't turn.

At our wedding I went down the aisle with Dad, then came back down the aisle with Jay.

"Mom!" she cried.

Nancy slipped into the first elevator, which was already full. Nomie followed her.

"Nomie!" Claire grabbed her sister's arm.

Nomie allowed herself to be pulled out of the elevator. "Mom?" she called behind her.

Their mother had her hand on the door, holding it for them, exhaustion and terror playing simultaneously on her face. "Honey?" she said, joining them in the lobby. The doors closed behind her. "What is it?"

"Oh God," Claire said.

Nomie's eyes were wide with fear.

"What floor is the office on?" Claire asked.

"The eighteenth." As Nancy spoke, Claire realized that

her mother had anticipated this problem. Her jaw was set, not for battle, but in resignation of a failed mission.

"That's too high!" Claire cried. "I can't go up that high."

"It's okay," their mother said. "I'll go up and explain."

"I don't want you to go." *If Mom went up alone in the elevator, would she come down?* Claire squeezed her hand.

"Nomie will stay here with you."

"Please don't go," Claire heard herself whimpering.

"Claire, honey. Come this way."

Tears blurred Claire's vision. Her legs dragged as her mother and sister steered her around the bank of elevators toward a waiting area by the walls of windows.

"Oh God, oh God, oh God," Claire said. The three of them crowded together on the edge of a black leather couch with a steep downward slope. Nancy handed Claire tissues. *Oh fuck,* Claire wanted to say, but she had never said "fuck" in front of her mother. "Oh my God . . . Oh my God!"

"Claire," Nancy said, touching her knee. "Can you sit tight with Nomie for a minute? I'll see if the doctor will come down to talk to you."

A doctor. She needed a doctor, yes. "Yeah."

"I'll be right back, I promise. Nomie will stay with you."

Oh fuck, she was talking about the shrink. Well, he would have to do. "Yeah," she said. "Yeah, okay."

Nancy's heels clicked away. Claire looked down at the tile, beige and black specks caged into silver-rimmed squares. Nomie's hand was on her back. "It'll be okay, you'll be all right," she said in a trembling voice. Without looking up, Claire could sense the mothers and daughters just beyond the window, with their red shopping bags, fresh off a train from someplace rural and wholesome, Kansas or Missouri, maybe, where husbands and fathers worked diligently to pay for mother-daughter outings to buy expensive dolls. Once, when

Claire was very young, when her parents were still together, they had taken a family vacation to St. Louis, traveling by train, and during the trip the train had jolted to a stop. They had waited there in the farmland for a long time. Years later Claire's mother told her that a woman had thrown herself in front of the train that day.

He went out onto the balcony: I saw him go onto the balcony and—

I didn't see him ask anyone for a cigarette, but I assumed he was going out to smoke. If I didn't see him with a cigarette, did I know he wasn't going out there to smoke?

When I locked myself in the bathroom, did I know already?

If I knew then, could I have—

"Here she is," she heard her mother saying.

Claire looked up. The man beside her mother was tall and thin, fiftyish, with a neat, U-shaped gray fringe encircling his head.

"Hello," the man said, extending his hand to Nomie, who had risen as he approached. "I'm Dr. Mercer."

"I'm Claire's sister," Nomie said, and motioned toward Claire.

Claire pushed herself forward, wobbled to her feet, and held out her hand. "Hello," she said. "I'm Claire."

"Oh, I see," he said, his handshake quick and firm. "Maybe we could spend some time alone, Claire, right here," the doctor said, looking quickly at each of the three women in turn.

"Of course," Nancy said. "We'll just be over there, Claire." She pointed past the security guard's podium in the center of the lobby to an identical arrangement of couches and low glass tables.

Claire nodded. She scooted over on the couch to give the doctor room. He set a shabby-looking leather briefcase on the floor and perched beside her. He was dressed in a manner that gave nothing away: blue suit, white shirt, red tie.

"So," he said, and Claire remembered those dreaded moments from childhood when the therapist would wait for her to say something. Thankfully, though, he interrupted the silence—the relative silence, for there were still shoes squeaking and voices bouncing off the high ceilings and a stream of people striding purposefully between the doors and elevators. "Now. I understand you're not comfortable going up to my office, and given what little your mother told me about your situation, I can understand why, and I'm sorry I didn't anticipate this myself. So I thought we could just talk here for a bit, and if you want to see me again, we can figure out a way to meet privately."

Claire nodded. "Give me a sec."

"Of course."

He waited while she blew her nose and wiped her face. When her sighs had shuddered away, she looked him square in the face. "What do you know about me? What did my mother tell you?"

"That your husband killed himself," he said, holding her gaze. "That he jumped off a high balcony at a party the two of you attended a couple of weeks ago."

Claire exhaled. She had been wondering how her mother, the whole family, had been telling the story; they had been careful not to tell it when she was present. The version the doctor had received was accurate, but incomplete. "It was a Valentine's Day party," Claire said. "Did my mother mention that?"

"No, I don't think so. Do you think that's relevant? His choice of day?"

"I don't know if it's relevant." The therapist smelled of

menthol and newsprint. The top of his shirt collar was slightly frayed. "I know it's embarrassing, though."

"Your husband's suicide makes you feel embarrassed?"

She cringed. "Do you think that we could use a different word?"

"Like what, 'ashamed'?"

"No, I mean to describe what happened."

"Oh. Instead of 'suicide,' you mean." He waited for her to nod. "How about 'death'?"

She sighed; he wasn't getting it. "I was thinking, like . . . 'incident' . . . or something like that. For the time being."

"Incident?" His eyebrows rose into roof peaks. "That seems like a bit of an understatement."

"I know, but I've been trying to think of another word that I can use for now. Something other than . . . the word you said."

"How about 'catastrophe'?" He paused, his gaze flickering from one of her eyes to the other.

"It feels like a big 'Fuck you,' " Claire blurted.

He nodded. "Like a big red valentine heart with 'Fuck you' written on it?"

She exhaled. "Yes." Now he was getting it. She considered telling him about the voice mail message, which seemed like a mitigating factor—Jay had wanted her to hear his heart, near the end—but she thought it would sound stupid. *Impossible,* he would say, *that someone could record the beating of his heart with a Motorola Razr.* Yet she believed she had proof.

"What about a note?" he said.

"A note?"

"A . . . catastrophe note." He cocked his head, as if asking for permission to be funny.

She smiled quickly, thanking him for treating her like a human being. "He left a binder."

"A binder?"

"Yeah. I guess there's all kinds of information in it for me, about our house and stuff." She shook her head. "I haven't read it yet."

He stared. "Has anyone?"

"Everyone's read it but me." She met his gaze. "I haven't yet, but I will."

His face softened, and then his voice lowered. "What are you afraid it will say?"

"That he blames me. That I wasn't there for him." She shook her head.

The doctor frowned. "Were you having an affair?"

"No, no. But . . . there are other ways you can let someone down. Getting wrapped up in my work, not being supportive enough, not knowing what to say . . . He was in despair, I think. He had these . . . spells . . ."

"Spells?" The therapist sounded almost mocking.

"Spells of depression."

He nodded. "Related to you?"

"I don't know. He'd had them for years. I thought it would always be that way. But that night, he didn't want me to go to the party—at least, he encouraged me not to go. I changed my mind at the last minute. I surprised him."

"Was he happy to see you?"

"I don't think so. He tried to act like he was, but in retrospect . . ."

"And he jumped anyway, even with you there."

She nodded.

"So it was clearly premeditated, since he had left a note. But you're wondering why he didn't change his mind after you showed up at the party. Why he didn't spare you."

She nodded, on the verge of crying again.

"Why he was that selfish," Dr. Mercer said, "or hurtful."

"Maybe he felt it was too late to change his plans," she suggested.

"But it wasn't, was it?"

"I guess not." Two young women had settled on the couch on the other side of the big glass table and were poring over their day planners. Claire was ready to leave. "I feel funny, talking here."

"Understandable. Me, too. Just one quick question, then we can end for now. Where's your father in all this? I see your mother and sister—"

Claire nodded at the window, where mothers and daughters with red bags were streaming by. She couldn't see past them to his car. "I think he's parked outside."

"I didn't mean literally."

"He didn't drive us here," she said, to make him understand that she wasn't being literal at all. "He followed us. He sits in his car on the street in front of my sister's house all day long. He's there in the morning when I get up, and he leaves when I turn out the lights."

"He's stalking you."

"I wouldn't call it that."

"Dads don't stalk their daughters, right?"

She shrugged.

"All right," Dr. Mercer said. "We won't get into this now. So, if you want to see me again, we should talk about how we can manage that."

"Do you have another office?"

"Nope. This is all I've got. But I can figure something out—borrow an office on a lower floor or something like that." He put his briefcase on his knees, snapped it open, and started rooting around inside. "Now," he said without looking up, "you may have noticed that I'm direct. That doesn't work for everyone. If you'd rather see someone a little more subtle, I can give you a referral. But given what you're dealing with, I think you should be seeing a therapist at least twice a week. Sound okay?"

"Um . . . yeah. I'll think about it. I should pay you for today, then."

"Well, I wasn't going to charge you, but your mother insisted, and she already paid." He smiled wryly as he handed her a sheet of paper. "She wanted me to give you one of these, too. It's an insurance form. She thought maybe you could get reimbursed."

Claire looked at the form, which had been copied so many times the type was grainy and crooked. He'd filled in Claire's name, and an amount for one session—$175. Next to the word "Diagnosis," he had written a number.

"What's my diagnosis?" she said, standing up along with him.

He cocked his head. "That's just for the bean counters."

She stared him down.

"There's a category called 'complicated bereavement.' I used that."

"Complicated?"

"Because of the circumstances. This is more complicated than ordinary bereavement—uncomplicated bereavement— because there's violence involved. Trauma. It's a little more like PTSD, if you know what that is."

"Like what soldiers get."

He nodded. "Exactly."

She could see her mother and Nomie standing across the hall, clearly trying to avoid looking at them.

"You're going to need some help with this, Claire. This isn't just grief you're dealing with here. You're going to have to reexamine your entire past."

"My past with Jay," she said.

"Your *entire* past."

She looked away again. "Do you want to talk to my mother?"

He smiled. "That won't be necessary. You're an adult."

Claire nodded. "Thank you. I need to . . . I need to think about things. So . . ."

"I understand. You think. It was nice meeting you." He shook her hand, turned, and was gone.

When they got home, Claire went up to the loft, shed her shoes and jeans, and went to bed. She stayed there all afternoon and into the night. Her sister brought her tea and peanut butter toast. Claire left them untouched: the smells were noxious, fatty and sour.

"Excuse me," Jay said, and left the kitchen.

I kept talking with Sally and Bart for a while, then rejoined the party. Across the room I saw the black drapes parting, a blotchy reflection, then the glass sliding away. Then a head, Jay's, I thought, then the glass sliding again and the drapes closing.

Out to the balcony for a smoke, I thought.

In the kitchen I helped Sally arrange fruit on a platter. We talked about locally grown produce. For how long? Too long.

I took the tray into the party and put it on the table. I looked for him. But in the living room, in the dining room, then back in the kitchen, I couldn't find him.

I saw the black drapes, closed. I didn't go to the balcony. Instead I went to the bathroom. The door was open and I turned on the light and went inside and locked the door and stared at myself in the mirror, and the whiteness was horrifying.

3

I n the days that followed, as she migrated between the bed and the couch, Claire began to see herself and Fang as kindred spirits. They lurked in the shadows of each other's lives, eating and dozing in separate corners, jolting to attention at the sound of the phone or, especially, the doorbell. When it rang, the cat would dart from wherever she had been sleeping and follow Claire as she sped down the hall and reached for the doorknob. They would both stare hard at the visitor—a delivery person with flowers or a gift basket, or a friend bearing food, trying to coax Claire into the fresh air for a walk. The cat would slink away while Claire dealt with the person as quickly as possible so she could get back to the couch and sleep.

Claire's cell phone rang often, sometimes several times an hour. She usually didn't answer it, but she was too superstitious to turn it off—not because she actually thought Jay would call her, but because she didn't want to miss the call if he did: a distinction so subtle, she knew, that it wouldn't make sense to anyone else except, perhaps, Pepper, Jay's mother, grieving in Boston with Jay's father by her side.

Since the funeral, Pepper had been leaving a message every few days in a tremulous voice: "Just checking in to see how you are doing. Hope to hear from you . . . when you feel like it, no hurry." A gift basket had arrived from Pepper and Tom, filled with teas, cookies, lotions, and soaps. Nomie had put everything away, and Fang began nesting in the empty basket. Claire hadn't called Pepper back, which she knew was cruel, but she couldn't help it. She was sure that Jay's mother's grief would swallow her up and leave her feeling even more inadequate and empty than she already felt.

Claire's friends called, too. They were not acting the way she had heard friends typically behaved in such situations. After an initial flurry of attention and concern, friends were supposed to abandon you, fearful of saying the wrong thing or getting sucked into a vortex of grief. But Claire's friends refused to leave her alone. An artist, she had a day job as a home stager in the real estate business, and like any nice person who lives in the same city for a while, she had acquired a wide circle of friends from different facets of her life. Now the artists, real estate agents, and high school and college friends had merged and organized, like a church or farm community; without fail, someone appeared on the doorstep at dinnertime with a warm covered dish. Nomie told Claire that her friend Ruth, a graphic designer, had created a website where sympathizers could sign up to deliver casseroles according to a schedule. Sympathizers—Claire found herself thinking of them this way, as if she were Adolf Hitler in 1930s Berlin and they her misguided followers.

She should be grateful. Secretly, though, she wished they would ignore her until the whole embarrassing mess blew over. She couldn't talk to people anymore, not truthfully, if she had ever had that ability. She sometimes welcomed her visitors inside and rewarded them with tears, petty little cloudbursts that seemed to satisfy them but made her feel, afterward, as if her whole body had dried up.

Since the incident, the only person she had talked to honestly, or at least started to be honest with, was Dr. Mercer. But she could not bring herself to schedule another appointment, to set that circus into motion again: the two-car caravan, the elevator, the tide of mothers and daughters with their big red shopping bags. The only way to go back would be to sneak out of the house without anyone knowing, but Claire couldn't imagine pulling that off. Besides, the idea of facing the therapist's uncomfortable questions again, and the next time for fifty minutes rather than fifteen, was terrifying.

You're going to have to reexamine your entire past, Dr. Mercer had said, with an emphasis on "entire." That sounded as if it would take a while. Until she found her way back to his office, she could get started on her own. Harry had confirmed with the life-insurance company that Jay had outlived its suicide clause, for which Claire could arguably feel grateful, and there was some sort of lump payment from the university, too, issued out of pity or paranoia, to tide her over. Jay's parents had paid for the funeral, evidently without any discussion between the families, as if following protocol, the way they had paid for the rehearsal dinner and her parents had paid for the wedding. There was no reason for Claire to scurry around on home-staging assignments to earn money, and the idea of returning to her art studio was unfathomable. She had time.

"I'm trying to find Orpheus Records."

Before Claire saw Jay for the first time, she heard his voice, low and scratchy. She was at the café on Long Street, scanning someone else's discarded *Red Eye* for celebrity gossip while she ate her sandwich and potato chips. The café was dead on that gray day; Claire often had the place to herself at lunchtime, which had made her worry that it would go out of business. She looked up to see hiking boots standing in a black puddle of melted snow—it was February, but the snow was left over from January. Her eyes moved up the back of a pair of jeans splattered with black slush and encasing sturdy-looking legs, up to nicely rounded back pockets, an olive green sweater with a hole at the hem, a navy blue scarf, and, finally, a gray knit cap pulled low around a head that looked especially large. She guessed that he was about her age, but that he wasn't one of the young fathers in the neighborhood—and not just because he didn't know where he was going. He wasn't as neatly dressed or as loud as the men Claire tended to see around here, type A's who were ostentatious about their involvement in parenthood, wheedling and throwing tantrums right along with their children.

"It's supposed to be across the street, but it's not," Jay continued.

"Yeah, yeah," said Andy from behind the counter. The gold hoop linking his nostrils bobbed. "You're right. There's no record store around here."

The hiking boots shuffled uncertainly. "Do you have a phone book?"

"Sure, sure." Andy fetched the Yellow Pages and watched with his usual crazed smile as Jay thumbed through it. Claire pushed her plate away and ran her fingers through her hair.

"See?" Jay turned the book around to show Andy. "Orpheus Records, 1828 Long Street."

"Yeah, right." Andy nodded. "That's weird, 'cause it isn't there. There's some record stores downtown that I could tell you about, though."

"Do you know when it closed?" said Jay.

"It's been closed for ages," Claire said.

Jay turned, pulling off his cap as he did. His hair, an indeterminate dull brown or steel gray, was not much longer than the stubble on his face. He wore glasses, wire rims. The glasses surprised Claire, and she realized she had already formed an image of the man in her mind, not necessarily of someone better-looking, but someone more sharply defined—with rosy cheeks, perhaps, a pale brow, and a light in his chocolate-colored eyes. The man before her was shades of gray, like someone sketched in charcoal.

"Yeah?" He looked at her sidelong, as if embarrassed for one or both of them.

"It was there when I was a kid," Claire said, speaking gently for fear of scaring him off. "We used to buy records there—on vinyl. It probably closed, like, twenty years ago. Is it really still listed?"

"Here," Jay said, striding toward her with the phone book.

The storefront had been a record store for a long time, Claire told him, until it became a travel agency. "Now it's a flower shop."

"You grew up here?" he asked.

She nodded. "My dad lived around here, anyway."

"Y'mind?" He motioned to the empty chair beside her.

"Please."

He sat down, hunched over the table, and watched her silently. His lips were pursed, almost as if he were holding back a laugh, as if they could already be in on a joke together. The night before, she had met forty different men during an evening of speed dating, a blur of "What do you do?" and "Where do you live?" Already she and this man had shared a longer conversational lull than she had experienced the entire night, but the silence felt comfortable rather than awkward.

But still, they should talk. "I remember the first record I bought at Orpheus," she ventured, thinking she should try to draw out the laugh at the edge of his lips. "The *Bugsy Malone* sound track."

He smiled, very slightly. Most people would think him aloof, she decided, but she would consider him shy until proved otherwise. (He turned out to be both. She herself could be both.)

"I'm Jay, by the way." He held out his hand.

She shook. "Claire."

They smiled, and just when she was thinking that it would be nice to find someone to be quiet with, he began to ramble. He told her that when he moved to a new town, he had a habit of checking out the local record stores. Being in academia, he had moved often, and he tended to get depressed when he was uprooted. Routines helped ease the transition. He said the word so matter-of-factly—"depressed"—that it had not seemed a thing to fear.

"The record store was right below my apartment," Claire said. She turned and pointed through the plate glass.

"You live across the street?" Jay said.

"And work. I have a studio in my apartment."

"Studio?"

"An art studio."

When he asked, she told him that she built dollhouses, not for children but as art.

"Are there people in them?" Jay asked.

"Sometimes." She was wary of telling him about her work. Usually men would look puzzled and then say something about Barbie dolls or tell her that they terrorized their sisters' dollhouses when they were little, pretending there was an earthquake or a mass murder. Sometimes she would meet a man who knew something about art, and they could get back on safe ground by talking about various male artists, and maybe Georgia O'Keeffe, while still seeming to talk about her work.

"Are they houses you've lived in?" Jay asked.

She paused. How did he know? "Sometimes. I mean, variations on them."

He smiled. "You don't like talking about your work."

"Well . . . it sounds stupid to me when I talk about it."

"I know what you mean. I feel that way about my work. I work with dollhouses, too, in a way."

"What do you mean?" she asked.

"More like puppet theaters. I build them."

He was an assistant professor of developmental psychology at the university, he told her, studying infant cognition. He and his colleagues had a laboratory—"The Baby Lab, we call it." Through birth records, they recruited babies as study participants. Parents, mostly mothers, brought their babies in every two months. They sat in chairs with their babies on their laps, facing a puppet stage. Behind the stage, research assistants showed "real" and "magic" conditions of various events: a ball rolling down a ramp or up a ramp, for example. The longer a baby stared at a magic event—a ball rolling up a ramp, a bunny disappearing seemingly into thin air—the greater the baby's surprise. "Their surprise tells us that they know something about how the world works, that they know we've violated the natural order of things."

"So . . . you're trying to find out how smart they are?" she asked.

"Well, sort of. We're looking at global intelligence. The point isn't to find out which particular babies are the smartest—though the parents always want to know how well their kids did—but to find developmental benchmarks, what most babies know at different stages. And it turns out that babies are a lot smarter than we think. Or than we thought."

"It must be fun," she ventured. "Having all those babies around." She wanted a baby: she had decided this so gradually over the past few years that she could not say when she knew for sure.

He smiled. "Yeah. The babies are the best part of the job."

He wanted to know about the record store, so she told him what she remembered. An old man and an old woman had worked there—old to Claire's adolescent eyes, anyway; they might have been only in their fifties. "I thought they were married, but it turned out they weren't," she said. Once, she told Jay, while she was browsing in the store on a Friday after school—"I must have been in junior high then," she said—the woman had asked the man about his weekend in an aggressive sort of way. "She made this big fuss about how she didn't have any plans, how she thought she would just cook some dinner and watch whatever movie was on TV."

"The Friday night movie," Jay said. "Remember the Friday night movie?"

"Mm-hmm. I felt certain that she had a crush on him and was trying to get him to ask her out on a date, and that he didn't have any interest." The word "date" hovered in the air. That morning, the speed-dating company had sent Claire a few matches via e-mail, but she didn't remember any of the men she had been matched with. Now here she was, meeting, by chance, someone interesting. Someone *possibly* interesting, possibly married, though she noticed there was no ring on the hands folded on the table.

Months later Jay had laughed when she told him that she felt embarrassed after describing the couple's romantic intrigue, that she was afraid he could tell she was hoping he would ask her out, too. *Silly girl,* he said, *I was already halfway in love with you by then.*

Only later, when she knew Jay better, did she tell him that she and Nomie used to call that business district Short Long Street when they were young because it was a short walk around the corner from their father's apartment. A second little shopping area, Long Long Street, was half a mile away, a tedious walk with a short-legged little sister, past apartment buildings decorated with white wrought-iron railings that looked prim and fussy, like metal doilies.

Their father had moved to Short Long Street when Claire was ten and Nomie was seven. After their divorces, the fathers of Claire's friends usually bought houses of their own in the same town or high-rise condos in downtown Chicago, or both. Douglas had broken with convention by renting an apartment in the next suburb south, the buffer between Wilmette and the city. Amid the houses full of families in that neighborhood, only lonely-looking single people lived in apartments: newly divorced men, widows and widowers, foreign graduate students who had wandered away from the university in the wrong direction.

After Nomie left for college, their father surprised them by getting a condo in Chicago, a two-bedroom unit in Lincoln Park. He said that as he got older, he wanted to be closer to the symphony. It hadn't occurred to Claire that her father could afford anything more than a shabby rental, or that he would prefer the city to the suburbs—that he had rented an apartment close by for his daughters' sake, to be near them and their schools. The Long Street apartment, Claire realized only later, had been a respectable choice for a man who did not care much about his own comfort and had decided not to date while his daughters were young. Just as Claire understood—as they all understood—that Douglas had not wanted the divorce, that he still, even today, was in love with her mother, she came to understand that he had chosen a second home that his daughters would find unobtrusive. After moving out, he had started calling the family home "your house" and his own place "the apartment." From a young age, Claire had known the difference between owning and renting.

She would not have rented an apartment on Short Long Street if her father had still lived around the corner. She would have felt pathetic, a single woman living so close to her father in a neighborhood overrun by couples her age starting families of their own. But after her father left, the three-block stretch became a part of family history. And so, two years before meeting Jay, when her apartment in Ravenswood was going condo, Claire looked at the place on Short Long Street, above what she remembered as a record store but was now a flower shop.

She was lonely in her new home on Short Long Street, but not unhappy. She was productive, and she had her routine. She worked on her art projects in her pajamas until one, then showered and went across the street for lunch at the café, followed by a walk around the neighborhood when the weather was nice. In the afternoon she worked on home-staging assignments; in the evening she went on dates or had dinner with friends.

Soon after moving in, Claire had ventured into the vestibule of her father's old building, one block down and around the corner from a pharmacy that was now an optical shop. When she was a child, the vestibule of the 1920s brick six-flat had reminded her of their church—cool and dark, its woodwork slathered in caramel-colored varnish that had dried in drips. Even the mailboxes, with their metal grating, looked like the window of a confessional. Claire knew she should not have been surprised that it had stayed the same for all the years they had been away—these old, well-built buildings never changed much, and there was nothing to disturb the space but the quick coming and going of residents—yet she was. Then she noticed a sign above the mailboxes warning that the area was monitored by security cameras, and suddenly alarmed, she slipped outside again. What violence had happened in that small, dim space?

Outside the café, Jay walked Claire across the street—followed her, she teased him later, for he hadn't asked if he could. "This is it?" he said in front of her door, and she realized he was talking about the former record shop, not her apartment upstairs. He pointed at the window of the flower shop, then reached for the door.

The florist was a thin older woman with the body and grace of a dancer, her gray hair pulled back into a short ponytail. Claire had seen her floating about the shop in black outfits, flowers outstretched in her hands like a ballerina, but had never spoken to her. When Jay asked, the woman told them that she knew the space had once been a record store, maybe ten years before, but she didn't know anything more about it. Her shop had been open for three years.

"We tried," Claire said when they were back on the step that led to both the flower shop and her studio, shuffling their feet against the cold.

"I have the phone number, though." He waved a napkin from the café in the air.

"Go for it." She smiled encouragingly, wondering whether he was a little obsessive or simply looking for an excuse not to leave her.

While he dialed his cell phone, she glanced through the glass-paned door at the staircase, its brown plastic runner leading up to her apartment. She didn't have a staging assignment that afternoon and had planned to work late into the night. She wanted Jay to ask for her number and go away so that she could be alone and happily daydream about him while she worked—whether they would fall in love, plan a wedding, start a family.

"Hi, is this Orpheus Records?" Jay's breath showed in puffs as he spoke. "Oh, okay. Uh-huh. Sorry to bother you." He hung up, stuffed the phone into his pocket, and kept his hand there. "Wrong number, the lady said. Woman," he corrected himself.

"Did she say if she's gotten calls for Orpheus before?" Claire held herself rigid to keep the cold from sinking into her bones.

He looked stricken. "I didn't ask. Do you think I should call her back?"

"Umm . . . maybe not."

"I shouldn't scare her, right? Or you, more importantly. I can be a little intense, I've been told."

"Yeah?" She raised her eyebrows.

"You're quiet," he said matter-of-factly. "Shy."

She nodded. Feeling an unexpected rush of emotion, she tamped it down.

"That's nice," he said, smiling shyly himself. "I like that."

Grateful, she felt she needed to give him something. "I always feel a pang when I think of that woman at Orpheus Records," she said.

"The one who was fishing for a date with her coworker?"

Claire nodded. "I felt sorry for her. She was old, or almost old. And she didn't even seem to care that I was there. I figured she must have liked him a lot to do that. And that she must have suffered in her life to not care if she seemed desperate."

"You have a tender heart." He was smiling at her, bemused.

Claire shrugged. "I don't know about that."

He asked her how else the neighborhood had changed since she was young. The post office, she told him, had always been there, and the ballet school, the bakery, and the branch library where she had read her way through the children's books. "The café used to be a drugstore, it even had a soda fountain, and the stationery store"—she pointed down the block—"was a dime store."

"A dime store." He smiled. "Now there's only dollar stores."

"And they're not the same thing."

He shook his head. "It must be cool to know a place so well."

She nodded. "Where did you grow up?"

"Boston," he said. "Boston-ish. Hey, listen. We shouldn't stand here in the cold."

"No?"

He shook his head. "I just read this research study. It wasn't in my field—it has to do with emotions, not babies—but I read it anyway. So in the study, a researcher met the subjects in the hallway one at a time, before the experiment, and she was holding a cup of either hot coffee or iced coffee, depending on the condition, and she asked the subjects to hold the coffee for her while she unlocked the door. And the people who were asked to hold the iced coffee said later that the research assistant seemed cold and unfriendly, but the ones who held the hot coffee thought she was warm and friendly."

"Uh-huh?" Claire said, a little stunned by the monologue.

"So," he continued doggedly, "because it's cold out, I started worrying that you'd associate me with the cold, subliminally, I mean, and then you wouldn't want to go out with me."

"Oh. Um . . ." She laughed. "What?"

"I guess I should ask first if you're married or have a boy-friend or—whatever." He frowned, then squinted down the street as if trying to remember where he had left his car.

She shook her head, stopping herself from telling him that she had been on forty dates with forty different men the night before. "You?"

He shook his head. "I'm not married, and I don't have a boyfriend."

She cocked her head.

"Or a girlfriend." He smiled. "Geez. Way to make a guy work for it."

"Sorry, sorry!" She laughed as she riffled around in her purse for a pen and paper.

"Hey." He pointed across the street at the café. Its interior walls were painted tangerine, and on that gray day the room shone into the street like a Chinese lantern.

"Pretty, right?" she said.

"Pretty," he said, smiling at her.

Before her father moved to Long Street, Claire sometimes had to remind herself, they had all lived together as a family—the dreamlike years of her early childhood. Her father had been a steady presence at home, giving piano lessons or practicing in his studio, dozing off in his green corduroy chair in the liv-ing room while classical music blared on the stereo, making snacks for the girls after school, building dollhouse furniture with Claire in the basement workroom. Their mother, mean-while, was a blur of perfume and lipstick, heels tapping fainter or louder on the sidewalk. Claire had never seen her parents argue, not before the divorce and not after. They kissed, but swiftly, self-consciously. She had always known her father loved her mother more.

One evening after dinner, while their mother was upstairs tucking Nomie into bed, Claire's father had taken a Sara Lee strawberry cheesecake, her favorite, out of the refrigerator, served her a large piece, and left the rest in its aluminum container on the table. It had not had time to defrost from the supermarket freezer, and the strawberries were crusted with ice.

"I'm moving out of the house, Claire," Douglas had said, watching her with concentration, his arms folded on the table. Back then he wore glasses with heavy black frames that made his eyes look small and all-seeing.

She shivered, whether from the news, his gaze, or the frozen strawberries she wasn't sure. She had imagined this moment, not knowing whether it would ever happen. She had pictured the four of them sitting together on her parents' bed, her father's arm around her waist, Nomie in their mother's lap, a box of Kleenex waiting to be emptied. In this cozy scene, she had imagined her mother telling them that she was leaving. Claire knew it was usually the father who moved out, but she had thought it would be different for their family.

If it was their father who left, Claire and Nomie would live like orphans. She would have to help her sister get dressed in the morning and do both of their braids.

"Your mother and I are probably going to get a divorce," he said, and Claire saw the sorrow in his eyes. "Your mom wants a trial separation, but I think it would be better if we just call it a divorce and try to come to terms with that, and then be pleasantly surprised if it turns out otherwise."

Claire nodded. It was their logic, his and hers: prepare for the worst and secretly hope to be surprised. While she swallowed back tears, he told her about the apartment he had rented nearby. Upstairs, Nomie began to keen, low and long, like a dog; then their mother's high cries started up.

Douglas put his head in his hands. Dutifully, Claire ate her cheesecake, wondering if their mother had fed Nomie gummy worms, her favorite food. Claire and their father, Nomie and their mother—that was how their family was aligned, before the divorce and even after. But when Claire felt she had waited a long enough interval to be polite, she excused herself and ran upstairs to cry with her mother and sister, who were hugging each other on Nomie's bed.

Claire was independent—people had said that about her before she met Jay, as if trying to spin a character flaw into an asset. She had never been with a man for longer than a year, which was suspicious for a woman of thirty-four, she knew. By her late twenties she had diagnosed her problem, which she understood to be common: she was indifferent to men who were attentive and drawn to those who were not. But just when she should have parlayed that knowledge into a search for an appropriate mate, she had gone to art school and given herself over to her work.

At age thirty-one, while helping her younger sister plan her wedding, Claire decided it was time. She joined dating websites and went on whatever blind dates her friends and her mother's friends plotted. Only after she started dating in earnest did she begin to panic. Somehow she hadn't believed that her single friends' complaint would be true for her as well: all the good ones were taken.

She gathered stories. Cumulatively, they made her despondent, but one by one she could use them to entertain dates who came later. Though Claire had been raised Catholic, one of her mother's friends convinced her to join JDate (the woman had a friend who had a daughter who met her husband, "a very nice Jewish man," there). Through JDate she met a Methodist lawyer who mentioned his hourly fee during their first date and called just before their second date to reschedule because his car had been repossessed. At a bar one night with a friend, she met a man who turned out to be ten years younger than she was; on their third date he asked her if they could lie to his parents about her age—he was afraid they would cut off his monthly stipend if they found out how old she was. At a friend's party a man flirted with her and asked her out, but he rushed through their first date and shook her hand at the end of it, only to show up the next week at her group art show with his mother, who bought a work by someone else. For six weeks she dated an attractive, funny veterinarian (who also happened to be a vegetarian) she had met on eHarmony, until the night he told her he realized that although he had recovered from the death of his fiancée several years before—the deceased fiancée being news to Claire—he had not recovered from the guilt he felt for falling asleep at the wheel and driving the passenger side of the car into a tree. He asked permission to call Claire after he went through therapy; even after she married Jay, she felt like a chump whenever she remembered that the man had never called. She had been on a first date with a man who recited the lyrics to "American Pie," his favorite song, during a lull in dinner conversation. Against her better judgment she dated an old friend, Frank, a heavy drinker who broke up with her after two weeks, saying, "I think it'll be better for both of us if I go back to worshipping you from afar."

There were stories men could tell about her, of course. She had let people she had no intention of ever kissing buy her dinner, just because she was hungry. After heartbreaks, she had dated too quickly, wasting people's time, waiting to see if she could learn to feel something for them. She had dumped a couple of men more than once.

In this manner, three years passed. She started to take breaks from dating, as if it were a job from which she needed a vacation, but she always went back to it. Women friends who were settled in solid marriages began telling her that love came when you least expected it, when you had finally given up, which Claire took to mean that they had given up on her and thought she should do the same: lower her expectations, learn to be happy with what she had. "You *seem* happy enough," a married friend said to her once; it appeared to irritate people that Claire needed a companion, just as they did—that she, too, was human.

Claire refused to give up. When she began looking for a husband, she had made a list of twenty qualities she was looking for. She took the list out three years later and crossed off seventeen. All that were left were "sane," "nice," and "cute," which she amended to "cute to me."

Claire and Jay had their first date on Valentine's Day. Not wanting to scare him, she hadn't said anything about the holiday when he phoned. But he had bought roses from her downstairs neighbor. Not only had he remembered Valentine's Day, it turned out, but he had blown off a work party to go out with Claire. "Didn't want to go anyway," he told her in the car. "Having a hot date was a good excuse." He didn't glance at her, but she felt herself redden.

He hadn't thought to make a reservation, though, and they were turned away at the first restaurant they went to, a French bistro near her apartment (it had been an organic food co-op when she was growing up), and they drove south, ending up squashed in a corner by the coatracks at an Italian restaurant in Edgewater that Claire had once been to many years before with Nomie. The waitress was overly solicitous, as if she knew they needed help, new acquaintances making stilted first-date conversation in a sea of blissfully oblivious couples.

"Maybe we should act like we're in love," Jay said, putting down the wine list, which he kept consulting and abandoning.

"Excuse me?" Claire said, buying time. A man saying the word "love" on the first date? This was new.

He pressed on. "To fit in. And, um, break the ice. Because if we were in love, you'd already know that I'm hopeless when it comes to picking out wine, and that if you want something you'll like, you'll have to pick it out yourself."

She took the leather-bound book from him. "Well, if we're in love, that means you know that I'm going to taste your food. I'll just stick my fork in without asking permission."

"Hmm. Well, if it's true—like, truly true love—"

"Truly true love?"

"—then you know I hate it when someone sticks her fork in my ravioli before I get to taste it myself."

"Well, of course I'd let you taste it first. That would just be rude, and by this point you know how considerate I am."

"Except when it comes to . . ." He eyed her, waiting.

She shook her head.

"I have to figure out your flaws on my own, I guess," he said.

"What flaws?"

The waitress approached, breaking the spell with a smile that said she was happy to see them getting along so well, and Claire, embarrassed again, pointed blindly at a not-too-expensive Chianti.

The last time she had eaten at the restaurant, it had been BYO—Claire had bought a bottle of wine at the liquor store across the street on her way to meet Nomie. The dining room had upgraded to white tablecloths since then, but the kitchen had let things slide, or else Claire's palate had improved. Back then, Nomie was a recent college graduate and without a boyfriend for the first time since junior high. A few months later she met Jim, whom she dated for four years, until she met Harry, who convinced her to dump Jim. In that brief window of time between college and Jim, Nomie had been angry and bitter—at their parents, at the world for leaving her alone and adrift—as Claire had never seen her before or since. During that era they had shared a series of clandestine dinners in which they revealed information and theories about their family.

"She told me that Dad was going to live somewhere else for a while, but he would probably be back," Nomie had said. Once broached, the divorce had proved to be an endless topic of conversation. The patio doors were open, and it was warm, the restaurant lit with strings of white lights and candles. Probably no one would have minded if one of them had started crying at the table, which had happened on other nights. "Mom said we'd be able to visit him after he left." Nomie frowned. "I had this idea that he was going to Dallas."

"Why?" Claire said.

"I have no idea. But I thought you and I would fly down to Dallas by ourselves and it would be our job to bring him back."

"I remember Mom going to a real estate conference in Dallas once."

"Maybe that's what I was thinking of," said Nomie.

"Dad told me that they were getting divorced," said Claire. "That they were *probably* getting divorced." She looked up at the ceiling, trying to get it right. "That he was moving out and they were probably getting divorced."

"Probably?" Nomie's teeth bared in a venomous smile. "That's nice. Not *too* confusing for a ten-year-old."

"The part that gets me is that they told us separately," Claire said. "Mom telling you upstairs, him telling me downstairs."

Nomie shook her head. "I know. So weird."

"I wanted to be up there with you guys." Claire started to cry, maudlin from the wine. "But I didn't want to leave Dad by himself."

"Oh, Claire." Now Nomie was crying, too. "Don't cry."

Arm in arm, they had stumbled back to Nomie's apartment, the studio in Edgewater where she had lived for a few years. Claire had slept on the foldout couch across the room from Nomie's futon. A cricket had gotten into the apartment and was chirping in the bedroom closet. It kept them awake, but they hadn't looked for it, for fear it would jump out at them.

After Nomie met Jim, she had gotten distracted and happy. It could take days for her to return Claire's calls, and her weekends were all booked up. When they did get together, Nomie didn't seem to want or need to talk about the past anymore. Their conversations about everyday life seemed superficial to Claire. Losing Nomie that way had felt like the dome of an observatory closing over a starry sky.

After their father moved out, Claire and Nomie began spending weekends at his apartment. The interior was large and airy, with wood floors and glossy, unpainted trim. Their mother helped him pick out modern furniture from a Danish furniture store nearby: blond, unfinished wood pieces with scratchy, rust-colored upholstery that pilled.

It seemed their mother was always traveling in the year after the separation, to San Francisco, Miami, and Boston. She brought back presents: clothes for Claire, and stuffed animals for Nomie, who named them after the cities they came from; a sheep named Miami had lasted into adulthood. Their mother said she was visiting clients, which in retrospect didn't make much sense, since she was a Chicago-area real estate agent. Then the trips ended, and for a while, instead of their father picking up the girls and taking them to his place on Friday nights, he picked up their mother, while Claire stayed home and babysat Nomie. "Your father's taking me out on dates," their mother would say to Claire with a wink, slipping hoops through her ears in the master bathroom. Their father's explanation was that they still had a symphony subscription, and it would be a shame to waste it. Claire would try to stay awake those nights, hoping for two sets of footsteps on the stairs, but her mother always came home alone. In the morning, their father would return to the house and pick up Claire and Nomie for the rest of the weekend.

It was obvious what had happened: Nancy had married too young, had children too soon, and gotten restless with her suburban lifestyle and her older, somewhat stodgy husband. Yet it was also clear that Nancy did not regret her first marriage. Like a woman married for decades to the same man, she still girlishly recounted the story of their courtship to her daughters. She and Douglas had grown up on the same block, but he was twelve years older. "I had a terrible crush on him as a girl," Nancy said. "He was so serious, so talented!" In his youth, before it became apparent that he would have to fall back on teaching, Douglas had been preparing for a concert career, and the sound of his piano, crashing through scales and Beethoven, carried into the street on summer nights when Nancy played outside with her friends. By the time they ran into each other at midnight Mass in the middle of Nancy's senior year in college, Douglas was known around the neighborhood as a "confirmed bachelor" (Claire's mother always winked when she said this). "He didn't remember me—I was just one of the Reilly girls—but he asked me out," Nancy said. They dated long-distance until Nancy graduated, and they were married by the end of the summer.

During their dinners together Claire and Nomie concluded that their mother had briefly fallen in love with someone else and that the affair ended badly. Nancy might have tried to put the family back together again, but for their father, the fear of losing her twice would have been intolerable. Through the decades, Nancy and Douglas continued to share a symphony subscription, meeting each other downtown for dinner and a concert five times a year. "It's our tradition," their mother said dismissively when Claire asked if her stepfather minded. "Robin understands." Implicit was the suggestion that Robin wasn't threatened, at least not anymore, by his wife's chaste outings with an old man, even if he had once been her husband.

At the end of their first date, Jay walked Claire to her door and kissed her against the front window of the darkened flower shop, where red Cupid silhouettes hung in the window and bouquets of unpurchased red roses languished. Hers, the lucky ones, were upstairs in a vase.

"Don't hold back with me," he whispered.

She flinched. It seemed he could tell that her mind was going a mile a minute, debating his obvious virtues (odd, ardent, open) and possible flaws (odd, ardent, open), deciding whether to gamble with their future by inviting him upstairs, trying to remember what was on her schedule for the next day.

"I won't," she said finally.

"Good," he said, and went back to kissing her.

She did invite him up, but when they were settled with wine on the couch, they talked about their careers. He told her he envied her for doing what she loved to do. He himself had planned to be a psychotherapist, not a research psychologist. "I chickened out," he said. "I took the easier path."

"You're still a psychologist," Claire said.

"Sure, but I analyze people who don't even know they're being analyzed and who can't benefit from it. Babies."

"Other people will benefit, though. Through your research."

He shook his head. "Yeah, but the babies don't give a shit."

She decided she liked him enough not to let him stay over; besides, she was drowsy from the wine and conversation. She walked him downstairs and made out with him again in the alcove.

"I love that you knew about Orpheus Records," he said. "I love that you had the answer I was looking for." That word again: "love."

"The record store, it's like a shadow," she said, looking at their reflection in the glass of the flower shop, two connected silhouettes. She was a little drunk and not sure what she was saying, but she liked that she wasn't censoring herself—that she was not holding back. "Like a shadow on a plate-glass window."

When Claire was in kindergarten, she had been hospitalized in February with what the doctors briefly feared was meningitis but turned out to be a very bad case of the flu. Her father had slept in a cot by her bed while her mother took care of Nomie at home. One day Claire's teacher visited and emptied a sheaf of construction paper hearts and store-bought valentines onto the bed. The valentines, tucked into translucent envelopes, were as small as playing cards and printed with cheerful bear cubs, bunnies, and cats. The smartest boy in the class had written his ABC's on his valentine. Others had scrawled their names, huge and spidery. Some had the teacher write messages for them: "Get well soon." "We miss you."

"We were terrified," Claire's mother told her later. "I still remember the sight of the doctor walking down the hallway to give us your diagnosis."

The knowledge that her parents had been united in the fear that she might die had tinged the experience with a rosy aura. Claire could still see the swirl of valentines, the reversible Red Riding Hood and Big Bad Wolf hand puppet belonging to her roommate at the hospital, and, when she got home, the cardboard farmhouse she played with on her bed.

Beginning in college and for a few years after, before she started building dollhouses, Claire had done a series of paintings of houses, including the cardboard farmhouse, her childhood home, her father's building on Long Street, and the apartments she lived in during college and after. First she painted the home's interior so that it looked like a dollhouse, cut open to reveal the furniture, the wallpaper, the residents, and their pets.

When the paint dried and she had lived with it for a while, she picked up a brush and began painting the exterior of the house—brick, stucco, trees, and sunlight—on top of its interior. Only an open curtain or a door left ajar revealed glimpses of the lives within. The finished painting reminded Claire of the back of a dollhouse, the outside wall that she and her friends had never paid much attention to when they played. The interior remained hidden, but she knew it was there.

It had been a gimmicky way of painting, one that attracted more attention for her technique than for the end result, but for several years the pitiless obliteration she committed with the second layer of paint had been one of Claire's great satisfactions. She had sold most of the paintings in the series or given them away to friends. In art school, she learned woodworking and started building dollhouses.

Only once had she returned to painting. For their first wedding anniversary, nine months earlier, she had painted the former Orpheus Records storefront for Jay. On the first layer, which Jay had never seen, Claire painted, in sepia tones, her junior high self inside the shop, lurking among the music bins near the window, and the older man and woman sitting side by side behind the counter. On the second layer she painted the flower shop and its owner, daubs of vivid colors and a streak of gray hair.

At first, when Claire gave the painting to Jay—they had been sitting on the living-room floor, tissue paper flying like Christmas morning—he hadn't said a word as his eyes darted across it. "I love it," he finally said, beaming. There were tears in his eyes.

A few months ago, Jay had told Claire that the new phone book had arrived at his office and he had looked up the listing on a whim. Orpheus Records was still there.

4

With no place to go in the morning, no compunction to be productive, no task but, Claire supposed, to grieve, she fell into a routine, a life of sloth and leisure that nonetheless had rhythm, structure. Nomie had moved into the coach house, stealthily, seemingly without discussion—though surely she and Harry must have at least touched on the subject—bringing over from the main house one afternoon a load of maternity clothes warm from the dryer, a bag of beauty products, and some baby books, which she stacked on the coffee table next to Claire's pile of untouched mail. Claire also helped her carry over not one coffeemaker, but two. Around eight every morning, while Claire feigned sleep, Nomie padded downstairs and brewed the coffee, decaf for her, regular for Harry and Claire. Then Harry would come by on his way to work, and Claire, listening to their murmuring voices, would drift in and out of sleep, the cat warming her leg. When she was sure Harry was gone, she would wait for the last drop of fatigue to dissipate from her body before sitting up. The cat would look at her, frank and insistent. *Today?* she seemed to say. *Today you'll bring him back?*

At the loft window, Claire sought out their father, back at his post, eyes glued to a book or the morning paper. Downstairs, baked goods waited on a plate—muffins, cookies, biscotti, slices of dense chocolate cake—selected by Nomie from the trays and boxes people had been bringing. The two of them would spend the morning reading magazines and listening to NPR, wordlessly honoring their mother's ban on daytime TV. Eventually Nomie, who was taking time off from her real estate practice, left to run errands; then Claire would shower, dress, take a nap on the couch, listen to the voice mail message of Jay's heart a few times, and wait for her sister to return with lunch. Claire's appetite had not returned, but she craved the presence of food. No matter how many casseroles and batches of cookies people brought, she still agreed when Nomie offered to go out for Thai food, soup and baguettes from Treasure Island, cappuccinos, or guacamole from the upscale Mexican place around the corner—made fresh, Nomie told her, by a young woman working at a rolling cart.

"Why don't you just have her roll that cart over here every day around noon?" Claire said to Nomie one day. "Save you a trip."

"It's no bother," Nomie said.

"I was *kidding*," Claire said, and then felt guilty for speaking sharply. Nomie had turned away as if she'd been slapped.

It was Nomie, not Claire, who always seemed to be on the verge of tears. Yet her panic over her pregnancy, her days of stockpiling Onesies and booties and hoodies, had passed. Claire wasn't sure if her sister had come to peace with motherhood or retreated into denial. She wondered if Nomie was glad—not that Jay was dead, exactly, but to have a legitimate distraction from shopping and nesting.

When Claire went into the kitchen during the day, she tried not to glance out the window at her father reading in his car. A transistor radio was parked on the dash, and she guessed that classical music—punctuated by the mild, soothing voice of the WFMT announcer introducing the pieces and reading ads for grand pianos and catering companies—filled the interior. Sometimes exhaust puffed from the tailpipe, presumably when Douglas needed a blast of warm air. Sometimes when Claire looked up, he was gone, and her breath would catch for a moment. She would steal glances at the street until he was back, usually within ten or fifteen minutes, eating a hamburger out of a wrapper or sipping coffee. Now and then Nomie brought him sandwiches and Cokes, which he accepted, though he turned down her invitations to come inside to warm up. Most afternoons, their mother stopped by the coach house. She would make a halfhearted attempt at tidying up the dirty dishes and clutter before offering to send over her cleaning lady. Before she came inside, she would join Douglas in his car. Claire would see her talking and smoking, her lit cigarette dangling out of the slightly lowered window.

"What do you think they're talking about?" Claire asked Nomie one time when they both happened to stop by the window and spot their parents in conversation.

"You, I suppose," Nomie said.

"I'm sorry," Claire said instinctively.

"For what?" Nomie's expression was genuinely quizzical.

Sorry that they're worrying about me, when they should be concentrating on you and the baby. Claire shook her head, keeping the thought to herself. Too painful to utter, it would be even more painful for Nomie to feel compelled to rebut.

A friend would drop off dinner in the late afternoon, and when Harry got home, the three of them would eat their charity meal in front of the TV. Nomie had been ordering innocuous movies on Netflix: *Ratatouille, March of the Penguins*; clearly she judged movies starring human beings to be too risky. By the time they were done with dinner, their father would be gone, leaving his daughters under his son-in-law's protection.

"Well, I think I'm going to turn in," Harry would say around ten-thirty, before kissing Nomie good night. There was never any discussion of her going with him. Nomie went up to bed soon after; Claire stayed on the couch through a couple of sitcom reruns, then joined her sister in bed around midnight.

Some nights Claire slept in bursts, trying not to disturb Nomie with her fidgeting. Other nights she slept hard and awoke with a stiff neck and pillow creases on her cheek, as if she hadn't moved all night. She had a monotonous recurring dream that she was being driven endlessly around a dark suburban subdivision by her new friend Britney Spears, who could not find her own house. Sometimes Claire awoke knowing that she had been with Jay in a dream, but she could never remember what had happened.

"Claire, how are you?"

It took Claire a moment to place the voice on the other end of her cell phone, and when she did, she wished she hadn't answered. But the area code on the display, 612, was unfamiliar, and the cat had given her a look when the phone rang.

Answer it, Fang seemed to be saying. *You never know.*

It wasn't Jay on the phone, though; it was his sister.

"Veronica, hi." Claire glared at the cat, who was now furiously licking her back. Claire had successfully avoided Jay's family since the funeral. When one of their names or a Boston number popped up on the display, she let the call go to voice mail. She felt as if Veronica had somehow tricked her. It was the middle of the afternoon, and Nomie was off running errands. Their mother had phoned to say she couldn't come by that day, but the girls should call if they needed anything.

"It's good to hear your voice, Claire." Veronica's own voice was as brittle as glass. "I'm in Minneapolis on business, so I was just thinking of you guys."

"Oh, uh-huh?" Claire didn't understand. She and Jay had never been to Minneapolis together. And were they still "you guys" if one of the guys was dead?

"You know, brick houses, crappy weather, cheese. Reminded me of my trips to Chicago."

So they serve a lot of Wisconsin cheddar at Charlie Trotter's, do they? Claire thought mechanically. Veronica was a consultant based in Boston who advised companies in bankruptcy—a vulture, she called herself without the trace of a smile. When she invited Jay out for expensive, multicourse dinners during her visits to Chicago, her excuse for not including Claire had been that she needed some heart-to-heart advice on men from her older brother. Jay would come home from these evenings maudlin and drunk, clutching his swollen belly and calling his sister a diamond in the rough. It was hard being the only girl in their family, he said, with a mother so different from her.

It was true that Veronica and Pepper were very different: Pepper was nice, and Veronica was a bitch. Claire's opinion about Jay's sister had been set when they called Veronica to tell her about their engagement. "Are you going to go on a crash diet for the wedding?" she had asked Claire (who had never weighed more than 135 pounds, or certainly never more than 140), quickly adding, "Not that you need to. I think it's totally crazy when women do that." But Veronica's shower gift had been a high-tech food scale that wasn't on the Crate&Barrel registry. She was a small, birdlike woman who dated meek, lumbering oafs and bossed them around until they left her in passive-aggressive fashion, like the one who sent his new lover to pick up his things from her apartment.

"How are you doing?" Claire said, wandering into the kitchen area, her father's car a red blob in her peripheral vision. She should be nice. Make an effort. Jay's family were no longer her kin, and she could be done with all of them soon, let the phone calls taper off gradually. Looking down, she saw that she was wearing her Christmas socks, white with red Santas. Jay had put them in her stocking the Christmas before last—socks inside stockings, a little joke. She used to wear the socks only at Christmastime, but Nomie had brought them from the house, and like a crazy old lady, Claire had put them on without registering that they were out of season.

"It's been hard," Veronica said, and paused to let a sigh sink. "I know I don't need to tell you that. I only lost a brother; you lost a husband."

"Well, I don't know . . ." Claire stopped herself from arguing with Veronica that on the relative scale of loss, life-long brother trumped recent spouse. Veronica had a knack for making self-effacing statements that Claire felt compelled to try to outmatch. Once, she had found herself bickering with Veronica about which of them was more short-waisted, and that turned into a debate over who was more farsighted. "She's perversely competitive," Claire had complained once to Jay, who responded that Claire must be as well, if Veronica was able to provoke her so easily.

He stood up for his sister: Claire knew that was supposed to be an admirable trait, but was it, really, if it made his wife feel small and petty?

"How are your parents?" Claire said now to Veronica.

"Oh, you know. Mother can't get through a sentence without breaking down, and Dad just worries about her. I think he's pissed at Jay."

"I'm sorry."

"Yeah, well. You know. Mother's always had a knack for sucking up all the emotion in the room and spraying it back all over everybody." She sighed. "She thinks maybe you blame her, or our family, for Jay's suicide. Since you apparently haven't been returning her calls. I said to her, 'Does everything have to be about you, Mother?'"

A muffling descended on Claire, not of sound but of focus, as if the coach house were closing around her like an enormous white comforter. She let her back slide down the kitchen cupboards until she was sitting on the tile floor, knees in front of her face. She had not heard that word, "suicide," spoken aloud since Dr. Mercer used it in the lobby of his office building the previous week. Beyond that, the phrase "Jay's suicide" sounded oddly familiar. Wings, she thought. There was a fast-food restaurant in her and Jay's neighborhood called Jamie's that sold "suicide wings." Jay used to bring them home sometimes, buffalo wings dripping with hot sauce, his idea of dinner for two. They'd slurp the meat off the bones in front of the TV. She thought of Icarus flying too close to the sun, wings dripping wax.

Blame. Veronica was saying something about blame. Claire replayed in her mind the last sentence she had heard: *Plenty of blame to go around.*

"What?" she said. She wondered if her father, in his own peripheral vision, had watched her sliding out of view. "I've been meaning to call your mother back."

"That'd be nice, Claire."

"And how about Timothy?" she asked, to keep the conversation from returning to the topic of blame. Timothy was

Jay and Veronica's older brother, a seemingly normal, well-adjusted man who kept his distance from the rest of the family. Timothy had come to the funeral with his wife, Gloria; they had left their two young sons in Florida. The couple had stuck to themselves but had been kind to Claire. At the wake, Gloria kept bringing her fresh glasses of water. As for Veronica, she had seethed quietly throughout the wake and funeral, clearly furious at someone—at whom, Claire didn't try to find out.

"Oh, who knows. Gloria doesn't let him call us. Now, about the shrink."

"What shrink?" How did Veronica know she had gone to see a shrink?

"Jay's shrink. Have you talked to her?"

"Oh. She was there. At the . . . wake. Didn't you meet her? She had . . . blond hair." Pretty, Claire thought.

"Yes, I did meet her." Veronica's voice was staccato. "Let me start over." Big sigh. "I set up an appointment to meet with her in a couple weeks, when I'm in town."

"You did?" Claire pressed her fingertips against her temples. "Why?"

"To find out what she knows."

"Knows . . ."

"About what was wrong with Jay. Aren't you curious?"

"I hadn't thought much about it. I mean, about what she might know." And she hadn't, at least not since seeing the therapist at the wake.

"Well, we are."

"She seemed . . . nice. Jay always said nice things about her."

"Well, nice didn't cut it, did it?"

"I'd rather not talk about this right now."

"That's fine, I understand. I'll be in Chicago soon. We can

talk then. Oh, and while I'm in town, there are some things of Jay's that Mother wanted."

"Things?"

"Report cards, high school yearbooks, that sort of thing. She'll tell you when you call. Oh, and maybe you can make a copy of the note for us."

Claire paused. "What note?" She knew, but she wanted to see if Veronica would say it aloud: *Be a dear and take your husband's suicide note over to Kinko's for me, will you?*

"Jay's suicide note. It would be helpful to have a copy."

"Why?" Claire said.

"For when I see the shrink, and . . . well, just to have." For the first time in the conversation, Veronica seemed to falter.

"Didn't you read it already?" Claire said.

"I read it." That was all she said.

There was a scrabbling noise behind Claire. She slid across the tile floor, getting out of the way of whatever it was, in time to see the cat hop from a barstool onto the granite countertop. Fang wove among the vases of dying flowers, nuzzling them until orange pollen streaked her whiskers like shooting stars; then she began nibbling the browning leaf of a wilting calla lily.

Feeling an odd sense of relief, Claire stood up and reached to stroke the cat's back, withdrawing when Fang gave her a mistrustful sidelong glance. She had never cared much for the cat, but it was Jay's cat, and now it was hers—not Veronica's, not his parents', not anyone else's. She found this oddly comforting.

"I'm not sure why everyone read that note," Claire said. "It's mine. It was written to me."

"Huh." The sound Veronica made was not quite a laugh.

"What?" Claire said sharply.

"No, nothing. It's just, like I said, no one blames you, Claire, but that note, it was . . . not the most flattering thing in the world."

"You didn't say that no one blames me." Claire looked out the window at her father, then stiffened and turned away: she had caught him looking at her—hadn't she? But when she looked back, he was facing forward again. Everyone had read the note but Claire, but she couldn't let Veronica know that. "You said—"

"I said there's plenty of blame to go around."

"Right."

"Do you dispute that?" Veronica said.

Fang hopped down from the counter. She moved quickly across the rug and began to heave, her body convulsing: *glug, glug, glug.*

"I don't have time for this," Claire said. "I've got to go. The cat's sick."

"Fang? Is he okay?"

"She," Claire said. "Fang is a she-cat. She'll be fine."

"Of course."

"I'm taking good care of her," Claire added stupidly.

"I'm sure you are," Veronica said. "Cats are easy, aren't they?"

Fuck you, Claire thought.

When she got off the phone, the cat was sniffing at the mess she had made: bits of dried lily leaf and some food. "No," Claire said, nudging Fang away with her foot. "No eating your own barf." Fang disappeared behind the couch.

Claire cleaned up the mess, then paced the room for a moment before flopping down on the couch. She dialed into her voice mail and listened to the beating of Jay's heart, thinking it would calm her, but it only drew her attention to her own heart, thumping away, riled up by Veronica. She hung up halfway through the message.

She glanced at the binder at the bottom of the pile of mail on the coffee table, then looked away. *Not the most flattering thing in the world.*

Claire imagined Dr. Mercer's regular patients dutifully, fearlessly riding the elevator to his eighteenth-floor office and being led on a guided fifty-minute tour of the past, learning insightful lessons and shedding tears at key points along the way, then turning over their checks and returning to their families incrementally healthier and wiser. And here was Claire, lying on her sister's couch in the middle of the day, avoiding her husband's suicide note.

"I've been trying not to rock the boat too much," she said into the open room. The sound of her own voice, small and hollow, surprised her. At first she thought she was talking to Dr. Mercer, but then she realized she was talking to Jay—apologizing for not reading his note yet. "Find a routine. You know how I am."

Tears rolled out of her eyes. She turned onto her side and closed her eyes.

She had always considered herself a creature of habit, a homebody at heart. After she married Jay and moved into the city, rather than feeling sorry for her single self, she had remembered her solitary routines fondly: her weekly walk down Long Street to the hardware store with a list of supplies for work, riding her bike to the farmers' market on Saturday mornings, cooking with the radio on that night, and falling asleep on the couch in the middle of a movie and a glass of wine. She had not traveled much; she felt homesick for her little studio when she was away.

After they married, there were new routines, nothing special, but special to Claire and, she thought—still thought—to Jay. They found a farmers' market in their neighborhood and cooked together on Saturday nights; she would fall asleep with her feet on his lap during the movie that followed. Tuesday afternoons, this past fall, Jay would bring his laptop to the café on Long Street after teaching his seminar and sit by the window. From her studio across the street Claire could look down and watch him work, and at dinnertime he'd come over and quietly watch her finish up for the day. But their Sundays together had been Claire's favorite: they went to the hardware store, then spent the day working on the house. They were both handy—Claire with her dollhouses, Jay with his puppet theater—and once they were homeowners, they started brainstorming and following through on larger projects together. They had built a hutch in a corner of the dining room and a cushioned headboard covered in a shiny dove-gray cotton for their bed. They had salvaged an iron bed from a junk shop, painted it white, and put it in the spare bedroom, which they planned to repaint, from baby blue to green. "A gender-neutral color," Claire had said to Jay, holding up swatches at the store, looking to see if he knew what she meant. He nodded. It was to have been a baby's room one day, but if she were to go home right now, she would find the pale green swatches still taped to a piece of white paper against the baby-blue wall.

"The cat threw up," Claire said, rising when Nomie came home with groceries from Treasure Island. "On the rug. I'm sorry. I tried to clean it up, but I think it left a stain."

Nomie paused on her way to the kitchen. Her mouth opened, then closed, then opened again. "There's something about the cat in the binder," she said before turning away.

"I'm sure she's fine." Claire chattered to hide her hurt. "She throws up all the time. Hair balls. Asthma. It's always been something with that cat."

Nomie hadn't mentioned the binder since Claire asked about the note the night she moved in. Nomie hadn't mentioned Jay or anything having to do with Claire's marriage, her former life—not outright, anyway. Instead she made oblique references: "The next time Harry and I go to your house, we can get your slippers for you," or "Let me know if there's anything you want to talk about, okay?"

"I got a call from Veronica," Claire said, leaning casually against the kitchen counter.

"Oh? What did she want?" Nomie closed the door of the fridge and pulled her hair back into a ponytail. Her belly yawned, pale and distended. Catching Claire's eye, she yanked down her shirt. Harry was the one who had wanted the baby, Claire recalled suddenly. Nomie hadn't felt ready, but he had talked her into it, just as Claire had tried to talk Jay into wanting one.

"I don't know," Claire said. "She's coming to town soon."

"Why?" Nomie said.

Claire paused, then shook her head. She wasn't ready to talk about the therapist yet—Jay's Dr. Hannah. "Business trip, I think."

"Hmm."

"Maybe she'll take me to Charlie Trotter's."

"Oh yeah?" Nomie said, perking up.

"Since Jay . . . she used to take him to nice places like that."

"Oh, right."

Claire had gone too close to the bone. "How are you feeling?" she asked, lamely changing the subject.

"Fine!" Nomie said. "I'm feeling fine. There have been

these . . . kicks." She moved over to the sink and turned on the tap.

"Kicks? Oh, like the baby kicking?"

"Yeah. It's kinda cool." Nomie smiled down at her lathered hands.

"Wow," Claire said. "I bet." But she couldn't bring herself to ask if the baby was kicking right at the moment—to expose herself to evidence of life moving toward them.

Fang threw up twice more that night, nothing but spittle: once while Harry was over and once as Claire was going to bed.

Glug, glug, glug, she heard in the night. Both she and Nomie stirred, but it was Nomie who rose to clean up the mess, as if the cat were their child and she had night duty.

After that, Claire couldn't sleep. *Blame,* Veronica had said, and that made Claire think of her thirty-sixth birthday, three months after their wedding.

"How far back does the blame go?" Jay had asked Claire. "Is some withholding cavewoman responsible?" They were celebrating at a Japanese restaurant, and he waved his fork, a spicy salmon roll impaled on the tines. He had said he felt pretentious using chopsticks, which Claire thought meant he was afraid of looking stupid. The restaurant was on Division Street and very hip: techno music pulsed, the servers looked like hookers, and the floors were a glowing frosted glass that made Claire feel as if she were in an igloo as she sipped her cucumber martini.

"Adam and Eve?" she offered. Jay looked at her fiercely as he chewed. He had been complaining about how his therapist not only attributed his depression to his parents, but occasionally would attribute Jay's parents' behavior to their own childhood wounds. This was not what Claire wanted to be talking about on her birthday, so she pushed: "Fred and Wilma?"

He leaned forward across the table. "I'm thinking of quitting," he said.

"You can't quit me," she said blithely. "We just got married."

"Quitting therapy."

She tilted her head, not quite a nod; it would be wrong to steer him in one direction or the other. "If you don't think it's helping . . ."

"She keeps suggesting I go on medication."

As if on cue, a siren seeped in from the street, or else from the speakers.

"I had this friend in high school," Claire said. "She had all kinds of ups and downs, until they put her on lithium or something, and after that she was fine."

The waitress arrived, her perky chest pointing toward Jay as she poured the dregs of a Sapporo into his glass.

"Lithium is for bipolar disorder," he said when the waitress was gone.

"Right," Claire said quickly. "I meant—" She reached for his hand. She couldn't let him align her with the therapist. "Would you see someone else?"

"I don't know." His expression was part defiance, part hesitance. "Are you worried I'd be complaining to you all the time?" He wiped his mouth with his napkin.

"No," she said with a start. He had a knack for reading her most disloyal thoughts. "But I don't always know what to say. I'm not a professional."

"I just want someone I can be totally honest with," he said.

"Aren't you honest with me?"

He paused. "I was talking about my shrink. Sometimes I find myself not telling her things."

"What things? Why not?"

He shrugged. "I'm not sure she can handle it."

"Handle it? That's her job."

"Or maybe *I* can't. Maybe I'm afraid of unsolicited criticism."

"Unsolicited?"

He smiled. "That came from work. All those 'revise and resubmits.'"

"What do you hide from your therapist?" she persisted.

"I don't know. Stupid stuff. Crazy thoughts. We all have them, right?"

"Sure," she said.

He reached over and nudged her arm. "You never share yours with me."

"Kesslers don't do that." She beamed, mugging for him.

He sighed. She held her breath, expecting a backhanded compliment or, worse, an open complaint, but he began to talk about work. "Writing those articles in the most tedious, restrictive format possible, only to have them rejected in the worst way possible, back to the drawing board—who came up with that term, 'revise and resubmit'?" he said. "The babies are the only joy, but then you have to deal with the mothers."

She exhaled, relieved; she had heard all of this a million times. She launched into her support speech. How frustrating to be a psychologist whose everyday interactions occurred on the surface of life. It had been courageous of him to get a Ph.D. in psychology, she said, with his parents pressuring him to get a law degree.

But he couldn't see past the cowardice, as he saw it, of choosing a research career over his dream of becoming a therapist—a "*real* psychologist. Seeing all these freaked-out parents day in and day out," he continued, "makes me wonder if we should even have kids."

"Happy birthday to me," she muttered, and started to cry.

This was how Claire complained: the feelings built up and the dam burst.

"I'm sorry," he said, getting up to comfort her. "I'm such an ass."

It was one of the oddities of being married to a sensitive man, a would-be therapist: he didn't mind when she cried in restaurants.

In the morning, Claire put out fresh food for the cat, but Fang stayed under the couch. Nomie went home to do laundry while Claire dug through the bag of pet supplies Harry had brought from the house. She rolled some fish-shaped treats under the couch like dice. Chin pressed against the floor, the cat lifted her lids to stare at Claire with filmy eyes, then began to growl in a guttural vibrato.

Claire sank onto the couch and looked out the window. Her father was there, face hidden by the *Tribune*.

"Look at me," she whispered, and waited a moment.

She allowed her eyes to light on the pile of mail from her and Jay's house. It was stacked neatly on the coffee table, a letter opener positioned optimistically beside it, winking as it reflected the overhead track lighting. She could see the binder's blue spine at the bottom of the pile.

She would work through the mail and figure out what to do when she got to the bottom.

The mail was neatly stacked in chronological order, the most recently delivered on top: condolence cards in white and pastel envelopes of various sizes. Claire sliced them open, putting aside a note from Sally: she could not bring herself to read that one yet. She skimmed the others one by one. "So sorry for your loss," "Words cannot describe," "Deepest sympathy at this difficult time," "If there is anything we can do," "It's so hard to know what to say." She was struck by that last phrase, "It's so hard to know what to say," which Hallmark had printed on the inside of a card from some college friends of Jay's, a married couple Claire had met only once, at the wedding, with the improbable names Marilyn and Mack. They had seemed nice enough and surely had managed to express sentiments appropriate to the occasion. And maybe it was true that near strangers would scarcely know what to say to their friend's widow under circumstances such as this; perhaps she should feel lucky that they sent any card at all. Still, it didn't seem . . . *appropriate* for them to call her attention to their discomfort. Claire's mother would disapprove, she was sure.

Suffused with a pleasant indignation, Claire set the condolence cards off to the side and made a mental note to shop for thank-you cards to send in response. The idea of doing something so efficient bolstered her mood. Next in the pile were credit-card offers, appeals for charitable donations, Jay's *Psychology Today*. She started a discard pile on the rug. Apparently Harry had been weeding out the bills and paying them.

A corner of red peeked from beneath the art supply catalog that rested on the binder: a valentine. Claire's heart began to pound.

It's nothing personal, the card might say in Jay's barely legible scrawl. *Please forgive me.*

Or: *Just kidding. I'm on an Alaskan cruise. Back next Friday.*

She picked up the envelope. It was from her friend Beth, who now lived in San Francisco but sent a valentine every year. The card was garish, a heart covered in red glitter. "For

My Beloved," it said on the front, and inside, a long, rhyming sentiment was printed in script. "Dear Claire," Beth had written above the poem, and below it, "I know you have a sweetheart now, but does he send you cards like this???"

Claire's mother and Nomie had divided up the task of spreading the news to Claire's friends. Beth had left a message on Claire's cell phone that seemed both sincere and urgent: "Claire? I heard what happened. I'm so sorry. Give me a call and let me know what I can do." They had met in art classes in college, and Beth had been good about keeping in touch, except when things were going badly in her own life. A few years earlier she had disappeared for a while after her brief, impulsive marriage to a man named Lyle, whom Claire had never met. Claire had returned Beth's call, but Beth hadn't called back. From her own embarrassing experience, Beth might have guessed that what Claire wanted most was privacy.

Claire set the card aside and brushed the glitter from her hands. The binder faced her, blue and blank. She picked it up.

A pair of green eyes stared up at her through the table's glass top.

"Ahh!" she shouted.

The cat. The cat was under the table.

"Fuck, cat!" she yelled, and dropped the binder back on the table.

Fang darted onto the rug and began to heave.

"Why always on the rug?" Claire yelled as she strode toward the roll of paper towels in the kitchen. "You're killing me here."

She managed to catch the vomit in a paper towel.

After the cat slunk away, Claire sat down again and stared at the binder.

"Goddammit," she said, and held her breath.

She turned the cover, expecting to see a neatly typed

suicide note on top, but instead there was a yellow tabbed divider that read "For Claire." Instead of turning the divider to the page beneath it, she flipped through the remaining tabs—"House," "Job," "Family"—until she got to "Fang."

Four typed pages followed.

Fang was a stray that Jay had taken in while he was getting his Ph.D. in Virginia, and she had always been sickly. There was an X-ray film of the cat somewhere in Claire and Jay's house, Fang reproduced in black-and-white shadows, the long, lean leg and rib bones outstretched as if in pursuit of a mouse X-ray. Once, at his place, Jay had held the film up to the light and pointed out the little flying-saucer asthma nodules nestled in the clouds of the cat's lungs. Every morning when he got up, Jay used to scoop the cat up, hold her like a baby at the kitchen table, pry open her mouth, and deftly push a steroid pill down her throat. A bit much, Claire had thought when she met him, but then again, wasn't it a sign that he would make a good father? Lately Claire had been mashing the pills in the cat's food, but the supply was running low, and she hadn't taken any steps to refill it, though there was the number to call, right under the "Prescriptions" subheading.

Under "Emergency care," Jay had written, "If Fang is throwing up and not drinking or eating, or if she has more than one asthma attack in a week, please contact Dr. Rochelle." The pages ended:

Claire, if you decide that you cannot cope with Fang, I understand. Please do your best to find her a good home. This request is of the utmost importance to me, even though I obviously have no say in the matter, and even though I suppose I deserve no say.

The utmost importance to me. That was his academic voice, the voice of his talks and papers.

Relieved to have a distraction, Claire picked up the phone.

"Fang," she said when the receptionist at the veterinary office asked for the cat's name. "Fang Monroe." It had not occurred to Claire until that moment that the cat had a last name.

Claire explained the situation, and soon Dr. Rochelle was on the line. "So Fangy ate a lily leaf?"

Fangy?

"Lilies are toxic to cats," Dr. Rochelle said. "Bring her in, and we'll do a blood test and give her some fluids."

"Toxic?" Claire said.

"They can cause kidney failure." Her tone sounded cheerful, unless it was resigned. "Throw out the flowers and come on over."

"Shit," Claire said after hanging up. She called Nomie at the main house to see if she would help her take Fang to see the vet. Nomie was silent for a moment; then something on her end screeched.

"Jesus Christ, what was that?" Claire's first, nonsensical thought was of the baby.

"The ironing board," Nomie said. "Or do you want to see if Dad wants to take you?"

"You're too busy?"

"He's just going to follow us, anyway."

"You're busy?" Claire said again. It was the first time Nomie had threatened to deny Claire anything since she moved into the coach house—or since ever, possibly. "Nomie, I'm scared. Please."

"All right," Nomie said after a pause. "I'll take you."

"Thanks." Claire hung up the phone quickly, for she had

started to cry. She couldn't lose the cat, not three weeks after losing Jay. Without the stupid fucking cat to take care of— without darling Fangy (she loved the cat and hated her at that moment)—there would be nothing left of their little family, no evidence that they had even existed. And if she lost the cat, too, it would mean there was something seriously wrong with Claire.

Only when she was up close to the vases, pulling out the flowers and stuffing them into a garbage bag, did Claire recognize the rotting smell that had begun to pervade the coach house. The flower petals were crusted and brown, the stems fermented into slimy yellow mush, the water a stagnant soup. Only the white calla lilies, the toxic lilies, despite their brittle leaves, were still hearty.

5

ang, her growl low and guttural, dug her claws along the floor as Claire pulled her out from under the couch, but when she was close to her carrier, she scrambled inside. After strapping the carrier into the back of Nomie's Outback like a car seat, Claire settled in beside the cat, letting Nomie drive. They pulled onto the street, and their father's car fell in behind them.

The wake had been on a Tuesday. Mourners trickled through during the day, mostly Claire's friends and Jay's students. In the evening, a line formed down the hall and out the door, as Jay's colleagues, school administrators, and more of his students filed by the closed casket in an endless, dizzying stream, a macabre version of the receiving line at their wedding.

At the end of the night, Claire waited with her mother and stepfather in their car for a path to clear in the funeral home's packed lot. From the backseat, Claire saw Jay's parents picking their way across the ice, pressed close together, a monstrous bouquet of flowers bobbing in Pepper's arms. Tom's tall, lanky frame and the bow tie peeking out of his overcoat made him look much younger than his age. Jay's parents had been married more than forty years, but thanks to Pepper's great, spilling bouquet and Tom's boyish looks, they looked like the king and queen of the prom.

If only we had known, Jay's mom had said earlier that night, rushing up to Claire at the funeral home, smelling so strongly of baby powder that Claire expected clouds of it to puff up from her when they hugged. *If only any of us had known,* she amended, perhaps because she was a lawyer's wife.

It seemed not too great a thing to ask of one's spouse—to choose to stay alive, Claire thought as she watched Jay's parents approach the car. Pepper and Tom had been able to give that simple gift to each other for all these years.

"Wait!" Pepper cried. "Wait, wait!"

"Oh dear," Claire's mother murmured from the front seat.

Nancy had always been the more sophisticated of the two mothers. For the wedding, Claire had chosen identical corsages for them, off-white roses and baby's breath. Nancy's looked elegant against her sleeveless tan shift, while Pepper's disappeared into the bright floral print of her dress, which had shoulder pads and looked, in the photographs, like a bedspread—Jay's description, expressed mildly and with a wistful smile; after years of therapy, his criticisms of his mother had lost their oomph. Now Claire's mother was superior to Jay's in a deeper way, Claire thought.

As Pepper and Tom approached, Robin lowered the window closest to Claire. "I didn't want to leave these," Pepper said, peeking in. Tom stooped over his wife, so that their faces fit into the open frame. Two lines of dried tears glazed Pepper's cheeks. Her customary coral lipstick, which usually suited her Irish complexion, had looked too bright in the yellow light of the funeral home, and now it was caked in the bite marks on her lower lip. "But there's no point in us taking them to the hotel. Here, please take them, won't you?"

Claire opened her door, and Pepper spilled the flowers into her lap. Immediately the stems wet Claire's legs through her dress. Jay, who had always said his parents were wealthy only because they were cheap, would have appreciated his mother's desire to recycle the flowers. Pepper had left their wedding reception with a couple of centerpieces, Claire remembered, though she and Tom were staying at a hotel then, too.

"Thank you," Claire said, bending to take a dutiful whiff. Despite their grotesque quantity, the flowers smelled like nothing much.

"We'll see you tomorrow," Nancy was saying. They still had the funeral to get through.

"See you then!" Pepper cried shrilly as she and Tom backed away.

"I need to stop at the drugstore," Claire said as the car edged through the alley. Inside the funeral home, she had felt the familiar, uncomfortable fullness in her abdomen.

"What do you need?" Nancy said. "Maybe I have it at home."

"I don't think so."

Expectant silence from the front seat.

"Tampons," Claire said.

"Oh, honey." Her mother sighed. The back of Robin's head was rigid. "You're right. I don't have any of those."

During the drive north Nomie reported that their father seemed to have lost them, but then on Sheridan Road she spotted him again. The vet's office was located on the border between Evanston and Chicago, on a stretch of Howard Street where drug dealers and police cameras carried on a dreary, decades-old standoff. Their father parked several spaces behind them and did not get out of the car.

After buzzing Claire and Nomie into the clinic, the receptionist stared at them, her doughy face blank, but she brightened when Claire set the cage on the counter. "Fang!" she cried, peering between the crosshatched cage bars. "Were you a bad girl? Did you eat a lily?"

"I didn't know they were toxic," Claire said. "We had a lot of flowers around."

"So you're Jay's wife?" A ceramic pin of a dozing gray cat was pinned to the woman's cornflower-blue smock.

"Uh-huh," Claire said.

"How's he doing?"

"Um . . ." Claire found herself savoring the myriad ways she could horrify this stranger.

As if she had read Claire's mind, Nomie edged up to the counter. "Actually, Jay passed away recently."

An invisible hand seemed to squash the dough-face flat. "Oh," the woman said, hand fluttering to her sunken chin. "I'm so sorry. I'll just get Dr. Rochelle." She rolled backward in her chair, and as she rose, her long skirt caught in one of the casters. She tottered briefly, then tugged herself free and disappeared into the back of the office.

"I hope that was okay," Nomie said in a hushed voice.

Claire nodded, unable to look at her. They retreated to the plastic chairs along the plate-glass window. Nomie peered out at the street while Claire stared inside the carrier resting on her lap. The cat looked glum, lying flat against the plastic floor of her tiny cell. "You're okay," Claire whispered. "You're okay, Fangy."

A small, pretty young Indian woman in a lab coat bustled through the door. Claire stepped forward and smiled. "I'm

Dr. Rochelle," the woman said, her expression grave as she extended her hand. "Martha told me about your loss. I'm so sorry."

It occurred to Claire that Rochelle was probably the vet's first name rather than her last. This was the type of informality vets engaged in, eliminating their own last names but bequeathing surnames to pets—Fang Monroe, for God's sake. But whether first or last, Rochelle seemed too romantic a name for the attractive, purposeful young woman who was ushering them into the exam room.

"Thank you," Claire said.

"Jay was such a conscientious owner," the vet said once they were in the small wood-paneled exam room. A waist-high table gleamed with a patina of claw and toenail scratches. The room's sole window, covered with black bars, looked onto an alley.

Owner? The doctor was talking about the cat, Claire realized, dangling in its little tree house at the end of her arm. She supposed it should be reassuring for her to meet these people who had known and liked Jay. Instead it seemed like a sign of deceit, a life he had hidden from her. How much did the vet know about Jay, anyway? Had they talked about anything in this little room besides the cat? Maybe he had been going around town treating everyone like a therapist, complaining about his marriage, Claire's failings as a wife.

"Well, he loved Fang," Claire said. "That's for sure."

Nomie sucked in her breath, but if Dr. Rochelle heard the stress on the word "Fang," her smooth smile didn't betray her.

"She's a good cat," the vet said. "She's had her share of health problems, but she's always pulled through."

"What life is she on? Seven? Eight?"

The doctor didn't respond as she gingerly pulled the puddle of cat out of the box and onto the examination table.

"You said lilies were toxic," Claire said, trying to recover from her lame joke.

"Yes, they are."

"Jay never told me," Claire said. "I'm not a cat person myself."

"Maybe he didn't know." Fang looked miserable, but acquiesced without growling as Dr. Rochelle turned her ears and eyelids inside out. "No signs of jaundice," the vet said. "We'll run some tests. If you don't mind my asking, how was she doing before she ate the lily?"

"Before . . . ?" Claire said.

"Since your husband passed away, I mean."

"Oh. Well, mostly she just sleeps. But that's not really unusual. I mean . . . you know . . . cats!"

"She didn't seem anxious?"

"Anxious?" Claire looked at Nomie, who only raised her eyebrows.

Dr. Rochelle's gaze was level, unamused.

"Well, um," Claire stammered, "she does this thing where she runs to the door when the bell rings." Claire didn't mention that she and the cat did this thing together. A term she had heard Jay use in reference to babies popped into her mind: parallel play.

The doctor nodded gravely. "She's waiting for Jay to come home."

"Yes," Claire said.

"She feels left behind. Depressed, I'd say."

"Yes." Claire let her eyes well.

"Her immune system might have been compromised by the trauma."

"The trauma," Claire echoed, rolling the word over her tongue, through her mind. She had liked Dr. Mercer's word better: "catastrophe." Or even Veronica's phrase, "Jay's suicide," as if it were something he owned, like the cat. A *cat-astrophe*, Claire thought, but refrained from saying.

"It's hard on pets when their owners disappear," Dr. Rochelle continued. "Obviously there's no way to let them know what's going on."

"Like children," Nomie said, reddening. "Like, they don't understand where . . . people go. When they go away."

Wait a second. Were they suggesting that Fang's trauma not only equaled Claire's, but perhaps surpassed it, by virtue of the cat's inability to communicate? *Jay is dead!* Claire imagined herself shouting at the cat. *He's not coming back! He offed himself!*

"Object permanence," she said. They stared at her, and Claire felt her own face flush. "That's what Jay studied in his lab. He would have babies watch something disappear and, um, see whether they seemed surprised, which would indicate that they, um . . ." Even Fang was looking up at her with an expression that seemed to say, *Will you get on with it already?* "That they, um, noticed when the thing went away in a way that it . . . shouldn't have." Jay's mangled body was probably rolling over in its casket right about now, but God help Claire, she needed to put a stop to this little coffee klatch on children, pets, and grief.

"Exactly," Dr. Rochelle said, as if Claire had made perfect sense. "So Fang's entire system is under stress right now. Assuming she pulls through this okay, I recommend that we explore some alternatives to help her through this difficult time. Changes to her diet, acupuncture, and the like."

"Assuming she pulls through? Meaning she might not?"

"Well, as I said, lilies are toxic." The doctor's expression was quizzical.

"I didn't know that, like I said." Claire's hands were trembling; she stuffed them into her coat pockets. "We don't normally have a lot of flowers around. The lilies were sent after Jay's funeral. Did I mention that he killed himself, by the way?"

The outburst had its intended effect: the vet was stricken for a moment, possibly ashamed. Then she ruined the moment by recovering. "I hope you're getting the help you need," she said, reaching to touch Claire's arm.

"It's hard to know what that might be."

"Well . . . I'm sure there are people to turn to. Support groups." With that, and a pat on the wrist, Dr. Rochelle sent the sisters out front to wait while she injected fluids and drew blood—"So she won't associate you with pain." But that would make us even, Claire thought. Within ten minutes Nomie had paid the bill and they were on their way home, the carrier buckled in, their father trailing behind.

Her mother had offered to run into Walgreens as they drove home from the wake, but Claire didn't want to be alone in the car with Robin. She felt guilty and embarrassed that through no fault of his own, he had ended up with a stepdaughter in such a fucked-up situation. So she went into the store herself, feeling conspicuous in her black outfit, hoping she might pass for a classical musician on her way home from a concert rather than a mourner.

She stood in the feminine hygiene aisle, dazed by the pink and purple boxes emblazoned with words like "pearls" and "satin." The organic tampons she usually bought at Whole Foods came in a cardboard box decorated with an amateurish sketch of sunflowers.

"Hey," a familiar voice said.

She turned. Her friend Frank stood in front of her, holding a twelve-pack of Miller High Life. He had shown up near the end of the wake, looking sharp in a suit, but in the past twenty minutes his shirt had gotten rumpled, his tie had gone missing, and he had put on a long wool coat with a frayed collar. Up close, she saw some whiskers he had missed in recent shaves, and his impossible, dun-colored hair was growing in all directions, so that she wasn't sure whether he needed a haircut or had just gotten a bad one. Yet seeing him gave her a jolt, just as it had when she saw him in the receiving line. He had hugged her longer than anyone and whispered in her ear simply, "I'm sorry."

"Hey," she said now. "Thanks for coming tonight."

"No problem," he said. "Whatcha doin'?"

She motioned at the wall of tampons.

"Oh," he said, grimacing. He was squeamish about certain things related to women: periods, affection, expectations. "You here by yourself?"

For a split second she tried to remember if Jay had brought her here, if he might be in another aisle or outside in the car.

"Hey," Frank said, for she was crying now.

She moved toward him. He set down his beer and held her. "Hey," he said. "Hey there." He was a small man, thin, and only slightly taller than she was, but he managed to envelop her, just as he had at the wake. She felt herself slipping, and then they were sitting on the floor.

"What do you want to do?" he said, cradling her in his lap. "Where do you want to go?"

"My parents are waiting for me outside."

She felt him tense up. "You're wet," he said.

"I'm not bleeding, you idiot. That's from the flowers. Jay's mother put all the fucking flowers in my lap. Oh my God!" Her voice caught, and she started to wail, an ugly animal sound. She grasped at him. "Oh my God . . ."

"Shh . . ."

"Don't shush me!"

"Sorry."

"And don't say 'Sorry'!"

"Sorry."

"Frankie," she sobbed.

"I'm here, sweetie. Let it out."

"Are you okay?" said a male voice somewhere above them. "Do you need anything?"

"We're fine," Frank said. "Just a little privacy."

Claire let Frank rock her until the sobs, like a summer thunderstorm, moved on as quickly as they had descended.

"I thought maybe I was pregnant," she said, her voice muffled in his shirt.

He sighed and shifted. "Jesus."

"I was hoping I was pregnant," she whispered.

"Claire—"

She grabbed him tighter. "Don't say it."

"I'm not saying anything."

"Frank, don't leave me!"

"I'm not going anywhere," he said.

"I need a drink."

"That can be arranged. Daiquiris?"

She managed to reward him with a laugh. To his embarrassment, that was what she used to drink when they went out. In college it had been amaretto stone sours, but they didn't seem to serve those outside of Big Ten bars, so after graduation she drank daiquiris for a long time. She and Frank had met freshman year in the dorms. She and her girlfriends from the fourth floor would take their wine coolers down to the first floor to watch movies with Frank and the other stoner engineers. Amid the crushes that developed, Claire fell for Frank, who fell for a pretty born-again Christian girl named Kristin who wouldn't have anything to do with him.

Six years later, when they were long settled into friendship and both living in Chicago, Frank decided he was in love with Claire after seeing a brief, unimportant boyfriend kiss her ear at a party. "I thought to myself, I want to kiss that ear," he told her the next time they were out at a bar together. "How did I never notice what sexy ears you have?" For half an hour he tried to wheedle Claire into letting him kiss her ear. Annoyed but strangely flattered, Claire, who hadn't had a sexual thought about Frank in years, finally relented. During the two miserable weeks of dating that followed, they behaved like an unhappily married couple: Frank's binge drinking had hardened into habit, and Claire found herself acting clingy and shrill. Terrible, they agreed, and went back to being friends, but with a newfound knowledge of each other as sexual creatures that, though useless and mildly frustrating, provided a certain familiar comfort.

But Frank hadn't liked Jay. "A little moody, no?" he'd said after they met at a party.

Their calls and e-mails had tapered off after that. "You'll always be the one who got away," Claire said, clinking glasses with Frank the last time the two of them went out, right after she and Jay got engaged. "You, too, kiddo," Frank had said. She hadn't seen him since.

He was here now, though, which was more than she could say for her supposed soul mate.

"My parents . . . ," she snuffled into his coat.

"I can talk to them. I'll tell them that I'll take care of you tonight." He said this with pride and a trace of defiance. "I'll take you out for a nice meal. I bet you're hungry."

"I want you to take me out." She liked the general idea of being with Frank, but then she thought about what that would mean in specific terms: crying in a restaurant, too much drinking in one or more dive bars, his cramped apartment smelling just like his dorm room all those years ago, like bong water and dirty laundry. And then when they woke up sober, he might be distant and gruff with her, as he was those weeks when they dated. Better for her to be tucked into clean sheets in her mother and stepfather's guest bedroom, no smell but fabric softener, no sound but the heat whirring through the vents at regular intervals.

"Let's go," he said.

"Frank," she whispered.

"What, hon?"

"It's so embarrassing." She looked up at him. "All those people tonight, they seemed so horrified. Like they didn't know me."

"Shh," he said. "You didn't do anything." There was sadness and a hint of fear in his eyes.

"What if I did?" She was still whispering. "Or didn't? What if I didn't do what I should have?"

"You didn't not do anything, Claire. There's nothing you could have done that . . ."

She wiped her eyes. "You don't know that."

"I could kill him," he muttered.

"You're too late."

"That asshole. Always beating me to the punch."

They left Walgreens together, Frank swinging the twelve-pack and the plastic bag containing the box of tampons Claire had blindly grabbed, which he had paid for, commenting, "Jeez, six ninety-nine for cotton and string?"

"Shit," Claire said, stopping in her tracks. She had just spotted her father parked in the space next to Robin and her mother.

"What?" Frank said.

"Nothing. Just—family. Everywhere." She almost approached her father's car to find out if there was something he wanted, but he wasn't looking at her, and that made her hesitate. Maybe he had told her mother he would come back to the house with them for coffee.

"I gotta go home," she said. "Take a rain check?"

Frank nodded, unsurprised: that was how they always had been with each other, making grand plans and then never following through. "I'll call you soon," he said. He handed her the plastic bag and pecked her on the cheek. She breathed in the smell of Old Spice and cigarettes.

"Was that your friend, um . . . Ted?" Nancy asked when Claire got back into the car, the flowers piled on the seat beside her.

"Frank. We ran into each other. Sorry." To her mother, Frank had just been one of Claire's college friends.

"Is he going to a party?" her mother asked.

"A party? Oh. The beer? No, he's going home, I think."

"Huh," Nancy said.

Robin swung the car back onto the street.

"Your father's behind us," Nancy said.

"I know," Claire said.

"What's he doing?"

"Dunno. I thought maybe you knew."

"We don't."

When Claire had arrived at the funeral parlor with her mother and Robin, her father had been the only family member there, pacing in a gray suit, his hair slightly damp, smelling strongly of soap. He squeezed her so hard that she thought he might break one of her ribs, then edged away. As the mourners started to arrive, Claire lost track of him. "Where's your father?" her mother said when a receiving line was forming. Nomie went to find him, and when they returned, Claire's parents wordlessly flanked her. She remembered standing with her father just outside the church on her wedding day, how he crooked his arm for her, also in silence, his expression sober as he prepared to escort her into her new life.

"So what do we think?" Harry stood at the kitchen counter looking from Nomie to Claire as he chomped on one of the pakoras someone had brought from Devon Avenue, his pink-and-green-striped tie tossed over the shoulder of his button-down shirt. "What's the verdict for poor old Fang?"

Nomie was stretched out on her yoga mat in front of the TV, watching a DVD for pregnant women. She had just debriefed him on their visit to Dr. Rochelle, leaving out the fact that the vet bill was $375 and that she had paid it with no protest from Claire.

Fang had retreated under the couch as soon as they got home, and Claire had been sitting on the couch ever since, the better to check on the cat. Dr. Rochelle had somehow inserted a pouch of fluid at the back of Fang's head, and beads of water were trickling down her back, Claire saw when she peered under the couch, which she did every ten or fifteen minutes. Fang would look at Claire piteously, then close her eyes.

"She looks miserable," Claire said. "We need to stay on top of this."

"I think she'll be okay," Nomie said. She was lying with her knees bent, head turned toward the muted TV, watching but not following along with the three women on the screen. They were in various stages of pregnancy: barely showing, convex, and about to pop. The most pregnant woman moved fluidly, perfectly synchronized with the others, without any awkwardness or apparent discomfort.

"I thought maybe the vet was trying to prepare us," Claire persisted.

"Prepare us for what?" Harry said.

She threw up her hands, exasperated. He knew what she meant.

"Maybe we should talk about how far we're willing to go down that road," Harry said. "Like, you said the vet mentioned acupuncture. What do we think about that?"

"We'll do everything we can for Fang," Nomie said. "Right, Harry?"

"Sure." He put his dish in the sink and sat down in the easy chair with a Corona. "Nothing but the best for old Fang."

"They should call it *cat*upuncture," Claire said.

"Maybe they'll give her a CAT scan," Harry said.

They grinned at each other. Claire missed humor. She missed Jay groaning at her corny jokes. "The vet's on Howard Street," she said. "So I'd worry about where they get their needles."

Harry looked at her blankly.

"For the catupuncture," she said.

"Oh yeah, right. Um, maybe they have a needle exchange program. For cats."

It didn't really make sense, but Claire smiled encouragingly. She used to feel sorry for Nomie, married to a man like Harry—solid and predictable, mystified by his wife's emotions and moods, and therefore, Claire believed, incapable of fully understanding her. But Harry would never leave Nomie.

"Are you going to take that staging assignment, Claire?" Harry said. He pushed the pile of opened mail on the coffee table, clearing a space for his feet. The binder, which Claire had put back at the bottom, poked out.

"What staging assignment?"

"Oh," Nomie said. She had raised her legs for a moment,

following the women on the screen, but lowered them again as she turned to Claire. "I was going to tell you. Remember that condo you were staging in south Evanston?"

"Yeah." Claire had arranged furniture at the model home on Valentine's Day. She had planned to come back the next day to finish the job.

"The building's about to go on the market. Rebecca was wondering if you want to take care of the finishing touches this weekend, or if she should."

"Oh," Claire said. "I was assuming she already took care of it."

"It might be good to get back to work," Harry said.

"Rebecca said they can manage if you don't want to," Nomie said.

They were both staring at her. Clearly this was a test they had devised when they were alone. A recovery test. She could already hear a buzzer signaling that she had answered wrong.

"Do you think Fang will be okay by then?" Claire said.

"If not, you could always cancel," said Nomie.

"Oh." So it would cost her nothing, at the moment, to please them by saying yes. "Okay. Why not?"

"Great!" Harry beamed and took a celebratory pull at his beer.

With that resolved, they all faced the silent television and fell into a stupor.

The women on the screen were like another species, Claire thought. They were pregnant and fit, industrious and passionate enough about good prenatal health that they had felt compelled to share their knowledge with other women. And they were also wearing very natural-looking makeup, or else they looked beautiful without any makeup at all.

Those women were at the top of the pyramid, Claire thought dreamily, and below them was Nomie. Lazy and neurotic, Claire's sister had nonetheless found a good man and was starting a family with him. She was not following along with the DVD, but at least she had good intentions.

Claire was on the bottom of the pyramid. Not only was she not pregnant, but she had no hope of getting pregnant, because her husband was dead. And not only was her husband dead, but he had killed himself. And not only had he killed himself, but he had jumped out a window on Valentine's Day. And instead of trying to work through her grief with therapy or yoga, Claire was sitting on a couch, breathing shallowly, fretting about the health of her dead husband's cat, and planning to skip a day of work because it sounded exhausting.

She heard herself snicker. Harry glanced at her, and she looked away.

Nomie suddenly sat up, cross-legged, and faced the TV with palms pressed together.

"Namaste," Claire said too loud, so that it sounded sarcastic, which she supposed, in retrospect, had been her intention.

It was a point in her favor, wasn't it, that she had wanted to get pregnant? Proof that after almost two years of marriage, she was committed to Jay. Or did it mean—did he think it meant—that she needed a distraction from him and his needs?

They had reached a deal before Christmas: Claire would go off the Pill, but they would not *try* to get pregnant; if it happened, it happened.

"I'm going to have to psych myself into this," Jay said the night they negotiated. They were curled on their sides, facing each other.

"Fatherhood?" she asked.

"Fatherhood," he said. "You make it sound like a Paul Reiser book."

"Who's Paul Reiser?"

"Who's Paul Reiser?" he said, incredulous.

"Yeah, who's Paul Reiser. Are you going to repeat everything I say?"

"Say I everything repeat to going you are?"

"But backward?"

"Backward but?"

She squeezed his ass. "It doesn't seem backward to me. It seems perfectly forward to me."

"*You're* perfectly forward," he said, pulling her close.

In the days between Valentine's Day and the wake, the possibility that she could be pregnant—*conceivably, get it?* she said to Jay in her mind—flickered before her. When Nomie delivered her datebook to her at their mother's house, Claire counted back. They had had sex for the last time six days before his death, after a Friday night date. It had been tender but not extraordinary, nothing to brand it in her mind, in retrospect, as the Last Time. What about in the weeks before that? She couldn't remember.

The morning of the wake, while putting on her first black dress, she felt feverish and wondered whether it was a sign of something other than grief and stage fright. But in the receiving line she gave up hope. One of Jay's colleagues, a professor named Alan who studied societal responses to physical handicaps, and his wife, a bovine-lidded, wide-hipped massage therapist named Sherry, had come up to Claire with odd half smiles on their faces—people couldn't seem to stop themselves from smiling, she had noticed. Alan and Sherry had been at Sally and Bart's party but had left by the time Jay disappeared: Claire remembered saying goodbye to them. They were probably disappointed that they had left early. Perhaps they were lying to people that they had been there when it happened, the way people sometimes exaggerated their ties to 9/11.

"You know, if you need someone to talk to, there are support groups out there, for . . . survivors," Alan said to Claire. His final word hung in the air between them for a moment, suspended in the eye contact that he stubbornly refused to break and the slight upward tilt that persisted in the corner of his mouth. He was proud of himself for saying this to Claire's face, she saw, rather than pitter-pattering around her the way others were doing. That was when Claire felt it: the familiar monthly sensation, a subtle, spreading warmth.

"What about the survivors of bad manners?" Claire said. "Do you know of a support group for them?"

Her mother rested a tempering hand on her arm. "The So-and-so's are here," she said. It would have sounded like an excuse to Alan and Sherry, but the So-and-so's were real people, the Soameses, neighbors from Claire's childhood. The Soameses, whose three daughters had been the best babysitters in the neighborhood, still signed "the So-and-so's" on their Christmas cards, Claire's mother had told her.

"Hi, Mrs. So-and-so, hi, Mr. So-and-so," Claire said to the couple, who looked as if they had shrunken and faded in the decades since her childhood. The So-and-so's were closer in age to Claire's father than to her mother, and they were old now, too, settled and serene; Claire had missed their entire middle age. They had moved to Deerfield, and their daughters, now middle-aged themselves, had their own families. Claire's favorite had been Trixie, who in those days had long brown hair parted down the middle. She brought over her Joni Mitchell albums when she babysat and let Claire and Nomie make forts out of the sofa cushions. How strange it must have been for Trixie to hear the news from her parents about the well-mannered, dollhouse-obsessed little girl she used to care for.

"Thanks for coming," Claire said. "It means a lot to me." And it did.

They kissed her on the cheek, both of them. Neither Claire nor her mother bothered to introduce Alan, whose eyebrows were raised expectantly, or Sherry, who blinked rapidly at the ceiling as if trying to pick up a background melody.

"Coming to bed?" Nomie said, rising from the sofa. Harry had left a while earlier, and Nomie had sat up with Claire watching sitcoms.

"I think I'll sleep here tonight," Claire said. The cat was still under the couch, and she wanted to stay nearby.

"Oh," Nomie said, hovering uncertainly above her.

"You could go home tonight, if you want."

"Really?" Nomie cocked her head.

"Sure."

"Maybe I will. If you don't mind."

"I don't mind."

"You can call if you need us."

"Of course."

"I'll be back in the morning."

"I know."

After Nomie left, there was no sound. Their father had driven away hours ago. Claire tried in vain to hear the cat breathing. Fang used to sleep under the bed, and some mornings they could hear her softly snoring.

Claire pulled the coffee table to the outskirts of the room. She brought a pillow and comforter down from the sleeping loft, found her phone, and made a bed for herself on the rug.

She stared under the sofa at Fang. The cat gazed out at her, glassy-eyed; then her lids lowered. Claire closed her own eyes for a moment, then opened them and found the cat looking at her. She dozed off for a bit, and when she awoke, Fang was still watching her.

Alan had e-mailed Claire about the support group he mentioned at the wake. It met on Thursday nights in the basement of an Episcopal church not far from campus. "You might see if it's helpful," he wrote. "And let me know if you would like to meet for lunch sometime. There might be some things I could tell you about Jay." *Jay thought you were an asshole,* Claire was tempted to reply. Jay called Alan a publicity hound with shallow, half-baked ideas. As proof, Jay periodically reminded Claire of the title of Alan's dissertation: "Paging Dr. Freud, Paging Dr. Phil: The Dawn of Public Psychotherapy and Censure." But she filed away the invitation in her mind, and she marked the meetings in her appointment book for the next two months in secret code: "SG, 7:30."

Claire dialed into her voice mail and listened to Jay's heart. *SHWEE-ohh, SHWEE-ohh, SHWEE-ohh.* She felt her own heartbeat settle into a slow, easy pace.

"I think your cat tried to kill herself," she murmured. "Did you know lilies are toxic to cats? I didn't know that. You should have told me."

The cat was watching her again, unblinking.

"Though maybe it's in the binder. Maybe I missed that part."

Claire stared back at the cat.

"I haven't read it yet. The note. But I will. I promise. If the cat gets better, I'll read it."

She saved the message and turned off the phone.

"I think she'll get better," she said. "I think I can save her."

6

Claire's car crunched into a snow-packed space in front of the courtyard apartment building. Reaching for the door handle, she saw her father through their car windows. Their eyes met briefly before he glided backward, parking in the space behind her. She got out, slinging her bag over one shoulder, and minced toward him across an ice patch.

He rolled down the window and smiled. "Hi, honey."

"Hi, Dad. How are you?"

"Okay. How are you?"

"I'm fine." Their chitchat felt as brittle as icicles in the thin, cold air. "I'm going to be working here all day on a model home. Finishing up a job I started . . . before. So you don't have to stay."

"Well . . ." He looked at his hand, flexed on the steering wheel. "We'll see."

"Please, Dad." She swallowed at the lump in her throat. "Take the day off."

He nodded. "Okay. I'll go."

She moved away, his window slid up, and he was gone by the time she reached the sidewalk. She forced herself not to look back.

Claire hadn't been at the model home since Valentine's Day, a day she had thought about only glancingly, like looking at the sun. Since then the developer appeared to have fallen on hard times. The lawn sign advertised condos starting at $227,000, down from $257,000 in February. It was an old, three-story brick building in a safe, quiet treelined neighborhood by the lake, with good schools and a Starbucks, but the real estate market was crashing, and the country might or might not be in a recession, and a few blocks away, brand-new condo buildings with parking lots and gyms were rising over the car dealerships and Oriental-rug shops. The world was stumbling along without Claire's attention. The economy, the war, the election: she heard about these things out of the corner of her ear, as her father used to say, when Nomie turned on NPR or when the news came on TV.

For two days Claire had kept a vigil above Fang, who stayed hidden beneath the couch. She would have continued to sleep on the floor, but after a night in her conjugal bed, Nomie had returned to the coach house. Claire felt obligated to join her sister in the loft at night, but she had trouble sleeping, and she tiptoed downstairs two or three times a night to check on Fang. She would stare under the couch, trying to figure out if the cat was alive. If the cat's eyes were closed, Claire would say, "Hey," and Fang would slowly lift her lids and give her a withering look.

But that morning, Claire rose early, in time to see Fang emerge nonchalantly from her cave, yawning and stretching. She flopped down on the carpet and allowed Claire to stroke her belly for a moment before nipping her fingers. While Claire watched, barely breathing, the cat sauntered over to her food bowl in the kitchen, sniffed, and took a few desultory bites. When she was done, she settled in the empty gift basket by the window, bathed herself, and went to sleep.

The realization that she could be alone on this day if she wanted to, completely alone, had startled Claire as she stood at the kitchen counter, where the vases of dying flowers used to be, stirring sugar into her coffee and watching Fang settle into sleep. Nomie was behind her at the sink, doing dishes, and Claire had tried to stay very still when the thought came to her, trying to hide the jolt it gave her. Today she would be alone. She would bring the binder to the model home, and she would get rid of her father. She would read Jay's note in privacy, with no fear of Nomie and Harry walking in, no surprise visits from friends "just checking in." No more excuses, she told herself. It was time.

Hammering had echoed through the apartment's courtyard in February, but now the workmen were gone, and the building's windows faced Claire with dead eyes. Sunporches jutted from the units, windows wrapping around empty rooms. Only the model home, a second-floor unit at the northern tip of the U, looked occupied; the rounded back of an easy chair that Claire had positioned was visible against the glass. Gretchen, the real estate agent working for the developer, had told Claire on the phone that only a few of the units had sold, and none were occupied. "We need a model home by spring. Everyone's got their fingers crossed that people will come out when the weather turns, if it ever does." Lowering her voice, she added, "Be grateful they paid you and Rebecca ahead of time. I think they've run out of money."

Inside the vestibule, Claire rescued the keys from the lockbox. The stairs were covered in paper, stained with footprints from work boots. The paper rattled as she jogged up.

She took her shoes off in the hallway and let herself in.

The radiators were hissing inside the warm apartment, which smelled like sawdust, the plastic shower curtain Claire had hung, and vanilla, though she saw that the bottle of vanilla extract she had left open on the kitchen counter (her mother's trick when there wasn't time to bake chocolate-chip cookies before a showing) had evaporated. Silly to have opened it so early—but then, she remembered, she hadn't known she would be away so long.

The police had forced Claire to remember the time she had spent with Jay that day—in the morning, and then at the party that night—but she had allowed herself to overlook the time they spent apart. Jay had taught a class, worked in his office, and stopped by the lab. Others had documented these facts, and no unusual behavior had been noted, though a few people said he might have seemed subdued. Claire herself had been alone at the model home until about three, arranging furniture. Then she had gone back to her studio, intending to work into the night and skip the party, but at the last minute, missing him, had decided to surprise him. She would have come back to the model home on the fifteenth to finish the job—to make the bed, hang pictures, and arrange vases—but instead she had walked into a very different life.

She moved through the rooms. The condo was as she left it: furniture placed, framed posters leaning against walls, boxes of decorations and books waiting to be opened. Someone, probably Gretchen, had been watering the plants, but there was a film of dust on the countertops and bookcases. It was a small two-bedroom, painted with the inoffensive colors Claire had selected—the bedrooms sage green, the bathroom lavender, the rest of it taupe. Their ironing board, hers and Jay's—a deluxe model, one of the few items he had requested for their gift registry—leaned against a wall in the master bedroom. The mattress on the queen-size bed was bare. The floors were polyurethaned blond hardwood, and the dusty countertops were granite; the refrigerator had stainless steel doors, and there were six burners on the stove, as if the inhabitants of such a small apartment might someday find themselves cooking six things at once.

In the sunroom, Claire looked up and down the street. Her father was gone. She was alone.

She took the binder out of her bag and placed it on the coffee table next to a roll of paper towels and a bottle of Windex. She sat down on the couch and looked at the blank blue cover.

She jumped up and pulled the tape off a sealed cardboard box.

In it she found books. Rebecca rented them by the yard from a local antiquarian bookstore that did a side business catering to interior designers and set decorators. For this home she had ordered a mix of mysteries, contemporary novels, biographies, and travel guides to conventional tourist destinations such as France, Italy, and Hawaii—books chosen to suggest to buyers that the home's future occupants would lead a leisurely life of literary escapism and international travel. Claire removed the plastic dust jacket from a coffee-table book on Tuscany and set it on the table underneath the binder, then started filling the shelves on either side of the fireplace with books.

Claire had started working for Rebecca several years earlier; they'd been introduced by Claire's mother. Rebecca had started her home-staging business to appease her husband after she had filled up most of their four-car garage with furniture and knickknacks that she didn't have room for in their house in Winnetka. "I quickly realized that I like the shopping part, and I like the meeting-with-clients part, but I don't like the pushing-the-couch-from-one-place-to-another part,"

Rebecca explained when Claire came for her job interview. Claire was hired on the spot after mentioning that Rebecca's living room, with its minimalist decor and cubist painting above the fireplace, reminded her of her favorite Thorne miniature room at the Art Institute: *California Hallway, c. 1940.* "I love the Thorne rooms!" Rebecca said. "I knew we would get along when your mother told me you built dollhouses. You know, all the best designers were obsessed with dollhouses when they were little, even the boys. *Especially* the boys."

In January, Claire had met Rebecca in her temperature-controlled garage to talk about the Evanston model home. As they moved through the narrow walkways between the carefully organized furniture, art, bins of bedding, and appliances, Rebecca gave Claire her profile of the type of people she imagined would buy the condo: "The wife is pregnant and desperate to get out of Wrigleyville, and the husband is afraid he'll become his father when he moves to Evanston, but down deep that's what he really wants." She instructed Claire to decorate in the style she referred to as Pottery Barn Blah, as opposed to North Shore Chintzy or Gold Coast Gaudy. Together they had picked out a bulky sofa with a rust-red canvas cover, framed posters of vintage Cinzano ads, mahogany cabinets and bookcases, and velvet drapes in neutral tones.

Rebecca had not come to the wake or the funeral. Remembering this, Claire stiffened, as if she herself had committed some rude offense that tactful Rebecca had chosen to ignore. Rebecca had sent flowers, though, and a sympathy card. "I'm so sorry. We'll talk when you're feeling better," it read, as if she had heard that Claire had a bad cold.

Now Claire opened another box: her faux-fur throw! She dragged the box into the bedroom, glad to have an excuse to be in a different room from the binder.

Rebecca had taught Claire that it was possible to cut corners when staging. A house was more attractive with minimal electronics, as long as there was a flat-screen TV on a wall to mesmerize male buyers. Kitchen counters should be kept clear of fancy appliances. The cabinets and fridge could stay empty, and dressers and closets could, too, aside from a neat stack of fresh white towels in the linen closet.

Rebecca had also taught Claire to make a bed without any sheets, but that was where Claire parted ways with her boss. When it came to the bed, Claire believed authenticity was crucial. It was not enough to toss a poly-cotton dust ruffle and comforter from Bed Bath & Beyond on a mattress and call it made. A bed could not look luxurious unless it actually *was* luxurious.

Everything in the bedroom box had to be ironed: sheets, pillowcases, dust ruffle, the crease where the faux fur had been folded. Claire opened Jay's ironing board, which was so fancy it didn't screech. It had cost $150 and had its own built-in electric socket. Veronica had given it to them, Claire remembered now; the food scale had been her shower gift. Claire filled the steam compartment and listened to the white noise of the steam as she stroked the first sheet. Jay used to iron in front of the TV. "I get inordinate satisfaction from smoothing out wrinkles," he had confessed to her early on, with sheepish pride and a smirk to show that he, a psychologist, knew how neurotic this sounded. But Claire had merely found it charming that he liked to iron.

That was the day she almost broke up with him, though not because of the ironing remark. It had been a bright, chilly Saturday in April, just a couple of months into their courtship. They had had brunch in Uptown and then crossed under Lake Shore Drive to walk by the lake, holding hands in his coat pocket. Clouds glided by like sailboats on the blue sky. A few joggers passed, then a middle-aged couple. The man leaned over his wife, speaking Russian or Polish to her in emphatic, even tortured tones. While he spoke, the wife gazed out at the lake with a look of intense concentration.

"That'll be us one day," Jay said, squeezing her hand.

"Yeah?" she said. "You jabbering away, me spacing out."

"Spacing out? She was listening."

"No, she wasn't. She was totally spacing out."

He didn't respond. Then, "What did you say?"

"Ha-ha."

They fell into silence, and in the silence Claire rewound his remark about the future and realized that he had decided he wanted to be with her forever. A wave of dread rolled through her. Maybe I won't love him, she thought. Maybe it won't be possible for me to love a man who wants to be with me forever. If she couldn't, she would have to conclude that it was impossible for her to love anyone who was good to her, for Jay was not only kind but funny and sexy, smart and strong. She might be doomed to always be attracted to men who were, to put it kindly, ambivalent: men who might love her but couldn't show affection when they were sober. Men who loved her but didn't actually want to spend much time with her.

Jay's hand was curled around hers.

She tried to reason with herself. She was scared because he was different. Every morning since their first date he had called her on his way to work—"Just checking in." At lunchtime some days the buzzer would ring, and she'd come downstairs, rubbing paint off her fingers, to find him with a bouquet he'd just bought from her neighbor, the florist smiling discreetly behind the glass. Jay had charmed her (Toni was her name) as well.

But thinking about how wonderful Jay was only made

Claire feel more panicked. Don't do anything rash, she told herself.

That night, she was supposed to meet his colleagues at a dinner party. For a moment she thought about breaking up with him immediately, to spare him the embarrassment of introducing her to people who would soon realize that she must have been thinking about dumping him, even as she held Jay's hand and feigned interest in their small talk.

An almost imperceptible unease lingered over her at the dinner party, where the men smiled at her benevolently and the women—professors, wives, and girlfriends alike—told her that they had never seen Jay so happy. A strange thing for people who had known him only a few months to say, she thought, welcoming the opportunity to feel suspicious. But he grew on people quickly, she conceded. If she blamed him for anything, it was his confidence that she was falling for him, too—which was petty and unfair, she knew.

In bed that night at her place on Long Street, she claimed to be too tired to make love. She awoke in the night, stifling hot, Jay's breath on her neck. The radiator was clanging.

"Hey," he said, stirring when she got up to turn off the heat. "What's wrong?"

She slid back into bed, facing him on her side. His body was so beautiful: the knobbed, sculpted shoulders, the concave shadow running down the middle of his chest.

"Tell me about your last girlfriend." She wanted to hear about someone else he had loved, someone who had loved him back. She wanted to hear how it was done.

"Okay," he said, propping his head on his hand, as if it were not a strange request for the middle of the night. He told her that he and Natalie had met during grad school orientation week in Charlottesville and stayed together for the five years it took them to get their Ph.D.'s. In the beginning the relationship had been tempestuous, but the passion faded over time, and then they both grew indifferent. They had rented a small house together, and by their last year of school they were sleeping on a mattress in the dining room so that each of them could have an office. "That last year, when we were writing our dissertations, there were days when we'd just run into each other in the kitchen. We weren't even sleeping at the same time."

"So . . . you didn't have sex?" The contours of his face were still unfamiliar and strange to her in the dark. She felt shy, and intimidated by his ability to be with someone for more than a year.

"No. That trailed off."

"Did you love her?" Claire asked.

"For a long time I did."

"What happened?"

"I guess the feeling just slipped away when we weren't looking."

"That's kind of scary . . . that you couldn't make it work, even though you were both psychologists."

He smiled. "I studied babies, and she studied organizational behavior."

"Does that scare you?"

"Organizational behavior?"

She squeezed his arm. "That you fell out of love like that."

"Not really. We both knew we'd have to go where the jobs were. We pretty much knew from the beginning that it would end."

Alarm bells were ringing in her head. "What if you had met me instead of her? Would it have been the same way?"

"C'mere." He pulled her close. "This is what it would have been like."

She squirmed. His whole body was warm around her.

"Let me go," she whispered.

He held her tighter.

She relaxed.

"See?" he whispered. "You can do it."

After he left in the morning, she missed him, and decided she had been wrong. She was, in fact, falling in love, but in a way that was unfamiliar to her. It was a calmer, subtler sensation than she had expected: quiet, secure, and then, finally, deep. For a while she missed the pang of wanting someone who might not necessarily call her in a timely manner after a date. But after a few more months she didn't miss the drama anymore, and she felt an embarrassed thrum of pride—embarrassed because it had taken her years to learn to do what so many people achieved naturally, without apparent effort: to be a couple. Yet she was proud that she had done it. Her heart had grown airy and expansive. So this was sustained happiness: a light, distracted feeling. She hummed through her days. Unhappy friends, single women, found ways to let her know they didn't think much of Jay, that *they* wouldn't have had him. They picked fights and retreated. She let them go. She didn't care.

Claire made the bed: mattress pad, fitted sheet, top sheet, blanket, comforter, pillows, cases. Feeling a little sick to her stomach, she lay down crosswise so that her feet wouldn't touch the clean bedding. She took her cell phone out of her pocket and listened to her husband's heart.

"The cat's better," she said to the empty room.

Being alone was overrated, she thought. She imagined calling Frank and inviting him over to the model home after work. She would order Thai food; he could bring beer. But she wouldn't know whether he had come because he wanted to be with her or because he felt obligated to attend to a grieving widow. And besides, it wasn't Frank she wanted.

By that first fall, it was obvious, though not discussed, that Claire and Jay would marry. Around Thanksgiving he began hinting about secret plans he was making for the end of the year. Just before Christmas he told her to dress up and pack an overnight bag for New Year's Eve.

He picked her up early on the thirty-first, wearing a jaunty wool cap and a charcoal-gray overcoat she had never seen before. He gave her a nosegay from the downstairs florist: a fist of pink tea roses tied with a ribbon. Like a bridal bouquet, she thought, but didn't say.

A heavy snowfall had been predicted, a foot or more. The earliest flakes were falling, large ones glowing fluorescent beneath the streetlights of Lake Shore Drive. They were quiet in the car. Tonight, she told herself. Your life is probably going to change tonight.

"Probably"—because she was old enough, had been foolish about men enough times to prepare herself for disappointment.

They dropped the car and their bags off at the Drake Hotel, where Jay had reserved a room, and took a cab to a French restaurant in Printer's Row that neither of them had been to before. Couples were flowing into the restaurant, shedding furs and down jackets into the arms of the coat-check girl, snowflakes evaporating in midair. A stick-thin, aging hostess in a purple sheath tucked Claire and Jay into a table against the far wall. A tall, hawk-nosed waiter with a long apron over his tux murmured something in French as he handed them their menus. Glasses of champagne appeared.

"To you," Jay said.

"To us," said Claire.

A spoon chimed. Champagne bubbles roiled out of the hostess's glass like witches' brew. The kitchen door swung open. *"Mesdames et messieurs! Attention, attention!"* shouted the bald, rosy-cheeked chef. *"Je vous remercie de votre patience!* Welcome to Edith's seventeenth annual New Year's Eve fete! It is lovely to see so many familiar faces and some new ones as well. Sylvie, my lovely wife, and I have prepared a very special night for you, which we hope you will enjoy!"

Claire had been expecting murmured voices, candlelight, delicate portions, carpeting to cushion Jay's knee. Instead there was a hubbub of voices, tinny accordion music, and scraping silverware. Faded plastic-framed posters of familiar photographs hung on the walls—the couple kissing on the street, the kid brandishing the magnum of champagne, the cyclist with a baguette in his basket. Most of all, there were roosters: on the seat cushions, the salt and pepper shakers, the teapots on the plate rail, and the crooked lampshades on the chandeliers.

"Do you like it?" Jay said, leaning across the table.

"Mm-hmm!"

Claire's disappointment was mild enough to be embarrassing rather than upsetting. After all, the night she had envisioned was a cliché. And the potato-leek soup was delicious, the champagne went straight to her head, and a sliver of French toast appeared, with a "complimentary foie gras garnish," as the waiter put it with a wink—the city council had banned its sale, so chefs were giving it away for free.

When they weren't eating, Jay held her hand across the table and looked around the room. The wine pairings made Claire lose track of the food. By the fourth or fifth course, a steamy cassoulet sweating beads of oil, she was rubbing his leg under the table with her calf. "What?" they said in response to each other's inconsequential comments about the food. "Excuse me?"

He was quiet, she thought, maybe nervous, further proof that he had something special to say. But he wouldn't propose here—God, she hoped not. Back at the hotel, he wouldn't have to squeeze between the tables and she wouldn't have to ask him to repeat himself, and they would both have sobered up a bit.

"And Jennifer and Robert," the woman next to Jay said to her dining companion, who was seated next to Claire. The woman, who looked to be in her mid-forties, wore gold-rimmed glasses and shimmery coral lipstick, and her short hair looked frosted. Too tidy-looking to be American. European.

"If we must," said the man. Claire had gotten a look at him when they sat down: sandy hair, a neat mustache, and a silk handkerchief tucked into the pocket of his tweedy brown blazer. He was about the same age as the woman—his wife?

"We must," the woman said. "We'll serve charcuterie, yes?"

"As you like," he said, sighing slightly as he leaned back in his seat. The cushion of the banquette compressed behind Claire.

The man and woman spoke English with different accents. Hers sounded French, and his sounded more like German, but a bit softer, maybe Dutch. *Can you imagine,* Claire wanted to say to Jay, *if we each spoke a different language and we had to communicate in a third?* She tucked the thought away to share with him later. For Jay seemed to be listening, too; his head was cocked, and his eyes were trained on the woman's plate.

He leaned toward Claire, smiling wryly. "We're pathetic."

"What?"

He shaded his mouth with his hand. "We should be having our own boring conversation."

Claire recoiled, hurt. "The tables are so close together," she said lamely, then waved her fork at a nearby hutch filled with rooster pitchers. "Funny place," she said.

"Funny?" Jay pulled at the knot of his tie, revealing the T-shirt beneath his dress shirt. Sexy, and in twenty years he would be more so. He was a professor with young women filing in and out of his classes. Claire would have to stay in shape for him as she aged: eat healthy, take long walks.

"You don't like it?" he said.

"No, I do!" She hadn't meant to criticize—not consciously, anyway. "It's not what I was expecting, but I like it. It's so . . . lively!"

"It's New Year's Eve," he said, frowning. "It's supposed to be lively."

"I know. Never mind. I don't know what I'm talking about."

"What were you expecting?"

"Um . . . I don't know. But this is great! We can be romantic back at the hotel."

"You don't think it's romantic," he said flatly.

"No," she said. "I do." She reached to squeeze his hand. He pulled back to saw at a piece of arctic char, which until then he had been slicing with the side of his fork.

"So, um . . ." She grasped for a new topic. "What are your parents doing tonight?"

"My parents?" He looked at her in disbelief. "I don't know. They're probably going to the club."

"The country club?" She hadn't met his parents yet. When he went home to Boston for Christmas for a few days, he had made whispered phone calls to her several times a day from his bedroom, as if he were being held hostage.

"Worst food in the world." His expression was deadpan.

"But not everyone can afford it, which apparently makes it edible."

"I guess all their friends are there," Claire ventured.

"Is it okay if we don't talk about my parents tonight?" His voice was sharp, and he turned away from her, focusing on the neighbor lady's plate.

"Sure," Claire said, looking down. Tears had rushed to her eyes, and she blinked them away furiously. He had never snapped at her before.

They passed the next two courses in near silence. Now and then Claire made little remarks to show him that she forgave him for snapping and she wanted him to forgive her for whatever she had done—"I've never tasted real truffles before, have you? The mushrooms, I mean, not the chocolate"—but he responded with grunts, scarcely looking at her. Next to them, the European couple droned on in a cryptic shorthand about their party: the food, the guests, and someone named Jelly, or maybe Gelée, unless that was just another item on their menu.

Just before midnight, after the checks had been dropped en masse and the tables cleared, Claire and Jay were herded with the other guests against the front windows. The waiters pushed some of the tables and chairs against the walls and carried others onto the sidewalk. Claire stared outside and sniffed her nosegay. Snow was falling steadily.

She clutched Jay's arm. "Is anything wrong?"

"No." He didn't look at her.

The lights dimmed, Sinatra started singing about Chicago, and a spotlight shone on a disco ball someone had strung from one of the chandeliers. The middle-aged patrons started to boogie, shaking their fists like crying babies.

"Do you want to dance?" Claire said.

"Do you mind if we don't?" he said without looking at her.

"That's fine."

They stood watching the crowd for a while, and then Jay turned and said, "Ready?"

"You want to go?"

"We can stay if you want."

"Not if you don't want to."

Finally he smiled at her, but tightly. "Let's do our own countdown at the hotel."

She nodded. It would be midnight by the time they crossed the Loop, she thought, but didn't say.

He fetched their coats. Out on the sidewalk, the European woman who had sat next to them was pacing, her arms folded across her chest. Her fur coat was short and swingy, probably not warm at all, revealing birdlike legs in iridescent panty hose.

"Excuse me," she said as they approached, "but I can't find my husband. You were sitting next to us. Have you seen him?"

Claire and Jay looked at each other and shook their heads.

"You're sure he's not inside?" Claire said.

"No, I looked everywhere. So did the waiters. He came outside to smoke half an hour ago. I don't know where he could have gone."

"Does he have a cell phone?" Claire said.

"I have our phone," she said. "We don't live in Chicago. We are staying at a hotel."

Jay had walked to the curb and was looking down the street for a cab.

"Do you want us to wait with you for a little bit?" Claire said.

"That's all right." The woman hugged herself. "Thank you. I'm sure he'll be back soon."

"Where are you staying?"

"The Hilton."

"On Michigan Avenue? Or in the Loop?"

The woman shook her head. "I didn't notice. My husband took care of everything. He has the room card."

"Was it a huge hotel on a big, long avenue," said Claire, "or was it a smaller hotel in a crowded area with lots of buildings around?"

"Smaller," the woman said. "It was by the train—the overhead train. It had a red awning."

"That's near our hotel," Claire said, though it wasn't, really. "Do you want to share a cab?"

The woman shook her head. "Maybe he just went to buy cigarettes and became lost."

"Shall we wait with you?"

She looked away, then turned back. "What? Oh. No, that's all right."

"Claire?" Jay said. He had a taxi waiting.

"Je ne peux pas croire que cela arrive encore," the woman murmured to herself, then paced farther down the street.

I can't believe this is happening again, Claire translated, word by word. Jay was holding open the taxi door. She ran toward him. "Good luck," she called over her shoulder. The woman didn't seem to hear her.

He's going to break up with me tonight, Claire thought when they were safely inside and careening away from the restaurant, away from the pathetic woman with her missing husband. The thought came from nowhere. It couldn't be true—how could it?—yet Claire was filled with dread.

Jay had reserved a corner room at the Drake, and Claire

gasped theatrically out the window at the slow-moving curve of traffic on the Drive, the festive strings of white headlights and red taillights. The snowy park shone blue under the streetlamps.

"This must cost a fortune!" She waited for him to embrace her from behind. "New Year's Eve!"

"I got a discount from my auto club." His voice was moving away from her. "I'm gonna brush my teeth."

Claire followed him, planning to brush along with him, but the door was closing in her face. "I'll be out in a sec, baby, okay?" he said.

She sat on the edge of the bed, waiting; on the slim chance he still planned to propose, she wanted to be fully dressed. She looked around for her nosegay and realized she must have left it in the cab.

Jay came out in his boxers and T-shirt and climbed into the far side of the bed. He didn't watch as she took off her dress. In bed, she curled up against him.

"Jay?" she said. "Is everything okay?"

"Mm-hmm," he said.

"Get my bra for me?" she said.

He rolled over and struggled feebly with the hook until it finally gave way.

New Year's Eve, a warm, quiet room in a nice hotel on a snowy night, bellies full of wine and rich food, and he did not want her: not as his wife, not even as his lover. She couldn't quite believe it.

"You don't seem like yourself," she ventured.

"I'm fine. Just tired. Let's talk in the morning, okay?"

"Sure." Turning so that he wouldn't see her tears, she lapped them with her tongue.

She must have fallen asleep, for she awoke in the night to hear him rustling. He was sitting on his side of the bed, hunched over, facing the floor.

"Jay?" Claire said. "You okay? You feeling sick?"

"I'm gonna go home," he said.

"What?"

"I'll take a cab. You can take my car in the morning."

"What are you talking about, Jay?"

"I can't sleep, Claire. I'm going home."

"You're breaking up with me? Right now?"

"I'm not breaking up with you. I'm having a rough night." He grabbed his overnight bag and pulled out some jeans. "I'm sorry. I'll call you in the morning."

"Tell me what's going on."

He stared at the carpet, his jeans bunched against his legs.

She joined him at the edge of the bed, hoping that the sight of her half-naked body would help. "I liked the restaurant," she said. "Really, I did."

"I know. You didn't do anything wrong." He reached to put on his socks. "This isn't about that."

"You can't just go home, Jay." She put her arm around him.

"Don't be upset." Still, he didn't touch her.

"Don't leave me!"

"I'm not, Claire. It's just for tonight. I can't sleep."

"You can watch TV."

"I don't want to keep you up. I didn't want to ruin your New Year's Eve, Claire. I'm sorry." He bent over and kissed her on the forehead. "I'm going to go home. I'll call you in the afternoon."

"There's a blizzard. There might not be any cabs."

He paused, clenching the sock he'd been about to put on.

"There's beer in the fridge," she continued. "Turn on the TV. I'll stay up with you. We'll have a little party and leave first thing in the morning."

"Please," he said. "Just let me go."

"I'll go with you." She found her bra on the floor and put it on.

"Claire, no." He rubbed his face. "Go back to bed. I won't go. I'll wait in the lobby if you want. I'll go for a walk."

She didn't believe him. He would find a cab and slip away, and she might never see him again. She didn't know why she thought that, except that suddenly all the rules had changed.

"I'll drive us home," she said.

"You can't drive in this weather."

"I learned to drive in the snow."

"Claire—"

"*Wait* for me!" she shouted. She had never snapped at him before, and it worked: he froze in place.

She sprang into action, moving efficiently but not so quickly that it would scare him. She dressed and packed her bag, throwing in the courtesy bottles of shampoo and lotion. He began packing his own bag as well.

Outside the room, empty champagne bottles and dirty dishes lined the hallway on room-service trays. Claire thought she heard a party down the hall, but when they passed, she realized it was only a New Year's Eve celebration on TV.

On the street, as they waited for the valet to fetch the car, snow fell in fat clumps. It seemed warmer than a few hours earlier, and there was no wind. The streets were white; plows had not come through yet. It was a blizzard disguised as a light snowfall. Around the corner on Michigan Avenue, cars moved in slow single file.

Jay did not protest when Claire headed for the driver's side of his car. Inside, he slumped against the passenger door. She locked them in and swerved slowly around the corner, then fell into the tracks of the car ahead of them.

On Lake Shore Drive, the snow was like a dry batter, six inches of uncooked pie dough. Immediately the rear window snowed over. Jay rolled down his window so that Claire could see out his mirror. Soon the wipers were crusted with ice, and Claire had to look for holes between the bars of snow covering the windshield. They crept by a van that had rear-ended a car in the right lane. One of the car doors stood open, no one in sight.

At the Fullerton exit, the SUV in front of Claire slowly fell away. She fishtailed at ten miles an hour, seeking traction. She jerked the steering wheel back and forth until finally the car swung into a cab's tracks and straightened.

Without daring to turn her head, she sensed Jay slumped against the seat and guessed that his eyes were closed. He was sleeping through this: she could not believe it. As they approached Belmont, she almost followed the cab onto the exit ramp, mesmerized by its tracks, but she recovered in time, guiding the stubborn wheels over the snowdrifts and into a new set of grooves.

"Where are the plows?" she said. One of the guys she had met online had told her there was a room at City Hall where snowplow drivers sat every day from October through April, watching TV and waiting for snow. Jay didn't answer.

She was behind a red car now. As they reached the end of the Drive, she stayed right to funnel onto Sheridan Road. They still had miles to go. Just after the turn, the red car slowed and stopped. "Fuck," Claire said. She pumped the brakes and stopped inches from the bumper. There was a good chance the next car turning off the Drive behind her wouldn't see her.

A young woman with long, curly hair hopped out of the driver's seat of the red car with a scraper and started brushing off her windows.

"Jesus Christ," Claire said. "What the fuck is she thinking?" Claire rolled down her window, scrubbed the mirror, and watched for an opening in the other lane. When it seemed clear, she pulled out. Behind her, someone honked. "All right, all right," she muttered. A Jeep was stuck behind her. Now Claire was half in one lane, half in the other. The young woman got back into her car, but instead of moving forward, the red car began rolling in reverse. Claire leaned on her horn. The car stopped, hesitating, then started creeping backward again until it was just a few inches from their bumper.

Claire leaned her head out the window. "Stop!" she screamed.

Miraculously, the car did stop. Claire was able to edge around it now.

"Stupid bitch!" she shouted out the window at the girl, who looked back at them—her window was down, too— with a stricken, blank expression.

"Jay!" Claire shouted when they had passed the car.

"What?"

She turned for a second and saw that he was leaning forward in his seat, eyes open.

"Pay attention! This is scary as hell!"

"We're almost home," he said. "We're fine."

After another block Claire couldn't see out the window at all: the windshield and the wipers were covered in an inch of snow. "I have to stop." She pulled over in the right lane, just before the driveway of a lakefront high-rise. Jay fished the scraper from the backseat and got out.

The back windshield was snowed over again by the time he returned, but the wipers were working. "Seat belt," she said.

The traffic grew sparse near Loyola, where the road turned west before looping north again. A group of college kids crossed in front of them, one of the boys holding up a hand as a stop sign. "Idiots," Claire muttered, coaxing the brakes. The boy helped along a girl who looked as if she could barely stand. Snow had matted her hair into dreadlocks.

After they passed under the El tracks, the car went into a slow skid toward a line of parked cars.

"Claire," Jay said.

"I know!" she said.

The steering didn't work, but the brakes eventually held, a few inches from a parked yellow cab.

She breathed: in, out, in, out. She waited for a car to pass, then turned the wheel all the way to the left, slammed on the gas, and skidded back into a pair of tracks. The car shimmied. The tires whirred, layered with snow-dough. The dough fell away, and traction returned.

"Okay," she said. "Okay now."

A low horn sounded behind them; in the mirror she saw the flashing lights of a plow. She pulled over to let it pass, then scuttled behind it. The plow straddled the two northbound lanes, pelting chunks of salt against the hood of the car. Hidden behind the plow, Claire felt safe.

"We're going to my place first," she said. "Then you're going home."

Jay didn't respond.

As they rounded the cemetery curve, the plow passed them going in the other direction, back into the city. No more cars were visible. The tires held their grip.

On Long Street, snow stood a foot high in the parking lanes. Claire hit the accelerator and plowed into the snow, then slammed on the brakes.

She put the car in park and turned the key.

The car—the whole world, it seemed—fell silent.

"Oh!" she cried. Suddenly she was sobbing.

"It's okay." Jay's voice was flat. "It's okay now."

"Don't talk to me!" she wailed. "Don't you fucking talk to me."

She didn't hear from Jay for four days, and then the doorbell rang. It was her florist, their florist, standing in the alcove between the doors, holding a bouquet of pale pink roses. After the blizzard, the weather had turned frigid, but Toni had not bothered to put on a coat.

"He asked me to tell you he's sorry," she said, and flashed a wry smile.

"How original," Claire said, accepting the bouquet, then felt rude when the woman shrank back.

When he called that night, she answered. She had been crying off and on for days, but the sound of his voice turned her to stone. Still, she agreed to meet him.

The next morning, they sat at a table by the window of the café on Long Street, keeping their coats on against the draft.

Black moods sometimes came over him, he told her, so bad he was almost paralyzed.

She let this sink in. "You could have told me sooner."

"I know. I'm sorry. It's not something I want to think about when I'm feeling good. And I'd been feeling so good with you." He sat low in his chair, looking up at her. "I had this heavy feeling coming over me the day before New Year's Eve. I knew what it was. I was hoping I'd feel better when I saw you, which has happened sometimes, but I didn't. It was the first time that seeing you didn't make me feel better. Which was kind of"—he shook his head, looking around the room—"hard. Then, when it seemed like you weren't having a good time . . ."

"For the record," she said, "I liked the restaurant, but I had this idea in my head that you were going to propose, and it wasn't really a proposal type of place, so I was just a little bit disappointed, but not that much. You overreacted."

He nodded. "Well, also for the record, I have been thinking about that." He glanced up at her. "Proposing. There was a plan in the works. *Is* a plan, depending on whether you still want there to be one."

"So . . . depression. Is that what you would call it?" She felt a strange sense of relief: she wasn't the problem.

He nodded. "Though it feels more like . . . almost like laziness, or . . . inertia. I get tired of pushing the stone up the hill."

"What stone? What hill?"

"When I have one of my . . . spells"—he looked at her sheepishly, acknowledging the quaintness of the word—"the thought that I'll have to take a shower every day for the rest of my life . . ." He gazed at her, beseeching. "I mean, don't you ever get sick of yourself? Doesn't it sometimes seem ridiculous that we have to live our entire lives in one consciousness, and there's no escape? Even when we dream, we dream about ourselves. Doesn't that just seem outrageous?"

"Um . . ." She vaguely remembered entertaining such thoughts in the darkest days of high school, while listening to the Smiths and Tears for Fears in her room, but they seemed beside the point now, adolescent indulgence. "I think everyone feels that way sometimes. Right?"

"Sure, I guess."

She wasn't good at this kind of talk; she was in over her head. In her family they didn't talk about feelings, and she had not acquired the habit as an adult. She asked him about medication. He said he had never found anything he liked. "I'd lose my libido, and I'd just feel kind of . . . flat. It's just never seemed worth it."

"How often does this happen?" she asked.

He shook his head. "It depends. Every three months, every six months."

"How long does it last?"

"A day, a week, a month. That depends, too."

"How are you right now?"

He shrugged. "I've been better. I've also been worse."

"Does anything help?"

"Therapy, sometimes. Talking. Working, keeping my head down, like when I'm writing a paper. Being around the babies at work. Being with you has helped a lot. I think it could help more, now that we're talking about it. I mean, if we . . . if you . . ."

"You abandoned me," she said. "On the drive home. We were in danger, and I was all alone."

He nodded. "I want to say that . . . I don't want to ever do that again."

"Don't want to, or won't?"

He looked at her sidelong, his mouth pursed into a bow. "Won't is a tough one."

"Not really," she said. "You just say it, and then you do it."

"All right," he said. "Won't. But I need you to not abandon me, either."

"Me? How have I—"

"I need you to open up to me. Be . . . vulnerable sometimes. So I'm not out there on a limb by myself."

Claire grimaced. "Okay," she said finally. "But we have to take it slow now." In her mind, though, she was already making plans. Maybe she could help him. Maybe—it was a sick little thought—this was what she had missed in their early months together. Uncertainty. Drama. The satisfaction of knowing that he needed her, and not just because he loved her.

He proposed two months later, at the café on Long Street.

He met her for lunch, as he often did, and when they were done with their sandwiches, he reached in his pocket and got down on one knee. Claire cried—because she was happy, because she was scared, and because he had surprised her and she hated being surprised. Across the room, Andy, who had brought them together by not knowing about Orpheus Records, grinned and bobbed his head at them from behind the counter.

The bedroom of the model home was turning a lunar blue.

Claire got up and looked out the window: snow. It was March, and it was beginning to seem like winter would never end.

In the bathroom, she splashed some water on her face.

She opened the binder to a blank yellow page with a tab attached.

"For Claire," the tab read.

She had planned to read the other sections in the binder first: Jay's advice about the house, his car, Fang, their finances and benefits. But as she flipped through them—"The car was once in an accident in 2000," "The broker who financed our loan was David Parkson," and so on—this idea struck her as impossibly tedious. Clearly he had tried to alleviate some of his guilt by being helpful, but the neat lines of type threatened to drive Claire into a rage.

She turned the yellow page. The note was double-spaced, like one of Jay's research papers. It was two pages long, half the length of the section about the cat. He had signed "Jay" at the bottom of the second page in blue ink, beneath the typed word "Love."

Dear Clairey,

I'm so sorry. I have let you down, just as I have let myself down, and everyone else. I have you, I have an interesting job, we have a nice home and a good life. And yet I feel myself going down deep again and it feels like I will keep on sinking forever. I know that each time I have come up for air again, but the next time I go down even lower and I know that it would only get worse. I don't know why I can't just be happy, like a normal person, but I can't. I don't know why you aren't enough to make me happy, because you should be. The only thing that brings me relief is the thought that soon this will be over.

I want you and others to know that there is no deep, dark secret that drove me to this. I have not stolen money, fabricated data, or had an affair. My only secret, maybe, is that I often feel worse than you might think. I love you very much, but it feels like my love has no connection to my spirit. I feel like there is a wall of glass between us. I made the mistake of thinking that marriage could cure me, that you could cure me. Maybe you made that mistake too. We tried, but I think we are not compatible in certain ways, and it has been frustrating to both of us. I have not been a good husband to you and I would not be a good father to our children.

I put together this binder for you months ago, after one of my spells, but I am writing this note the day before Sally and Bart's party. I have grappled with this decision for a few days and now I feel certain it is the right one. When I think about their balcony, it is just too tempting and I'm consoled by the knowledge that you will not be there. Please forgive me that it happened on Valentine's Day. It is true that my heart is broken, but it has always been that way. That we couldn't repair it together is my fault, not yours.

Claire, you are a beautiful person. You have the gift of contentment, something I have always admired about you. I hope you will be able to forgive me and find peace. Eventually you will find a man who is solid and not so needy.

I've put together some information to help you cope with things. Keep in touch with my family if you want to, if not that's OK. Be good to Fang, she will miss me. Try to get over me as fast as you can so you can start a family and forget about me.

Love,

Jay

She reread the letter twice, then closed the binder and sat in the darkening room for a long time. Finally she went to the window. The street was filling up as people returned from work, and her father's car had returned.

The women at the dinner party: What had they said?

"We've never seen Jay so happy."

Or was it, "We've never seen Jay happy."

For the life of her, she couldn't remember.

She took out her phone and looked through her wallet for the business card Jay's therapist had given her at the wake. Hannah Ackerman, that was her name.

Claire hoped the woman would be gone for the day, so she could leave a message, but she answered on the third ring.

"Dr. Ackerman?" Claire said. "This is Claire Kessler. Jay Monroe's wife. Yes. I was wondering if we could talk."

7

C laire wasn't sure whether it was Nomie's snoring, which seemed to be getting worse as the pregnancy progressed, or her own nerves that kept her awake that night, but at least she didn't oversleep. She was out of bed at six, and by seven she was hustling down the block to her car. Success: her dad hadn't arrived at his post yet. She had never known exactly what time he showed up— he was always there by the time she rose—so she had left earlier than was necessary. She didn't want him following her today.

As Claire drove north on Lincoln, the streetlights flickered and dimmed; buses trundled up to groggy-looking commuters. Jay's therapist had an office in her home in Lincoln Square, a neighborhood northwest of Nomie and Harry's house and not far from Claire and Jay's house, farther north. A block from the doctor's place, Claire lingered at a Starbucks, staring at the only reading material she had with her, her datebook. In addition to the therapist's address and the time and location of Nomie's doctor's appointment, there was another notation in the day's rectangle: "SG, 7:30." The support group Alan had told her about was having its weekly meeting that night. She was simply too busy, she thought with satisfaction as she slashed an X through the notation and circled her sister's appointment.

Claire got back into her car and drove around the corner. Dr. Ackerman lived on a side street behind the folk-music school where Claire had once taken a voice class, back when she was single and trying to be around people, any people, and where, soon after they were married, Jay had taken a couple of guitar lessons before deciding he was too uncoordinated to enjoy the hobby. The therapist lived in a sprawling three-story house, its wood panels painted light blue with white trim. In the center of the frost-laced yard squatted a primitive snowman, a pile of dirty white lumps impaled with sticks. There was a woodpile on the big front porch, along with a couple of wicker chairs and a swing. Through the front windows, which were framed with lace curtains, Claire glimpsed bookcases and an archway leading to a softly glowing room. Drapes covered the second-floor windows, and in the small third-floor window tucked in the eaves, there was a reflection of the softening sky.

It was the kind of house Claire had hoped she and Jay could graduate to when their family grew, maybe when they needed room for a second child, though they would have had to live in a cheaper neighborhood. Ten years earlier, when Claire lived in a studio apartment nearby, the houses and two-flats were owned by white middle-class families who had been rooted in Lincoln Square for decades, some descendants of the German immigrants who originally settled there. Hispanic families and white kids like Claire, recent college graduates, had lived in the larger apartment buildings. Then the market exploded, yuppies started buying and rehabbing, and the square was spruced up with a fountain. A baby boutique, a gourmet cooking shop, and an ever-changing assortment of trendy restaurants took their place alongside the lonely German shops that sold stodgy, overpriced shoes and women's clothing.

When Claire returned from the model home the previous evening, feeling spacey and oddly calm, she had sneaked the binder back onto the coffee table in the coach house. She didn't tell Harry and Nomie that she had read the note, but she did tell them about the appointment she had made with Jay's therapist. Dr. Ackerman had seemed solicitous on the phone and suggested that they meet early the next morning. Seeing Harry's and Nomie's alarmed looks, Claire effectively blocked a flurry of questions by saying, "I feel it's something I should do." After Nomie offered to drive her, Claire said, "I feel it's something I should do on my own."

She was wondering whether she could go through life keeping people at bay with variations on the phrase "I feel it's something I should do . . ." when Harry said, "Speaking of appointments, you're still good for tomorrow, right?"

"Tomorrow," Claire said, stalling. She was sitting in the armchair with the sleeping cat on her lap. After surviving her self-poisoning, Fang seemed to have decided that Claire would be her new primary caregiver; she followed her around the house during the day, just as she used to follow Jay, and no longer ran to the door when the bell rang. So much for Dr. Rochelle's theory about trauma, Claire thought, and Jay was wrong, too: Fang didn't seem to miss him very much. Secretly Claire gloated. It was nice to be needed, if only by a cat.

Harry and Nomie, side by side on the couch, looked at Claire as if waiting for her to disappoint them.

"The doctor's appointment," she said. It came back to

her. A few days before, Harry had found out that he needed to go to a meeting in Milwaukee, so he had asked Claire to go with Nomie to her latest checkup with her obstetrician. Claire didn't understand why her sister needed someone to go with her, but remembering how she had wheedled Nomie into going to the vet's office with her, she didn't ask. "What time was that again?"

"Twelve-thirty," said Nomie.

The doctor's office was in the professional building of an outdoor shopping mall to the north, Harry reminded her. "On the fourth floor."

"Right," Claire said. He had made a point of stressing that detail the first time it came up as well, the message being: no elevators, no excuses. "Not a problem." She would be a model of big-sister responsibility. "I'll drive." Pushing it, maybe, she added, "I won't let you down."

At that moment a small patch of skin on her face began to tingle, just outside her right ear, as if it had fallen asleep. She tapped the spot lightly as Harry rose from the couch and rinsed his beer bottle in the sink.

"Great. Thanks." He touched Nomie's shoulder. "Are you coming?"

She reached for his hand and let out a fake-sounding yawn. "I'm so tired, and it's so cold out."

Harry studied his wife for a long moment, his eyes darting over her features as if he would not see her for a long time and needed to memorize them.

"Maybe you should go, Nomie," Claire said, suddenly chilled.

"That's okay." Harry stooped to give his wife a swift kiss. "Call me after your appointment. Let me know what you find out."

"I will." Nomie reached up for a hug.

Claire looked away, rubbing at her ear. The tingling had gone; now the spot was numb.

"This spot on my face has gone numb," she said.

They pulled away from their embrace and looked at her.

"What do you mean?" Nomie said.

"I don't know. It's just kind of . . . numb. Right here." She rubbed the spot.

"Can you hear okay?" Nomie said.

"Yeah."

"Your speech isn't slurred," Harry said.

"Well, I stopped after the fourth martini," Claire said. Nomie gave her a wan smile, for which Claire was grateful. In fact, there had been a conspicuous absence of alcohol in the coach house during her stay. Harry brought over a couple of beers each night, but not enough to share. It was insulting, Claire thought. She was a codependent, not an addict. Wasn't that obvious by now?

"Maybe you can ask Nomie's doctor about it tomorrow," Harry said.

For a second, Claire hoped she had had a ministroke, not serious enough to do any lasting damage, but authentic enough to make Harry feel guilty for dismissing her ailment.

It was 8:20. Claire had been parked across the street from Jay's therapist's home for twenty minutes. Ten minutes until their appointment.

This is what it's like to be my father, she thought.

Her coffee had gone cold—she had been afraid to drink much of it for fear that she would have to ask to use the therapist's bathroom—and she didn't have an appetite for the muffin she had bought. The engine was idling to deliver heat and NPR, the voices low enough to be incomprehensible and therefore soothing. Some of the mix CDs Jay had made for her—part of her musical education—stuck out of the storage slot in the dash, but she didn't dare listen to music these days, especially not songs chosen by Jay. She rubbed the skin by her right ear: still numb.

A rickety-looking staircase zigzagged up the north side of the house. "Come up the side stairs to the third floor," Dr. Ackerman had said on the phone. Jay had told Claire that his therapist had a home office that was separate from her living quarters, but for some reason Claire had pictured an annex tacked onto the first floor, a sort of renovated shed. The staircase railing looked slick from melted snow.

Two floors, not twenty-three or even eighteen, Dr. Mercer's floor. Jump or fall off that top landing, and you might break your legs or your spine. You might be paralyzed, but you'd probably survive.

Mercer had said he could meet with her on a lower floor. Claire imagined going back for a second appointment and telling him that she had gone to see Jay's therapist after reading his suicide note.

Why? he would ask. *What did you hope to find out?*

I don't know. Maybe why he went ahead with it. He said he was consoled by the fact that I wouldn't be at the party. But then I ended up going, and he did it anyway.

So he was pretty determined.

I don't know. Maybe it was just a cry for help.

Cry for help, cry for schmelp, she imagined Mercer saying. She had the idea from their single, brief meeting that he would be irreverent with his patients. She yearned for someone to be irreverent with her. *What, maybe he thought he'd survive a twenty-three-story fall?*

I'm saying, what if it was a fleeting impulse?

A fleeting impulse? Your husband didn't just leave a suicide note. He left a suicide binder.

Time's up, she thought, glancing at the clock, ending the session as abruptly as shrinks did in the movies.

It felt sneaky, climbing up the side of a near stranger's house, but then again, the doctor might feel as if she knew Claire already, having heard the story of Jay's marriage unfold week by week. Therapists probably formed mental images of the people in their patients' lives; you couldn't help it, even if you knew the picture you painted wasn't accurate. You might decide that someone's wife looked like your former college roommate, or a famous actress, or your cousin, or a composite of all three.

Claire had not looked like herself the night Dr. Ackerman met her. Before the wake, her mother had taken Claire into her dressing room and made up her face, holding her chin steady, just as she had on Claire's wedding day. Within the fog of medication, Claire had recognized that her mother had skill. Nancy gave her face a polished, airbrushed look that made her appear prettier than she actually was and thus lent her dazed expression a tragic undertone appropriate for the occasion. But at the funeral home, as the guests filed in and the family members assumed their places before the coffin, Claire felt a sheen of oil rise on her face and some itchy bumps flare up on her jawline. When it was over, as they gathered up their things in the "family room," she had glimpsed herself in the mirror, beneath a fluorescent bulb: an aging, weary woman with dark parentheses framing her mouth and the pouchy beginnings of jowls.

Today she wore jeans and a black turtleneck sweater, studiously casual. She had blown and brushed her hair dry. She was wearing her black boots with the spiky heels, the ones Jay used to say were sexy, and her black coat with the lamb's wool collar, which attracted at least one compliment per day. She had slathered on moisturizer to prop up the slack skin alongside her nose, dotted concealer on the dark circles under her eyes, and put on some green eye shadow she found in Nomie's makeup bag.

"These boots are hard to walk in," she thought, humming nervously (Jay had put Nancy Sinatra on one of her mixtapes, she remembered) and clinging to the railing as she climbed, though someone (the therapist's husband? And what would *he* look like?) had applied tread marks to the steps. No windows to peek through on the side of the house. When Claire got to the top, she faced a white screen door.

"Let yourself in when you get here," the doctor had said, but there was a bell, and Claire couldn't help but ring it. With a mother like hers, there was no way she was going to enter a stranger's house unannounced, even if it meant disturbing someone else's—no, someone's; *Claire* was not a patient— session.

The door swung open and Debussy floated out, a difficult étude Claire's father used to practice. Dr. Ackerman's mouth was smiling, but the rest of her face was taut. "Hi, Ms. Kessler."

"Claire. Hi."

"Claire, please, come in. Did you have any trouble finding me?"

"Finding me": an odd turn of phrase.

"No, not at all," Claire said. "I used to live around here, a long time ago."

Their soles creaked over the slanting wood floorboards as the doctor ushered Claire into a room that was more a front parlor than a waiting room: there was a flower-print couch and a rocking chair, and an antique sewing machine stood against the far wall. A stack of coffee-table books sat on the coffee table, along with a box of Kleenex. On the floor was a pastel-colored rag rug just like one that Claire had seen in Rebecca's garage—vintage Pottery Barn Kids. The walls were a soothing peach. She and Dr. Ackerman had the same taste, Claire realized with dismay: they both liked soft colors, worn antiques, a cozy room where one could curl up with a book in the afternoon and nod off.

"We've only been here a few years, but we love the neighborhood," Dr. Ackerman said, her smile still rigid as she took Claire's coat and hung it up in a closet by the front door. "Great coat." Check, Claire thought. The therapist's hair was darker than Claire remembered, more of a honey color, but her eyes were the same brilliant, false green, and maybe even more striking in the airy room. She wore a long-sleeved pink T-shirt, pressed khakis, and tan suede moccasins; the pale colors and the woman's slight frame made Claire feel dark and heavy in her black sweater and jeans. They were closer in age than Claire had thought. Jay had described his therapist as middle-aged, but he had exaggerated, perhaps for fear that Claire would be jealous to find out he confided weekly in a woman who was not much older than she was and, objectively speaking, prettier.

"Thanks."

They stood together, looking at the room. "Um," Dr. Ackerman said, motioning toward the seating area, "please make yourself comfortable. Can I get you some tea?" She was already moving down a narrow hallway. Apparently it was a self-contained apartment, a pied-à-terre.

"Maybe just some water." Claire felt relieved; it seemed

the woman was going to confine her to the waiting room. She didn't want the doctor to act as if she were there for a therapy session, and it would have been strange to be in the room where Jay had confided his most private thoughts each week.

"Great."

After Dr. Ackerman disappeared from view, the floor creaking lightly under her moccasins, Claire sat down on the couch. The therapist would have to cope with the awkwardness of conducting their conversation from a rocking chair.

She continued her appraisal of the room. There was an old bookcase against the wall, painted a distressed orange and filled with a collection of 1950s-era salt and pepper shakers: pairs of boys and girls, ducks, piglets, and Thanksgiving turkeys wearing Pilgrim hats. Above the bookcase, small framed watercolors of flowers hung low and haphazardly, along with a small collage made of lace imprinted with someone's tiny script. There was a needlepoint sampler, too, in a peeling golden frame. The cross-stitch read:

> *Hours fly*
> *Flowers die*
> *New days*
> *New ways*
> *Pass by*
> *Love stays*

Absurdly, Claire's eyes filled. She looked toward the door, wondering if there was time to sneak out.

Through the blur of tears she saw a familiar image encompassed in a square. She wiped her eyes on her sleeve and looked again.

It was the painting she had given Jay for their anniversary, the painting of the flower shop on Long Street, beneath her studio, where Orpheus Records used to be.

Claire stared, disbelieving.

The painting sat unobtrusively on an old-fashioned telephone table, propped against the wall. She got up and stooped over it. In the painting, a shaft of yellow light cut a diagonal across the plate-glass window of the flower shop. Bunches of spring flowers, tulips and daffodils, slouched in the windows. She had painted the florist in a white shirt, bending over her wares, her girlish ponytail belying her age. Claire's own mailbox was visible just outside the front door, with its little taped-on scrap of paper, her name illegible on it in red—her way of signing the painting.

"You recognize that."

Claire turned, startled. Dr. Ackerman was standing in the doorway with a mug in one hand and a glass of water in the other. The ice in the glass was tinkling: her hand trembled. She set the drinks down on the coffee table.

"Jay gave that to me," the doctor said. "Maybe you know that."

"It's mine," Claire said.

The woman froze. "It was yours?"

"I painted it."

"You painted it?" Dr. Ackerman tottered for a moment on one foot, then caught her balance. "I don't understand. I thought you built dollhouses."

"I do. I used to paint, though. I painted this for Jay for our first anniversary. This shop had special meaning for us." Claire felt a strange need to provide evidence, as if she were the one who had stolen something, not this woman, or Jay, or whoever had been the thief.

The woman sank into the rocking chair. She motioned to the couch, but Claire didn't move. "Jay sent that to me the day he died. It arrived two days later by UPS, from his office."

"I gave it to Jay," Claire said. "He hung it in his office. He said he wanted to be able to look up at it during his day and think of me." Months earlier, the last time she stopped by his office, the painting had been hanging to the right of his desk, directly in his line of vision.

The woman shook her head as if clearing it. "There was a note with it. He said he wanted me to have the painting as a token of his appreciation for the work we had done together."

Claire couldn't move away from the painting. "He didn't tell you that I painted it?"

Dr. Ackerman shook her head. She was leaning forward, her hands clasped together tightly. "I didn't know. You'll take it when you go. It's yours." Her cheeks had flushed, making her look even prettier.

Claire looked her right in the eye. "You didn't mention it at the wake."

"It didn't seem like the right time. I called the officer who had questioned me, and he came and looked at it—the painting and the note. I didn't hear from him again. I guess I thought they would tell you."

"They didn't." But of course, Claire had had no dealings with the police after the first couple of days; her family had shielded her.

"I'm sorry." Again the doctor shook her head. "When people are contemplating suicide, they sometimes give things away."

Finally Claire sat down on the couch. "No one else got anything," she said. My husband committed suicide, and all I got was this stupid binder, she thought. "Did he say anything else? In his note to you?"

The therapist shook her head. "It was very brief, just a sentence or two. I can show it to you, if you want."

Claire shook her head. "There wasn't a photo with it, was there?" she asked.

"No. No photo."

"So. He knew for sure it would be that night, then. It wasn't just an . . . impulsive act."

"That's how it appears. He left a note for you, yes?"

"He could have thrown that away the next day if he changed his mind—it was in his office. But the painting, that was already in the mail."

"I see what you mean. But . . ." The doctor seemed to reconsider whatever she was planning to say. "I suppose you have some questions for me."

Claire focused on the salt and pepper shakers in the bookcase. Shopkeepers and collectors had shepherded these pairs through the decades, making sure they were not separated, simply because they were jolly and sweet. "I heard that Jay's sister made an appointment with you."

"Veronica. Yes, in a couple of weeks." The doctor looked across the room, possibly at the painting, then back at Claire. "I'm afraid there's not much I can say to either of you. Client confidentiality, it doesn't go away after death."

"Right." Claire picked up her glass of water. She was afraid to take a drink for fear the lemon slice floating on the surface would flip onto her nose. The therapist lifted her mug and blew on it gently. They both set their drinks down without tasting them.

"As much as I'd like to speak openly with you if I could," Dr. Ackerman said.

"I don't know about Veronica," Claire said, "but I'm not

here to . . . threaten you or anything like that. I mean, you offered to meet with me."

The woman took a deep breath. "I understand. I . . . I imagine we've both been looking back and wondering what we could have done differently. One thing I've wanted to tell you is that I did *not* think Jay was suicidal." She said this with a vehemence that Claire had not expected. "He . . . struggled. As I think you know."

Claire nodded.

"He could be very depressed." She looked steadily at Claire, her green eyes piercing. "I'm concerned about violating his privacy."

"Jay's dead." Claire's gaze landed on the line in the sampler that had almost made her cry: "Love stays." It seemed mocking now. "People who kill themselves don't get to have any privacy." Because that sounded petty, she beamed at the woman, her best Cheshire cat grin.

"The therapeutic bond, it's, well, sacred, in a way," Dr. Ackerman said.

"Jay and I had a sacred bond. We stood up in a church." Not the right tack, Claire guessed, too late: this woman would know that Jay was an atheist. Psychology was his faith, something he practiced in the next room, once a week without fail. "We signed a license."

"He must have tried to explain himself in his note to you. Do you want to talk about that?" Dr. Ackerman asked.

"I'll tell you if you tell me." Claire flashed her fake smile again.

The doctor's eyes narrowed. "I told you what he wrote in his note to me. It's the details of what was said in this room that are private."

"This room?"

"Yes. In my office."

"I thought it was a waiting room."

"No, this is my office," the woman repeated, sounding a bit testy. "Why did you think that?"

"Therapists usually have waiting rooms. They did when I was a kid, anyway." She assumed Dr. Mercer did as well, in that sleek high-rise.

"I wish I did," Dr. Ackerman said, warming into a smile, the first genuine one Claire had seen from her, "but there isn't room up here in the attic. My clients have to wait downstairs in their cars. But with our kids, it helps to work close to home."

"I wanted kids," Claire said. "Maybe Jay told you that."

The woman's face jerked slightly; then she regained her composure. "I hope you do have that chance, with someone else, if that's what you want."

"I wanted kids with *Jay*." Sensing that she sounded like a stubborn child, Claire tried to soften her tone. "But I don't think he was ready, even though he said he was. I mean, *obviously* he wasn't ready." She heard herself snort.

"I'm sorry." Dr. Ackerman's hands were clenched tightly together, as if in prayer. "I wish I could help you somehow. I truly do."

"I feel like it could have been a cry for help," Claire said in a rush. "An impulse, I mean. Something he might not have done a week later. A day later."

Dr. Ackerman stared at her.

"I had a message from him." Claire pressed forward before she could lose her courage. "On my voice mail. He tried to call me on his way to the party that night. I wasn't going to be there. Maybe he called because he wanted to be talked out of it. But I didn't hear the phone ring. So he left this . . . message."

"Can I ask what he said?"

"He didn't say anything. It's just a noise. I think it's his heartbeat. I think he recorded it for me for . . . some reason. Maybe you could listen to it," she said, and realized this was why she had come. The message still meant more to her than the note—the bewildering, clichéd note with its walls of glass and broken hearts. She wanted someone else to hear the message, someone who knew Jay well enough to confirm that she was right: that near the end he had wanted Claire to hear how valiantly he had struggled to stay alive.

The therapist nodded, so Claire took out her phone and dialed. As the sound started up, she turned on the speaker and set the phone on the coffee table between their untouched drinks.

SHWEE-ohh, SHWEE-ohh!

Dr. Ackerman hopped up and turned off the Debussy. She sat down again and looked across the room as she listened. Her fingernails were bitten down to the quick, Claire saw, and the skin around them was cracked and lined with dried blood.

SHWEE-ohh, SHWEE-ohh, SHWEE-ohh, SHWEE-ohh!

Amplified in the cozy, feminine room, the sound was sinister rather than soothing, much different from how it sounded when she pressed the phone to her ear. Quickly Claire retrieved the phone and turned it off. "It goes on like that for a few more minutes."

"You thought it was a heart?" Dr. Ackerman said.

"I heard his heart once. When he got an echocardiogram. I was in the room."

"But a cell phone . . . it's not an echocardiogram machine."

"So you don't think it's his heart."

"Well, to me . . ." The woman cocked her head and paused, looking at Claire as if wondering whether to go on. "Honestly, to me it sounds like someone walking. Like pants swishing together. He might have had his phone in his pants pocket, and maybe he dialed you by accident. I've done that sort of thing myself."

Claire remembered the pants Jay had worn to the party. Tan corduroys that would have swished together when he walked. With a gray-blue sweater, brown shoes. His coat had been found in the pile on Sally and Bart's bed and searched. Claire hadn't seen it again, but she had been given his keys. Jay's cell phone had smashed, and his glasses, too. His wallet, stained with blood, had been searched and thrown away.

"Maybe I'm wrong," the doctor said, "but I just don't think a phone would magnify a heartbeat like that."

"Okay," Claire said, tucking the phone back into her purse. "Fine. Anyway. Thanks for your opinion."

The woman nodded.

The rug, the salt and pepper shakers, the sewing machine, the pale peach room with its soft morning glow, maybe even the adorably bad snowman: it was all set up for comfort, for the intimacy of this woman's clients—even the word "client" was chosen in favor of the condescending "patient." The entire tableau was staged as deliberately as a model home, and Claire was an outsider here, too.

"You saw him, what, a few days before he did it?" she said.

"Three days before," said the doctor. "That Monday morning."

"Was this where he sat? Where I'm sitting right now?"

The doctor opened her mouth, but didn't speak immediately. "Yes," she said finally. "That's where he sat."

Claire looked down at the rag rug. "Did he say anything about the closets?"

Silence, and then Dr. Ackerman said, "I'm not sure what you mean."

"We were supposed to redecorate the closets that weekend." Claire didn't look up. "The Sunday after he died. We had these . . . terrible closets. The bar in my closet had collapsed, and my clothes were in a heap on the floor, and so, maybe a month before—before the party—we went out and ordered this organization system for all of our closets."

She paused, listening for a stirring of recognition. Nothing.

"We loaded all this crap into the car," she continued, "and brought it into the house, all these shelves and brackets and stuff, and left them in the guest room, which we were remodeling. We liked to do home improvement stuff together on Sundays.

"Jay kept saying we'd work on it, but then every Sunday he'd blow me off to work on a paper or something. And then he had a bad week, and I thought he was having one of his . . . spells. But he seemed to come out of it, and that Sunday, the day before he saw you, I told him I was frustrated with him about the closets, and that I missed spending Sundays together, working on our projects, and he got kind of defensive. He said we could work on them the next weekend, which was the weekend after the party.

"So I'm asking you to tell me whether he told you about that, and maybe complained about me nagging him, and if you think that could have pushed him over the edge. Because, you know, he had this thing where . . . when he was feeling low, the thought of doing something really tedious, like the thought of taking a shower every day for the rest of his life— that was something he said to me once—it could just send him into despair."

Claire looked up. The color had left Dr. Ackerman's face; she was a study in sepia tones.

"You're asking," she said, "whether I think Jay killed himself because you asked him to help you organize your closets?"

"I know you can't tell me. But I'm asking you to tell me anyway. I promise I won't sue you."

Now it was Dr. Ackerman who looked down, at her hands, splayed on her knees. "He was feeling low when he saw me. Not suicidal, it didn't seem to me, but low."

Claire held her breath.

"He didn't say anything about your closets," the doctor said.

Claire exhaled. "Did he say anything about me?"

Silence, and then: "He loved you, Claire. I believe that."

Look at me, Claire thought.

"He . . ." The woman met her gaze. "You mentioned that you got frustrated with him. Maybe you found him needy. Emotionally needy."

Claire stopped herself from nodding. She needed to be a statue. She couldn't do or say anything that might make the woman hold back.

"Jay had a deep need to communicate," Dr. Ackerman said. "Communicate and connect. I can imagine that might get exhausting, especially for someone who isn't used to men being so open."

A chill ran through Claire. "What do you mean by that?" *I think we are not compatible in certain ways . . .*

"I was trying to get him to accept people for who they are. I wanted him to appreciate what was good in his life."

"Was I good in his life?" Claire was crying now.

"I think you were. I believe, as he did, that you are a good person."

"But was I good for *him*?"

Silence.

"Was I the right person for *him*?"

Silence.

"Was I right for *him*?"

The woman handed her a tissue. Claire didn't take it.

"I can't answer that," the therapist said.

"Only Jay could, right? Well, he killed himself, so I guess I have my answer."

"I don't know if it's that simple. If anything, Jay was trying to escape himself."

Claire glared at the therapist. "You know, he talked to me about quitting therapy. Quitting *you*."

Claire watched with satisfaction as the woman's green eyes filmed over with tears.

"He wasn't sure you were helping him. He wasn't sure you were *right* for him." She kept going, transitioning from fact to fiction: "He thought you might mess up our marriage. Sometimes things were worse between us after he saw you."

The doctor nodded once. "He and I talked about him leaving therapy at different times." Her voice caught. "I was one of the people he was never . . . never quite satisfied with."

"I'm going to go now," Claire said, standing up. She grabbed the tissue the woman had offered her and wiped her eyes, blew her nose. She wasn't going to sit and listen to the therapist describe her own private pain.

"Do you want me to call someone?" Dr. Ackerman rose as well. "Your father?"

"What do you know about my father?" Claire's eyes darted to the window: branches barbing puffy clouds.

"I—what? I just thought maybe a family member—or your mother? Your sister?"

It was creepy, the things this woman, this stranger, knew about Claire. Week after week she had committed it to memory and accepted her check. "I'm fine. Can you get my coat?"

"Of course." She didn't move. "But I feel strange. Should we talk some more?"

Claire shook her head. "No more talking. No more!"

"Can you give me a number where I can reach you? I'd like to follow up with you."

"Don't worry, I'm not going to kill myself."

The doctor sighed. "I know. I know you won't." She went to the closet and got Claire's coat, then held it open just as Jay had done at nice restaurants. Claire flailed about for the armholes and finally shrugged the thing on.

The doctor reached for the painting. Before handing it to Claire, she paused. "It's very pretty."

"It's not meant to be pretty," Claire snarled. The woman knew nothing about the darkness underneath the cheerful top layer.

"Skillful," Dr. Ackerman amended. "You're talented, that's all I'm saying." She handed the painting to Claire.

"He gave it to you," Claire said darkly, even as she accepted it.

"Listen." To Claire's surprise, Dr. Ackerman gripped both of her arms. Her face was just inches away from Claire's, her green eyes bright and piercing. Green means go, Claire thought. "We need to get through this, you and me. We can't let this do us in. You understand?"

How dare this woman lump their pain together? Claire pulled away, tears clouding her vision, but Dr. Ackerman held her grip.

"I'm going to be checking in on you," she said. "Your job is harder than mine. You're going to need help. Are you getting help?"

Claire shook her head.

"Get help, Claire. There are good people out there who can help you. Or go to church. Or try a support group. You need other people, do you understand?"

"I'm already in a support group, actually," she lied, not

knowing why she cared what this woman thought of her mental health.

"That's great." The woman gave Claire's arm one more squeeze, then released her grip and opened the door.

"Take care of yourself," she heard Dr. Ackerman say as she clattered down the stairs, bump bump bump, the painting clenched under her arm. By the time she reached the sidewalk, her boots smacking against the slushy pavement, she was sobbing.

In the car, she tossed the painting onto the backseat. She didn't wait to stop crying before pulling out onto the street—the doctor might be watching her from the window.

Without thinking, she drove north on Lincoln instead of south. When she realized where she was going, she didn't stop herself. She turned right on Leland, left on Damen, crying while she drove, great big boo-hoo-hoos, and stuffing cold chunks of muffin into her mouth.

A few more turns, a few more minutes, and she was kicking up gravel in the alley behind her and Jay's house. She hit the garage-door opener on the visor. After the door rumbled up, she swerved into the empty space next to Jay's car—Jay's car, holy mother of Christ. The tennis ball he had hung from the ceiling to tell her when to stop bounced violently against the windshield as she hit the brakes. She shifted into park, lowered her window, and clicked the device. Behind her the door rumbled shut, enclosing her in the dark with the engine's hum.

8

She had gotten into the garage and lowered the door without seeing the house, without seeing neighbors. The idling engine was loud, like factory machinery, as if it were doing more than just running in place.

She let out a final sob, turned the key, and yanked it out of the ignition. Hitting the garage door opener, she stumbled out of her car and past Jay's car, and stooped to slide under the rising door.

Claire whimpered as she ran in the alley, heels crunching over the snow-patched gravel. She slowed down a few garages away and bent over, hands on her knees. Her heart was pounding.

A squirrel, squatting by a neighbor's fence, was watching her. Clenched in its teeth was something silvery pink with a fluttery little tail. Claire stared back. The squirrel was clutching a Hershey's Kiss wrapped in pink foil. A special Valentine's Day edition, thrown out in the trash.

"Drop it," she said. She took a menacing step toward the squirrel, thinking of Fang and the lilies, dogs and chocolate.

Still staring her in the eye, the squirrel hopped sideways, then scuttled under a chain-link fence with the candy in its mouth.

Claire paced, arms crossed against the cold, blinking back tears. Not even a squirrel, she thought. I can't even save a fucking squirrel.

She went back to the garage, lowered the door, and turned on the overhead bulb. As she passed through the narrow space between the two cars, she glanced inside Jay's, an ancient Saab with bad heating. Someone had cleaned it: no papers and books cluttered the backseat; the fast-food litter was gone. She had never seen it so tidy.

When she met Jay, Claire had been single for so long that the idea of living with someone "full-time," as she thought of it, and for the rest of her life, was beguiling, but struck her as bizarre. By the time they were engaged, she had grown fond of their back-and-forth pattern—one night together, one night apart; one night his place, one night hers. She liked her nights alone, and she noticed how happy she and Jay were to see each other after a day or two apart.

And she had fears. Since New Year's Eve, Jay had not had a major episode that she knew of, but at times he was distant and distracted. For three days in February he contacted her only by e-mail, saying he was busy with work, and didn't answer her calls, only to pop up again, acting as if nothing was wrong. Sometimes he spent hours complaining to her about work, and she got bored. Twice he canceled plans, saying he wouldn't be good company. If they were married and living in the same home, what kind of company would he be then? Before he proposed, she wondered if they should live together for a while, but she decided she was too old for that: she wanted kids. She was thirty-five. There was no time to waste.

"Maybe we could get a two-flat, and I could live upstairs and you could live downstairs," she mused to him the morning after they got engaged, as they lay in her bed talking about their future. She was only half kidding. "We can go to our separate corners when we get tired of each other."

He had looked hurt, then wary. "I don't get tired of you," he said. "Do you get tired of me?"

"I don't get *tired* of you, but you know, it's sometimes nice to have time alone."

"What about when we have kids?"

"Well, then we'll merge."

"I see. A marriage, then a merger." His eyes flitted across her face. "You're used to living in two places."

"You mean my parents' divorce." He was psychoanalyzing her again.

He nodded. "Even before the divorce. Remember how they broke the news to you?"

She wished she hadn't told him.

"You and your dad downstairs, your mom and Nomie upstairs?"

"You can't blame everything I do or say on my parents' divorce."

"But look at what you do in your work. You build houses and divide them into boxes. You compartmentalize." He waved his arm in the direction of her work space at the other end of the long room.

"I don't buy all that stuff," she said. "These . . . theories."

"But if the shoe fits . . ."

"It doesn't fit that well."

"Too tight or too loose, Cinderella?" He lifted her hand and tugged at her engagement ring. It was as sparkly as it was supposed to be, but too tight. Once he'd put it on, she hadn't been able to get it off, and she felt panicky whenever she thought about that.

"You're the one who seems to need space," she said, turning from her side onto her back. "When you don't call for a couple days and, you know, cancel plans."

"That's because of my problem," he said. "I want to spare you."

She faced him. "How can you spare me if we live together?"

"I'll figure something out," he said. "Maybe I should see my therapist twice a week, or find a different shrink. And . . . open up to you more, if you can take it."

More? she thought. "Sure. Bring it on."

He chuckled. "On their wedding day, the bride hopes the groom will change, and the groom hopes the bride will never change. Did you ever hear that?"

She shook her head. "I'm not trying to change you. I just want you to be happy."

They reached a sort of compromise: Claire would move into Jay's condo and keep her apartment on Long Street as an art studio. "You can run off to your studio when I drive you nuts," he said, "but at least I'll know where to find you."

On a Saturday in June he asked her to join him while he tried on tuxedos for the wedding. After they settled into his car, he pulled a blue silk tie out of his back pocket, held it by both ends, and moved it toward her head. "Hey!" she protested, ducking, but when he promised a surprise—"a good one"—she let him blindfold her.

After a fifteen-minute drive, he parked and removed the tie. They were sitting in front of a bungalow with cream-colored stucco. Pansies were growing in the window boxes, and a FOR SALE sign was stuck in the tiny scrap of lawn. And there was Claire's mother, leaning against the railing.

"Where are we," Claire said, "and what is my mom doing here?"

Jay took her hand. "I think an artist who builds houses should live in a real house. What do you think?"

"Um . . . wow!" She squeezed his hand.

Her mother, who it seemed had helped Jay with his secret housing search, took them on a tour. The place had curb appeal, but the owners had not bothered to stage the interior or even to abide by normal household conventions: they kept their books in the kitchen on shelves made of planks and concrete blocks, and the linen closet was stocked with cans of organic food.

"Wait till you see this," Claire's mother said, opening a door in the hallway and yanking the string attached to the bare bulb.

A baby's crib was wedged into the back of the narrow walk-in closet. A bare coat rod extended overhead, and a Winnie the Pooh print hung on the rear wall. Stuffed animals were piled in a heap on a high shelf. Claire spotted a pacifier in the crib.

She shrank back. "Their baby sleeps in the closet?"

"Arguably, a baby might like sleeping in a small room," said Jay, the infant expert, but without much conviction. "Though it's kind of sad there's no window."

"They use the second bedroom as a family room," Claire's mother said with icy irony.

They moved on, seeking out friendly touches to distract them from the bleakness of the baby's closet. In the living room, the fireplace was framed with Dutch tiles painted with windmills and milkmaids. Throughout the house, the molding had been stripped down to the wood, and the kitchen island was an eco-friendly bamboo. But what really persuaded Claire that they should buy the house, beyond its good bones and her desire to make Jay happy by pleasing her, was the idea of liberating the baby from its cave.

"We'll be happy here," she said, squeezing Jay's hand after they were back in the car, and he smiled in agreement. It was a promise, of sorts.

Soon after, at her bridal shower, Claire overheard her mother say to friends that Jay had been ready to put down earnest money before consulting Claire about the house. "Nuh-uh, I said to him," Nancy said. "Not a good idea. My daughter doesn't like surprises, I told him."

That had brought Claire up short: the idea that Jay almost bid on a house without consulting her. It was a sign of romanticism, yes, but also recklessness. Yet he had restrained himself, deferring to his mother-in-law-to-be's superior knowledge of her daughter. That was the important thing.

Claire got back into her car, unbuttoned her coat, and unwound her scarf. She would not be able to go into the house today—she wasn't anywhere near ready for that—but getting as close as the garage had to count for something.

He's gone, she thought. The clean car was a clearer sign of that fact than his coffin had been. A clearer sign than the voice mail message or the painting on the therapist's telephone table. A clearer sign even than his suicide note.

"He's gone," she said aloud.

She rubbed the numb spot by her right ear, thinking. How could the therapist be sure it wasn't Jay's heart on the message? She fumbled in her purse for her phone. As soon as she took it out, it rang. She screamed and tossed it into the air. "Mom," the display read after she fished it from the floor of the car. Her eyes filled at the sight of the word.

She cleared her throat and answered. "Hi, Mom."

"Claire, hi. Where are you?"

"I'm . . . running some errands. I got up early today."

"Oh. Well, good. But your father's worried about you."

He must have noticed her car was gone. She should have anticipated that. "Can you call him back? Tell him I'm fine?"

"I don't understand why you two can't call each other."

"Mom, please? I gotta go. I'm in line at the bank."

"What are you doing at the bank?" Her mother sounded concerned.

"The ATM." No one stood in line at the bank anymore. "Just call him, will you?"

Nancy's voice softened. "Hon, are you sure everything's all right?"

"Yeah, fine! I'll call you later."

"All right, then."

After hanging up, Claire dialed her and Jay's home phone number and waited through the rings. If it had been summer, she might have heard the phone through open windows, across the small yard to the garage, but not now, not in March. Then she heard her own voice, self-consciously jaunty, higher than she always expected it to sound, telling her to leave a message for Claire and Jay.

Following the beep, she slid her phone under her sweater and placed the receiver end underneath her bra, by her heart.

She stared straight ahead and breathed, waiting.

There was not much in the garage. Lined up against the wall were the lawn mower that Jay used on Saturday mornings, playing the part of the proud homeowner; the toolbox Harry and Nomie had given them as a housewarming gift; an old easel of Claire's; and some paint cans with dried drips that matched the walls of their rooms—the upstairs bath (pink eraser), the living room (velvet leaf), the kitchen (crushed orange).

Claire took the phone out of her shirt and hung up. After waiting another minute, she dialed into their home voice mail and listened to the message she had left. She heard a loud rustling of fabric against microphone. Then she did hear a heart, but much fainter than Jay's message, no more magnified than the soft *thumpa-thumpa* she would hear when she pressed her ear against his chest on lazy nights when they were lying on the couch.

He had not been trying to tell her anything. He hadn't even known he had called her. She had mistaken the swishing of her husband's pants for the beating of his heart. That was how well she knew him, in the end.

Claire was not supposed to have gone to the party.

The hosts were Jay's colleague Sally, who ran the Marriage and Family Lab at the university, and her husband, Bart. Married more than forty years, they had thrown their first annual Valentine's Day party decades ago, after one of Sally's single graduate students complained she'd been working so hard studying other people's relationships that she would be alone for the biggest date night of the year. The party was always held on the night itself, never loosely on the weekend before or after, Sally told Claire at a dinner party during the winter holidays. "It's as bad as New Year's Eve," she said, "but maybe worse, because Valentine's Day blindsides people right there in the middle of February, the most depressing month of the year in Chicago."

Jay had skipped the party his first two years in Chicago, both times to be with Claire. The first year, they went on their first date; the following year, still gingerly recovering from the New Year's debacle, they spent the holiday holed up at a bed-and-breakfast in Union Pier. Jay had been to

Bart and Sally's apartment during one of his recruiting visits, though. "Swanky," he told Claire. "A view of the Drive like you wouldn't believe," which, though she didn't say it, made her think of their suite at the Drake on New Year's Eve—the snowflakes so large and bright they looked plastic, like sit-com snow; food and wine churning in her stomach as she absorbed the fact that he was not entirely who she had thought he was.

When the party invitation came, a heart-shaped card in a pink envelope, Claire assumed they would both go. She wasn't looking forward to it, but she didn't dread it, either. A Thursday night event was simply inconvenient. Most Thursdays she worked at her studio until she got tired, while Jay did the same at his office. Then they would meet at home and throw together some pasta, open a bottle of wine, and watch a DVD of one of the HBO shows they were juggling. Instead she would have to put on tights and a dress, lipstick and mascara, and be a faculty spouse: amiable and witty, but careful not to outshine her husband, who would be up for tenure in a few years.

Not that Jay had ever coached her. But the way he said "They loved you" and squeezed her hand after they left her first department dinner party showed her how important it had been to him that she had his colleagues' approval.

The week before Valentine's Day, Jay had seemed moody, quiet and subdued. He stayed late at his office, then fell asleep on the couch in front of the TV, and Claire guessed that one morning very soon he would crawl into bed and not get up. But the storm blew over: he was buoyant on their Friday night date, at dinner and then at the Green Mill, where they sat in a booth, half listening to the jazz, whispering in each other's ears for fear of being shushed by the floor manager.

That night she watched Jay grimace in ecstasy, eyes shut, as he clung to her.

"I love you," he said afterward. "I'll always love you. You know that, right?"

"Of course," she said, smiling. He worried about the strangest things. "I'll always love you, too."

But on Sunday, Jay said he had to work again, and Claire scolded him about the closets.

"Next weekend, I promise," he said. "I've gotta get going on this new project. Ari is waiting on me."

"What kind of project?" she said, softening. She liked hearing about his experiments: the benign ways he and his colleagues tricked babies into revealing just how smart they were. And she hadn't actually minded the husband-and-wife tension about the closets, so typical, so mundane: she thought he was being lazy and inconsiderate, and he probably thought she was a nag. It was the kind of problem she could mention to her friends, rolling her eyes.

"A revise and resubmit," he said, stooped over in the hallway as he pulled on his boots.

"An article?"

He nodded.

"I thought you said a project."

He looked up at her blankly. "Right. An article project."

"I thought you meant a research project. Hey," she said, "by the way, Sally's party is on Thursday, right? Did you RSVP?"

"Oh yeah," he said as he tied his laces. "I told them probably I'd just come on my own."

"Why? I can come."

"It's not a big deal. I know you like to work late on Thursdays. I can do the witty and charming thing on your behalf."

"It's Valentine's Day," she said, slightly hurt. In the past he had always wanted her to go to work functions with him.

"It's not like it would be romantic," he said. "A big party like that."

"Well, I guess. We could celebrate next weekend."

"Sure," he said, and rose to kiss her goodbye.

Claire leaned the painting against her steering wheel. Anyone with taste would find it competent but unremarkable: a simple image of the proprietress of a flower shop, stooping over her wares on a bright spring day. The brushstrokes were swift and sure, melding with the subject matter to suggest a smug understanding between artist and viewer that the world was a peaceful, sunny place where people wanted for nothing. It was the kind of painting that would sell in a vacation town in Door County, Wisconsin, but Claire would not have wanted anyone in the River North gallery district to see it.

She ran her fingers over the stippled bumps of the flower buds, the S-curve of the owner's gray ponytail, trying to identify the raised contours of the hidden layer of paint.

She had made this painting for Jay for their one-year anniversary because she needed to tell him a story about their marriage, as she understood it, in the best way she knew how: glossy contentment on the surface, with something darker and sadder lurking underneath.

She had been excited and distracted in the month or so before Valentine's Day: she was trying something new in her work. Maybe that was why she hadn't pressed harder to find out why he didn't care if she went to the party with him.

In the past she had built her dollhouses from memory,

conjuring up images of homes she had lived in or visited. The further back in time she traveled, the easier it was to convey the mood of a piece. She relied on the remembered details that had floated to the surface and remained there for years: the broken cap on the banister in her childhood home, which she and Nomie were always knocking off when they played; the valentines swirled on her hospital bed when she was in kindergarten; the strawberry patch in the garden of the home in suburban Paris where she had stayed on a high school exchange trip. She tried to build her dollhouses and dioramas around just a few important objects so they wouldn't become too cluttered or specific.

For the first time, she was working on a dollhouse modeled on her current home. Her and Jay's house was a living organism, always changing, with a hundred seemingly important details in each room to sift through mentally. Building a model of it felt like trying to paint a portrait of someone who refused to sit still.

When she decided to start the project, a month earlier, she had found herself sketching a floor plan of the house viewed from above, rather than her usual construction, a dollhouse open on one side. She had tried to explain what it looked like to Jay as they were having dinner at a bistro near their house. She told him it would open from the top so that the viewer could look down into the partitioned rooms.

"It's kind of like a rat maze," she said.

He gave a short laugh and stared at her. "That's funny."

"What?" But in a split second she realized what he was thinking.

"You feel like a rat in a maze at our house," he said. "Trapped."

She looked away and shook her head, stung. "No I don't. I love our home."

"I know," he said quickly. "I'm sorry."

Mercifully, he began to tell her about rat mazes, which it turned out he had worked with in graduate school. She gave him a pen, they pushed their dishes aside, and he began sketching on the butcher paper. "This is your basic rat maze," he said, drawing a partitioned box with a starting point and an end point where the cheese was placed—"Food pellets, actually." Next was a maze shaped like a hollowed-out letter T: "The experimenter puts different types of food, or even other rats, at the tips of the T. Then they put a rat at the base of the T to see which choice it makes—whether it prefers right or left, chicken or beef, mommy or girlfriend," said Jay. Finally he drew a water maze. The experimenter would place a rat in a tub of water and time how long it took the rat to find a hidden platform.

"Hey!" he said. "Have I ever told you about the visual cliff?"

"I don't think so." They were hunched over the table, knees pressed together, as if they were the only two people in the bustling restaurant.

"That's done mostly with babies, though it's been done with rats and other animals, too."

"Babies? Human babies?"

"Yeah." He sketched a large block. "Imagine this platform is about waist-high. It's draped in a checkerboard cloth, and there's a piece of Plexiglas covering it. But the Plexiglas extends over the edge of the platform by a few feet, see? So you put a baby that has just learned to crawl on the checkerboard block, and then you have Mom stand at the other end of the Plexiglas."

"Okay . . ."

"Because the Plexiglas is clear, the end of the platform looks like a sheer drop, see? Even though it isn't. That's the visual cliff. So babies will crawl up to the edge of the cliff, but they won't go over it, even if Mom is standing on the other side calling to them."

"They think they're going to fall?"

"Yeah. See, this experiment showed that humans have depth perception at a very early age. Depth perception, plus a self-preservation instinct. The babies don't want to fall off the cliff, even if it means being alone."

"Huh. Which would you rather do? Fall off the cliff or be alone?"

He smiled and shrugged. "Fall off the cliff. You?"

She smiled back. "What do you think?"

She watched him hold himself back from making a pointed remark. "I think opposites attract," he said, and kissed her. He started drawing a picture of the Skinner box, "which is not a maze, either, but very important in studies of learning . . ."

She took a sip of wine and folded her arms on the table, content as she watched her husband make funny little drawings, and happy that he was content, too. Together they had wandered into one of her favorite zones in their marriage: a moment when she learned something new about him or he took interest in something she was saying, just when it seemed they knew everything about each other. She felt relieved, too. They had averted danger. He had dropped his remark about her running away.

Because of something that happened on a night early in their marriage, her art studio on Long Street—the reason they met—had become a sore subject between them.

They had come together in the kitchen of their house after work. Before either of them even reached for the light switch, they embraced and started telling each other about the day, swaying as if music were playing, talking into each other's shoulders. She told him about having lunch with her mom, and then a meeting with a difficult staging client, a woman in Winnetka who had called Rebecca's supply of furniture "trashy." Jay told her he was still frustrated with his coauthor's work on an article that a top-notch journal had asked them to revise and resubmit. "I don't think they're going to want the paper," he said.

"I was talking about that with my mom," Claire said.

"Talking about what?"

"How you get stressed about work, but you probably don't have to worry about tenure, since you've already got so many papers published."

"You told your mom I get stressed?"

"Mm-hmm. Just, you know, that it sometimes makes you feel . . . low. She sympathized. She said you're a worrier, like my dad." They were still swaying.

"She sympathized with you or with me?" He pulled away and pushed up his glasses, which had slid down his nose while they hugged. It was dusk, and his face was shades of blue-gray in the dark apartment, like a grainy photograph.

"With *you*."

"You told her that I feel low? What else?"

Claire shook her head. "Nothing." She hadn't told her mother or anyone else about his depression, in so many words. She had told some of her friends that he could be melancholy and moody, but that was all. Jay had never asked her not to talk about it, but she hadn't wanted anyone to know, fearful that someone would try to talk her out of being with him—and, she had to admit to herself, embarrassed. Ashamed. "That's all I said, that you get low sometimes. Because of work, I said."

"Great," he said, backing away. "Now what's your mom going to think of me?"

"That you're a normal guy with normal problems. C'mon, everyone gets stressed."

"Okay, but I don't want you talking to your mom about me like I'm some kind of . . . specimen."

"I don't do that."

"It's not appropriate in a marriage. And it's not really fair, either, considering." His eyes narrowed appraisingly.

"Considering what?"

"Considering you don't open up to me the way I open up to you."

Her heart was thudding. "Just because I don't talk a lot?"

"The fact is, Claire . . ." He turned away from her, pacing a few steps, then looked back. "Sometimes I feel like I don't even know you that well."

She recoiled. "What do you mean? You know everything about me."

"I don't always know what's in here, though." He clenched his fist and pressed it against his chest.

"Well, if we didn't spend so much time talking about your problems, maybe you'd know me better."

"Nice," he snarled. "Very supportive. I didn't know I was such a burden."

"Stop being an ass," she cried.

"*I'm* being an ass?"

That was when she walked out of the house and drove to her studio, thinking he would leave her now or she would leave him—she was too confused to know what had happened, to know which one of them had more of a right to be angry. For an hour she paced and sketched at her studio, feeling like she should be calling someone for advice, but not knowing who. She had people she considered good friends, she realized, but no true confidantes in her life. The word "divorcée" ran through her head—*dee-vor-say, dee-vor-say*—until it sounded like nonsense syllables.

When he showed up at her studio, she wouldn't buzz him in at first; he had to wheedle his way in over the intercom. "Why don't I have a key to this place?" he shouted when she let him in, but then he held her on the couch as she cried. "I'm sorry," he whispered. "I do know you. I know you're as open as you can be. It's not fair to want to change you. I know from the way you kiss me, the way we are together." The hopefulness in his voice told her that he was trying hard to convince himself as well as her. He was like the bride in his adage, hoping for change, she thought, and she was like the groom, wanting things to stay the same.

"But you can't walk out on me," he said. "We're married now. It's okay for us to argue. You don't need to be afraid."

"I know," she blubbered. "But you need to not say mean things to me." Not having had much experience getting angry in her life, she found she sounded like a child when she did. "I don't know how to do this."

"I know," he said. "Shh, shh. I'm sorry."

She didn't know then how bad it would get. She didn't know that during their year and nine months of marriage he would be immobilized six times. She kept a tally in her mind.

The first time had been on their honeymoon. He had been solid through their wedding, a perfect, loving groom buoying the stressed-out bride. But when they got to Maui, he crashed, spending the first few days in bed with the drapes closed. Claire had tiptoed around him, but by the end of the week she had broken down in tears and yanked his arm, trying to pull him out of bed. After a fight, he had rallied, at first gruffly going through the motions of beach walks and dinner on the patio, then suddenly coming to life, full of remorse. The last few days had been shaky—literally, she had seen both their hands shake as they fumbled with the room card or made grave promises over margaritas—but the undercurrent of secrecy, of barely averted disaster, had been thrilling to Claire in a shameful way. She had thought, stupidly, that she was the reason he got out of bed that day.

"Tell me what it's like," she whispered to him on the plane ride home. Her head was resting on his shoulder.

"It's hell," he said, "but it always passes. I guess it's like what people say about migraines or childbirth. You forget how bad it is until it's starting up again. That may be the worst time, actually—waiting for it to come on."

After that, the spells came every few months, regularly enough to be part of the fabric of their marriage. Six months passed without one, and she began to hope that they were safe, but then he grew irritable and began sleeping late, and once again they were in the thick of it.

Jay's family knew about his illness, and a couple of his friends who lived in other cities, but no one in Chicago did. Somehow he managed to hide it from a department full of psychologists. At his worst, he called in sick to the lab or to his classes. Family emergency, he said once. Food poisoning, he said another time into the phone. ("That shuts people up real quick," he said darkly when he hung up.)

The last spell had been three months before his death, in November. Slowly, over a period of days, he grew silent, then nearly mute. For a week he barely got out of bed and ate only when Claire brought him food. He left the house once, for his therapy appointment, and when he got back, he crawled into bed fully dressed. When Claire asked him what she could do, if there was anything she could get him, he said no, that he just needed to sleep.

As she had in the past, she thought about calling his therapist for advice. She thought, not seriously, about calling his parents and telling them to deal with him. She thought about yelling at him to get up. But she had tried that before, and it hadn't worked in Chicago as it had on Maui. Instead she kept up her usual routine and treated Jay as if he had a bad case of the flu. She brought him soup. She lined up glasses of 7-Up, orange juice, and water by his bedside, re-creating the cheerful grouping of fluids her mother had placed by her childhood sickbed after her hospital stay.

At night she lay beside him. Usually he was a restless sleeper, muttering and jolting awake, but during his spells he did not seem to move at all during the night.

One morning in early December he rose before she did. She padded into the kitchen and found him washing the dishes. He had showered, shaved, and put on a clean shirt. On the radio, two men were complaining about the Bears.

She wrapped her arms around him. "Feeling better?"

"Much." He turned around and, grinning, waggled his soapy hands at her.

"Stop!" she said, and started to cry.

Each time, there had been a day like that, so predictable that she thought their lives would always be this way. Claire would cry, Jay would apologize and console her, and then they would have a sober conversation about steps they could take to alleviate his problem. They joined a gym, wondering if endorphins would help, but then Jay got busy with work and they stopped going. Claire nagged him about finding a psychiatrist and trying different meds, and he said he would think about it, but she didn't know if he had. And after each recovery, there would inevitably be a night when Claire worked late at her studio and fell asleep on the couch. Jay would chide her gently the next day: he knew it wasn't always easy, living with him, but they were married now. She couldn't live like a single person. They needed to spend as many nights as possible together, he said, because you never know how many you have left.

Claire got out of her car, took the toolbox down from the shelf, and set it on the hood of Jay's car. She found the package of razor blades in the tray, underneath the hammer and screwdrivers. They had bought them to scrape fresh paint off of windows. She put the toolbox back on the shelf and took the box of blades back to her car.

She had not seen him much the last few days. They both worked late, then met up at home for takeout or leftovers in front of the TV. They didn't talk much and were too tired for sex—at least, she thought that was the reason. "I miss you," she whispered to him in bed that Wednesday night.

He stroked her hair in the dark. "Miss me? Silly. I'm right here."

The next morning, he was up early, saying he had meetings before the lab opened. Half asleep, she heard him rushing around.

"Hey." He stooped over her, smiling, before he left.

She propped herself up on an elbow for a kiss, which was deeper and longer than she had expected.

"Hey," she said, smiling. She opened her eyes to the sight of her lovely husband, fresh-scrubbed and neatly dressed.

"I love you." He cupped her head in his hands and kissed her on the forehead. "Very much."

"I love *you*," she said. "Very much."

Only when he was bounding down the stairs did she remember. "Happy Valentine's Day!" she called out.

"You, too!" he called back.

She worked at the model home that day, then went to her studio to work. After Jay had told her about rat mazes, she changed her idea about the piece. Rather than partitioning the house as it actually was, she extended the walls, adding dead ends where there were none and narrowing the hallways in a manner she thought looked menacing. The corridors opened up to just three rooms: the kitchen, the bedroom, and the living room.

That afternoon, Claire used her jigsaw to fashion a piece of wood into the curves of the green love seat she and Jay sat in together when they watched TV; then she glued a scrap of kelly-green velvet onto it.

She sat the couch in the middle of the living room and saw that it overpowered the bed in the next room; she had used a lathe to form the ripples and craters of tossed-aside sheets and blankets. She paused, debating which object was more important in their lives: the bed, where they slept and made love, or the couch, where Jay sometimes slept and where they sometimes made love, but also ate dinner, watched TV, and talked until late in the night.

See, she said to Jay in her head, *I do think about our marriage, just not in the way you do.*

She checked her watch: it was six-thirty. Jay would be getting ready for the party. She felt restless suddenly, and wanted to be with him. She didn't like surprises, but he did. She would work a little longer and show up at the party. A Valentine's Day surprise.

By that point he had already placed the binder on his desk and sent the painting to his therapist. The struggle was over; there was no turning back. He could have returned the binder to his shelf the next morning, but he couldn't get the painting back. He would have had a hard time explaining that, especially to a psychologist.

He must have left the voice mail message by accident when he was walking from his car to Bart and Sally's. Later, Claire learned that he'd parked several blocks away.

It was getting cold in the garage.

Claire had planned to get back into her car, but she realized that she wouldn't have room to work sitting behind the steering wheel. She had never liked sitting in the passenger seat of her own car, the few times Jay drove it and she rode: it made her feel antsy and out of control.

She had his keys, she remembered. Someone, maybe Harry or her father, had given them to her. They were at the bottom of her purse.

She retrieved the painting from her car, then unlocked the passenger door of Jay's car and got in.

The interior had been vacuumed and cleaned. There was not so much as a penny or a gum wrapper in the well between the seats, and an unpleasant, synthetic strawberry smell hung in the air. But underneath the chemicals she could still smell Jay: a dark citrus scent like burnt oranges and cloves, a little like the Swedish glogg that Sally had served at the party, but with a bitter, musky undertone.

At Sally and Bart's, the doorman ushered Claire to the elevator without calling up to the apartment first. "Enjoy the party," he said.

Inside the apartment, familiar faces milled among vases of red roses. Votives shimmered, casting shadows on the rose petals that covered the tabletops; it was as if they had all crashed some young man's elaborate proposal scene. Jay noticed Claire, did a double take, and moved toward her, smiling, though not as widely as she had expected. He looked cute in his blue sweater, a Christmas gift from her, and his new black-framed glasses. He had gotten them a month earlier, but they still surprised her every time she saw him after an absence, expecting the old wire rims.

"Hey! What are you doing here?" He kissed her swiftly, tasting slightly of beer.

"Happy Valentine's Day!" She took his hand. "Surprise!"

"Happy Valentine's Day. This is a surprise." He kneaded her fingers distractedly. "Okay, then. Welcome!"

There wasn't time for her to dwell on his lack of enthusiasm. He led her into a pack of people drinking glogg, steam rising from the glass mugs. The persona Claire used with this crowd rose up out of nowhere: arty, and therefore cool by default. Friendly, but slightly detached. Bemused. It wasn't something she would ever admit aloud, but Claire loved being part of a couple. For so many years she had arrived at parties alone, offering up her guacamole or bottle of wine, moving from person to person, careful not to talk to married men for too long or to stand alone by the chips. Now she was insulated from seeming predatory or pathetic. Now she was part of a team.

As the wife of a nontenured professor, she had expected to be at a power disadvantage with these people, not anticipating that many of them were frustrated creative types who would treat her with a mixture of envy, respect, and condescension. When they were a little drunk, an inordinate number of the psychology professors revealed to her that they dreamed of writing a novel, being a photographer, or playing the cello professionally. What went unspoken was that unlike Claire, they had opted for financial stability. Also unspoken: they thought her lucky, shrewd even, to have found a man who could support her flaky artistic career.

Alan, one of the Marriage Lab professors, had been there, and Sherry, his cow-eyed wife. Jay and Alan continued a debate they had been having before Claire arrived about the percentage of parents who regret having children. Jay argued that the figure was close to seventy percent; Alan said it was only ten percent and that Jay was falling for bullshit Ann Landers statistics. Not liking the side Jay had taken, Claire listened to Sherry tell her, as she had at several other department parties—her eyeballs rolling freakishly in all directions—that she, too, used to be a painter, when she was in college, until she decided to go into massage therapy to pay the bills.

Claire squeezed Jay's hand. Taking the cue, he said they needed to get her a drink.

In the kitchen, Sally was splashing vodka and rum into the pot of glogg on the stove, "in case I accidentally boil the booze away." She was in her seventies, and stylish for a professor: she wore vintage Chanel suits to her classes, and that night she was wearing a red taffeta shift, quite possibly from the Jackie O era. Thanks to her ramrod posture and black pumps, she appeared to be six feet tall. Her husband, Bart, a portly man with a white mustache who was retired from doing something with investments (possibly only managing his inheritance), was spooning salmon mousse onto heart-shaped phyllo puffs.

Sally kissed Claire on the cheek and handed her a mug of glogg. "Wonderful to see you. Both of you. Finally you made it to one of our parties!" She told Bart that Jay and Claire's first date had been on Valentine's Day. "So, a red-letter day for them," she said with a wink.

"How long since the wedding?" Bart asked.

Claire and Jay looked at each other. "A little under two years," said Jay.

"Remember our early years, Sal?" Bart asked.

"I try not to." Sally's face had a girlish flush from the steam rising from the pot.

"We went into counseling," Bart said. "This was the fifties—no one went into counseling!"

"We were pioneers."

"Leadbelly. Or Ledbetter. That was the good doctor's name."

"Dead for centuries, I'm sure," Sally said.

"We should pay a visit to his grave on our fiftieth anniversary," Bart said. "Lay some tulips."

"Don't give him too much credit," Sally said. "He used to fall asleep, remember?"

"He did, he did. Even worse, he told me to stop going to Cubs games. Can you believe that? He actually had me bring the tickets in to our sessions and rip them up in front of him."

Sally raised an eyebrow at Claire and Jay. "He had been drinking."

As Bart paused to look at his wife, a spoonful of mousse dripped onto the floor. "During our sessions?"

"No, dear, *you* were drinking. I'd come home from work, and my new husband would be sitting on the sofa in the dark with a bottle of Scotch."

"I only drank when they lost."

"Which would have been fine, if you were a Yankees fan."

There were lots of problems a couple could have, Claire remembered thinking, there in the kitchen. Alcoholism, disinterest, infidelity—all of these things were worse than occasional bouts of depression, she told herself, no matter how severe.

"Naturally, given her profession, Sally dragged me into therapy," said Bart.

"We talked about maintaining perspective."

"It's only a game, and all that crap."

"Excuse me," Jay said, and he was gone.

Claire turned, surprised and a little embarrassed that he had left the conversation so abruptly. "So, it worked?" she said to their hosts.

"Mind over baseball," Sally said.

"Actually, Claire," Bart said, "I think it was just a matter of growing up. I said, 'Oh, okay. Those are the rules? Well, I'm a baseball fan. I know about rules.' And that was that."

"Has it always been that easy?" Claire said. "Like, with any kind of problem that comes up? Mind over baseball?"

They both shook their heads. "Oh no," Bart said. "Definitely not."

"This wasn't such a deep issue," Sally said. "This was just baseball."

"We've passed over rougher ground since then, let me tell you," said Bart.

Settled in Jay's car, the painting leaning against the dash, Claire took out one of the razor blades and touched it lightly against her fingertip.

She slid the blade along one of the top corners of the painting, trying to get under the upper layer of paint. She had applied a sealant over the first layer for exactly this purpose, but in her mind, she had anticipated that she and Jay would perform this ritual together on some distant anniversary.

On her first try, both layers came off, leaving a clean white spot of canvas. She tried again, more gingerly, and managed to separate a strip of the pinkish top layer from the sepia tones underneath. Then the top layer broke off, the chip falling into her lap. She started over again, working chip by chip.

The top layer of paint came off most easily if she shaved it off. She scratched lightly, using the blade like a nail file. The sepia tones surfaced, reminding her of the jigsaw puzzle of the pyramids that she and her father had labored over together at her mother's house during the earliest days of mourning.

After Jay had left the kitchen, Claire mingled with several different small groups. She spotted him a couple of times through the crowd, standing silent and unsmiling in a clutch of grad students. Claire stayed where she was, with a gaggle of professors who were making fun of a professor in the sociology department whom she didn't know. Above everyone's heads, the black velvet drapes against the far wall parted, revealing an impressionistic reflection of the party on glass, shadows bobbing on spots of rosy light. Then the reflection gave way to the gray-white sky, heavy with snow. Claire thought she saw her husband's round, closely shaved head moving through the opening, onto what must be the balcony—she had a fleeting image of him walking into nothingness, unharmed for a few steps, like a cartoon character, or a baby crawling on Plexiglas—before the glass door closed again and the black drapes fell into place.

Startled by a burst of communal laughter, she excused herself and wandered away from the group. Jay bummed cigarettes at parties sometimes, only one or two, not enough that she had to worry it might become a habit; he didn't even hold a cigarette properly, pincering it between his thumb and forefinger like a joint. She had wondered, vaguely, if he was alone out there on the balcony or if he had joined someone, and if he had put on his coat. It was freezing outside.

Tired of the career talk, Claire returned to the kitchen. Sally was alone, arranging strawberries and raspberries on a platter along with some pound cake, and Claire was glad to put down her glogg, which had gone cold, and pitch in. The impressive state of the February berries got them talking about the craze for locally grown food. "Slow food, my foot," Sally said. "They turn up their noses at mangoes from Mexico when some kids in this city can't find anything but Cheetos and Yoo-hoo in their neighborhoods."

How long was she in the kitchen with Sally, enjoying their mutual, if uninformed, indignation about food snobs? Awhile. Ten minutes, maybe fifteen. Claire had been in no hurry to leave. She might not have thought about Jay at all.

"Take this to the table for me, will you?" Sally said finally.

Claire moved slowly through the room with the platter and made space for it on the dining table. She looked around. Jay should have been back from his smoke, but she didn't see him. The black drapes hid the balcony from view.

She was tired suddenly; she had a low tolerance for crowds and wanted to go home. She went to the bathroom to get away from the people and the noise. As soon as she was shut up in the quiet, bright room, she felt frightened.

He must still be on the balcony, talking to someone, she told herself. Or chatting with someone in a hallway.

She leaned in close to the mirror that covered the wall above the sink. The skin beneath her eyes was sagging, as it did when she was tired; soon enough it would look like this all the time. She reapplied her lipstick, which had worn away in the center.

He was somewhere in the apartment, anyway. Object permanence. When a bunny puppet seemingly disappeared into thin air, a six-month-old baby would stare and stare, knowing this was impossible.

Out in the party, the music stopped. The chatter and the laughter diminished to a murmur.

The shower curtain was ugly, a pattern of gold and black streaks. Seized with fear, she pulled back the curtain. The shower gleamed, stark white and empty.

Thinking of the European woman who had been abandoned by her husband on New Year's Eve, Claire took out her cell phone and saw that there was a message waiting. She dialed into voice mail, and that was the first time she heard it, what she thought was the furious beating of Jay's heart.

Her own heart was pounding. She saved the message and disconnected.

It's safe in here, she thought, not knowing why. I should stay here.

But she left the room.

The apartment had become almost as bright as the bathroom had been. Everyone faced the front door, as if someone were standing there giving a toast. Two police officers stood in the doorway, a man and a woman, flanking the doorman. The three of them were talking to Sally and Bart in hushed tones, their heads bowed together. The party had been too loud, Claire thought with an odd sense of relief. It was a weeknight, and neighbors had complained.

Claire looked in vain for Jay, then turned toward the dark hallway. She would search the rest of the apartment.

"Claire," Sally said behind her.

She kept moving down the hallway.

"Claire," Sally said urgently, touching her back.

Claire turned around.

Sally's mouth was open; Claire could see the gold fillings in her back teeth. "Have you seen Jay?" Sally's voice was bright with panic. "Is he here?"

"I don't know," Claire said, stalling. She couldn't admit to Sally, to everyone, that she had lost track of her husband. "What do you mean?"

"Come here," Sally said, steering her into a bedroom. The bed was piled with coats. Claire looked around the darkened room for Jay, but it seemed to be empty. Sally led her to an easy chair away from the window. Far below on the street, sirens were whining. "You stay here," Sally said. "Don't move. I'll be right back."

She left and shut the door without turning on a light.

Claire sat dutifully. She would stay in that room for as long as they would let her.

Claire brushed the painting's shavings from her lap. She had finished. The flower shop was gone, replaced by Orpheus Records.

She had painted the record shop as she remembered it from that Friday afternoon when she had wandered in after school. Details, whether real or false memories, had risen to the surface as she worked. The woman who hinted, or so Claire had thought, about a possible date with her coworker was tall and wore her white hair in a bun. The man, his eyes downcast, a pencil in his hand, had a gray mustache and was wearing an argyle sweater. Claire remembered the pair in sepia tones, faded and dull, so that was how she painted them. In the foreground, her own hand with its bitten fingernails grasped the edge of an album in a bin. She had been a girl already familiar with the ways adults could hurt each other, a girl who maybe even expected love to turn out badly.

After painting the first layer, Claire had put sealant over it and taken a photograph of it. Then she had dipped a brush in pale blue and started painting the sky reflected in the flower shop's plate-glass window.

On their first anniversary, along with the painting, she had given Jay the photograph of the first layer. After he studied it, one corner of his mouth twitching with happiness, he told her he would hang the painting in his office but that he was going to hide the photo.

"What's underneath, that's our secret," he said.

"Our secret," she said, pleased.

Claire looked over at the empty driver's seat. Leaving the painting on the passenger seat, she got out of the car and went around to the other side. She sat down and pressed her face against the seat, breathing in Jay's smell. Shuddering, she closed her eyes and began to cry.

9

Claire had forgotten about her sister. By the time Nomie called to ask if she was coming to pick her up, it was too late, 12:05 already. The obstetrician's appointment was at 12:30, and the office was a half hour away.

"Shit," Claire said, wiping her eyes. She had dozed off in Jay's car at the end of her crying jag. "Nomie, I'm so sorry!"

"That's okay!" Nomie sounded both chipper and on the verge of tears. "I don't even know why Harry wanted you to come. I'll drive myself, no problem. Or maybe Dad will want to come with me, since . . . he's just sitting there. Maybe he would like something to do."

"I'm still coming," Claire said. "I'll meet you there." What had she said to Nomie and Harry? *I won't let you down.* Jesus.

At the mall in Skokie, she shuffled in her wobbly boots from the ice-slick parking lot to the professional building, its entrance tucked unobtrusively beside the Banana Republic storefront. She had passed the building hundreds of times, for this had been her childhood mall, but had never been inside.

Swinging open the glass door, she faced an elevator's blank panels. Fourth floor, she reminded herself. There had to be stairs. Whirling around, she barged through the only door in sight. Success.

On the fourth floor Claire emerged into a maze of gray-carpeted, low-ceilinged hallways. She had forgotten to ask Nomie the name of her doctor, and the appointment would have started fifteen minutes ago. Claire would either have to call her father to see if he was there or find the office on her own.

As she scuttled through the halls, she imagined Jay sketching her from above on butcher paper, a rat frantically seeking its reward. She easily eliminated Dr. S. Neilenberg, D.D.S. The next door, belonging to Dr. P. Coulos, was locked, though she could hear some tinkly piano music playing inside. Cracking open the door of Drs. T. V. Pilsen and J. L. Shrestons, she leaned into a waiting room filled with white noise, as if she had poked her head into the center of an enormous seashell. She took in a framed poster of two empty Adirondack chairs side by side in the setting sun, a basket of miniature Hershey bars, and an issue of *Psychology Today* atop the stack of magazines on the coffee table. She herself could not have staged a more prototypical therapist's office, she thought as she retreated without a sound. SKOKIE VALLEY OBSTETRICS & GYNECOLOGY, the plastic plaque alongside the next door read. DR. R. DRESSNER AND DR. T. KAPLOW.

Well, well, Claire thought, there you are. She pulled open the door to reveal her own parents sitting against the far wall of a crowded but hushed waiting room, their heads close together, their knees touching.

Women of childbearing age, many visibly pregnant, were seated around the perimeter of the room. There were a few men as well, and two little girls sitting side by side with their heads stuck in books. As Claire walked in, people looked up, glancing at her face, then her belly, before looking away. First trimester, they might have decided.

"Claire," her parents said in unison. Relief softened the tension in their faces, but neither of them rose to greet her. Their family was not big on hugs. Jay had been a hugger. Claire had had to get used to all those hugs, and now she would have to get used to not hugging again.

"You're both here," she said to her parents. "Is everything okay?"

"Fine," Nancy said. "Nomie's in with the doctor. Your dad drove her. He called me, and I was free, so I was able to meet them. We weren't sure when you would get here."

Claire's father shrugged apologetically. "I was thinking maybe she'd want a woman here with her, instead of her old dad."

"She didn't want me, either, as it turns out," Nancy said with a quick smile. "But it's a good time to catch up with your father." She patted his knee, and he smiled back.

Pregnant women sat on either side of her parents, so Claire squatted to their level, eager to get back in their good graces.

"Thanks, Dad," she said. "I'm really sorry."

"It's okay, honey." It was strange to see her father close-up, just as it had been yesterday in front of the model home. Even past seventy he was still a handsome man, with his long face and gray eyes. His hair had turned white years ago. A fine network of burst blood vessels outlined his nose on both sides, possibly new, a reaction to stress or lack of sleep. Not alcohol, though; Claire's father had never been a drinker, and she knew he wouldn't become one now, not when he felt he had to be alert for her.

"I had an appointment this morning," she said. She calculated that in their family, the word "appointment" would be suggestive enough of the possibility of an uncomfortable conversation to ward off questioning. They might even infer that she had gone downtown to see Dr. Mercer for a second time. "It went longer than I expected." That was a lie, but what was she supposed to say—that she had been sitting in her and Jay's garage for several hours?

"With Jay's therapist," her mother said. "Nomie told us."

Claire nodded, dumbfounded. It wasn't like Nomie to tattle; she might truly be pissed. "That's right."

"And?" As usual, Nancy was perfectly put together, a crisp white collar pointing out of a mint-green cashmere sweater, her camel-hair coat folded on her lap. Her hair was the same wheat color it had been for Claire's entire life. Claire knew she herself probably looked like a fright—lipstick long gone, mascara smeared under her eyes.

"It was fine," Claire said.

"Fine?" said Nancy.

"Maybe we could talk about that later." Claire let her voice get testy.

"Fine!" her mother exclaimed, holding up her hands.

The room was warm. As Claire stood to remove her coat, blood rushed to her head and a sour odor rose up from beneath her sweater. "I'll just sit over there," she muttered, and retreated to an empty seat against the opposite wall. Her parents glanced at her, then ducked their heads together again, resuming the conversation she had interrupted with her arrival.

Claire felt as if she had been sent to her room, something that had never happened to her as a child. She had been a good girl then, well-behaved to a fault. Did this one mistake, forgetting to take her sister to the doctor, cancel everything out?

She looked away from her parents. Above the pregnant women and their family members, the waiting room's white walls were covered with framed photos of babies, creepy and semipornographic. There were babies disguised as sunflowers and bunnies, a baby peering out of a hole in a chicken egg, a dangerously premature infant dozing naked in a man's dirty old work boot, and—perhaps most frightening of all, Claire imagined herself telling Jay that night—Céline Dion snuggling a shut-eyed, inexplicably green-haired newborn baby in her bony lap.

Claire had been fighting a smile as she thought of telling Jay; now she felt it fade. The photographs might be the kind of sentimental kitsch people only liked once they were pregnant or became parents. She, too, might find a baby sleeping in a work boot adorable if she were expecting.

But not all of the pregnant women in this room were happy, Claire reassured herself. Jay had told her about research that proved it: people overestimated the long-term impact of positive events—such as getting married or having a baby—on their happiness, not recognizing that seemingly less important factors, such as a long commute or a lack of social connections, could have an even greater effect. The woman sleeping in the seat next to Claire's father, for instance, with the *People* magazine splayed atop her very large belly. Her mouth hung open, and her head was canted against the wall at an unnatural angle, as if she had just been shot. Her skin did not glow, her straight brown hair looked greasy, and acne was sprayed like freckles across her cheeks. More important, she was alone. No attentive husband for her, following the pregnancy every step of the way.

"They say we have a set point of happiness that we return to throughout our lives," Jay had said. This was on one of their early dates, too early for Claire to have been concerned. "We have our ups and downs, but we eventually level off."

"That's depressing, isn't it?" Claire had said. "If nothing we do will make us permanently happier, even just a little bit?"

"Look at it this way: if you were permanently happy, you wouldn't feel the need to reach for the next big goal—your next gallery show, or a fulfilling relationship, for example." He grinned; she blushed. "If you were happy all the time, you'd never get out of bed, see?"

Slowly, the woman across the waiting room from Claire opened her eyes and looked directly at her, her gaze cool and appraising. They stared at each other for a long moment, and then the woman set aside the *People* magazine and began to stroke her large belly.

Her face burning, Claire averted her eyes to her parents' knees, which were still touching. Their voices were lost to her within the room's low murmur.

"Claire Kessler?" A slender young African American woman in pink scrubs was standing in the doorway that led into the office.

"Yes?" Claire said, jolting to her feet. Nomie must need her. Maybe there was bad news, she thought, and almost cried with gratitude that she wanted this not to be so. She wanted Nomie to be all right, and her baby, too.

"Follow me, please."

"I'll be right back," Claire said to her parents, registering their stricken faces as she approached the woman.

Through the door and down the hall they went. "Your sister's in here," the woman said, pausing with her ear to a door. She knocked lightly, and a woman's voice told them to come in.

The room was dim and hushed. Nomie was lying on the

examination table in a lab gown that had fallen open to reveal her rounded belly and her bikini underwear. A woman seated before the ultrasound monitor was moving a wand over her stomach.

"Hi!" Nomie said, smiling broadly.

"Hi! I'm sorry I'm late."

"That's okay."

The receptionist left, pulling the door closed behind her.

"You can have a seat by your sister," said the ultrasound technician, an older woman with tightly curled hair.

Claire perched on a chair next to the head of the examination table and smiled at Nomie. "How's it going?"

"Good," Nomie said, beaming. "So, we found out it's a girl."

"Oh!" Claire's throat seized up. She herself had wanted a girl, but she hadn't known her sister evidently had, too.

"You can't tell from the picture right now," the ultrasound woman said. "She's moving around too much. But we figured it out a minute ago."

The wriggling image on the screen made Claire think of a prehistoric fossil being unearthed: seemingly disconnected limbs and a rib cage as delicate as a fish bone floated in and out of view. "Oh!" she cried, for there was the face coming toward them: alien-like, yes, with a skull as broad as the moon, but the child's pinched expression made it look—made *her* look—irritated, and thus human.

"She's beautiful," Claire said.

"Thanks." Nomie took her hand. "Thanks for being here."

Soon it was time for Nomie to dress and talk to the doctor. Claire went back to the waiting room, which had thinned out a little. She took an empty seat next to her father.

Her parents watched her expectantly. "How is she?" Nancy said.

"She's good," Claire said, holding back tears. "She's awesome."

"And the baby?" her dad said. "Did you see it?"

"Awesome, too," Claire said, careful not to use a pronoun. This was Nomie's news to share.

After a while Nomie came out, but she held the door open and beckoned to Claire. "I hope you don't mind," Nomie said when they were back inside the office hallway, "but I told the doctor about that thing you have, with your ear."

Claire shook her head, confused. "What thing?"

"Do you still have that numbness?"

"Oh." Claire reached to touch the spot by her ear. "Yeah. Why?"

"I asked her if she'd talk to you about it."

"She's an obstetrician, right?" Jesus Christ, was Nomie going for an Olympic medal in sisterly martyrdom? Even Claire had forgotten about her weird little ailment.

"Just—come here." Nomie took Claire by the arm and led her down the hall. Claire obeyed, cowed by her sister's exasperation, so unlike Nomie these days.

They entered an examination room, where they found the doctor leaning against a counter, flipping through a magazine—O, Claire saw when the woman tossed it on the counter. "Hi!" she said, smiling, a short, middle-aged woman with a careworn face, her black pageboy shot through with strands of wiry silver. Nomie introduced them, and the doctor extended her hand, which was smooth and cool when Claire shook it, as if carved out of soap.

"Now," the doctor said, once Nomie had slipped out the door and Claire had settled uncomfortably on a metal chair. "Your sister was worried about you. You've got some numbness?"

"I'm sure it's not a big deal. I feel silly even talking about it."

"I don't normally do this sort of thing, but Naomi felt you were too busy looking after her to worry about yourself."

As if, Claire thought.

"So I just thought I'd ask you a few questions. Wouldn't be kosher for me to actually examine you, but I can give you the number of a specialist if it doesn't seem like a total emergency."

"Um . . . okay." An obstetrician taking interest in her face wasn't the strangest thing that had happened to Claire lately.

Dr. Dressner rattled off a list of questions: Did Claire have any pain, loss of hearing, loss of smell, loss of taste, blurred vision, a family history of strokes or MS?

She answered with a series of noes.

"Do you grind your teeth at night?"

"Um . . . I don't know."

"Show me where it's numb." Claire touched the spot. The doctor leaned in and rubbed it. "Feel that?"

"No," Claire said.

"And no pain."

"No. Nothing. No sensation."

"This area we're talking about," Dr. Dressner said, "that's where the trigeminal nerve is. It kinda branches out into the face like an octopus." She spread out her fingers and wiggled them. "Like a sideways octopus, if you can picture that. Now, there's something called trigeminal neuralgia, but if you had that, you'd know it. That's when there's a blood vessel pressing on the nerve. They say the pain is unbelievable." She rolled her chair back to the counter that served as a desk and picked up her pen. "They call it the suicide disease."

"What?" Claire felt the blood rush to her face. "What did you say?"

The doctor looked at her blankly. "Pain. Intense pain?"

"No. The part about suicide."

The doctor sucked in her breath. "I shouldn't use that term. They call it that because the pain is so excruciating that, well, people who have it sometimes just . . . give up. But what you have, numbness, that's different. That's a new one on me. I'm going to give you the number of a neurologist. He's here in the building."

"Do you think I'm going to get it? The tri—the suicide disease?"

The doctor shook her head. "I'm out of my element here, but I don't think it's something you have to worry about, I sincerely don't. It's probably just a fluky thing. Bodies are weird!"

The room fell quiet, the only sound the scratch of the doctor's pen as she wrote the neurologist's name on her prescription pad.

"Did Nomie—Naomi—did she tell you anything else about me?" Claire heard herself stammer.

"Anything else . . ." The doctor looked up.

"Like—that—my husband killed himself recently?"

The woman wheeled around on her chair. "I'm so sorry."

Claire nodded. "So when you said 'the suicide disease' . . . it threw me."

"Yes, yes, of course. Bad choice of words. There was no reason to mention that." She rubbed her eyes. "Listen, it might not be appropriate for me to share this with you, but then again, it probably wasn't appropriate for me to call you in here in the first place, so what the heck." She hunkered down, elbows on knees, hands clasped, and looked Claire straight in the eye. "My brother killed himself. When we were in our twenties."

"Oh." Claire's hand rose to her mouth. "I'm sorry."

"So I know." She nodded, up and down, up and down, until Claire was nodding along with her.

"Yes," Claire said.

"You're feeling guilty? Angry?"

"Yes." Her eyes filled with tears, and her face grew hot.

"And then angry for feeling guilty, and guilty for feeling angry"—her head bobbed back and forth—"and you feel guilty when you're not angry, and so on." The doctor handed her a tissue.

Claire dabbed at her eyes. "Yeah."

"How long ago did it happen?"

"Um . . . about a month ago?"

"So you still don't really believe it. And there's the things people say. Or don't say. A lot of *not* saying anything, right?"

"Right." She let out a sigh. "A lot of not talking about it."

"Are you on any meds?"

Claire shook her head.

"Therapy?"

"Sort of . . . not right now. I need to find someone. I know I should do that."

"I can give you names, if you like. And you might try a support group. They're not for everyone, but you could give it a shot."

"There's a group I heard about," Claire said. "It meets tonight, actually."

"Oh! Well, that's good. I mean, maybe. Hard to know." She pursed her lips and stared at Claire. "I remember this one thing someone said to me that kinda helped—and it might have been the only thing."

Claire nodded, waiting for the pearl of wisdom.

"Just—to remember it was one really bad day in his life, one really bad day that made him do something really stupid. That one day doesn't cancel everything else out."

"Yeah."

"Y'know?"

Claire nodded; she couldn't speak.

The doctor pointed at the side of Claire's face. "I wouldn't be surprised if that just went away on its own, as mysteriously as it came."

"Thank you. I should go, I know you're busy."

"It's no problem." They both stood up, and the doctor passed Claire another tissue. "Do you have any children?"

"No, but—" She caught herself from saying, *No, but we're trying.* "No, but I want to," she said.

"Well, maybe someday you'll come back and see me for something I actually know something about. How old are you?"

"Thirty-seven." That was almost enough to make her start crying again.

"Plenty of time. Don't believe the hype. There's Match.com if you want to do it the old-fashioned way, but there's all kinds of other options. And in the meantime, you can practice by being an aunt."

Claire forced a smile. "Yeah, it's exciting."

The doctor sighed. "Well, you must have mixed emotions. But it'll be nice to have a little one around." She leaned in close and held Claire's arm. "And don't tell your sister I said this, but being an aunt, that's the ideal scenario."

The last time their nuclear family had shared a meal, Claire thought—just the four of them, without Robin, Harry, or Jay, the male interlopers who followed—might have been twenty years ago at this very restaurant, a coffee shop on Ridge Road. Today they had been given a booth, and Claire and their father had slid in on one side, Nomie and their mother on the other, just like old times, and though it was drafty by the window, Claire didn't care. Across the aisle, by the counter with its built-in stools, cream pies and glasses of Jell-O parfait revolved in a case, exact replicas of the desserts she and Nomie had watched spin lazily when they were young.

"So," Claire's father said, looking up from his laminated trifold menu. "Here we are again, at the good ol' Ridgeway."

Their mother grinned. "Hasn't changed a bit, has it?"

"They still have francheezies on the menu." Nomie giggled. "That was our favorite. Remember, Claire?"

"Yup." A hot dog filled with cheese, wrapped in bacon, and deep-fried. Claire swelled with pride. When her mother proposed lunch, it was Claire who suggested the Ridgeway. Before the divorce, they would come here for dinner when her mother didn't feel like cooking; and even after, before Nancy married Robin, the four of them would still sometimes meet up, as if nothing had changed. "I was thinking of ordering one. That and a chocolate milk shake."

"Oh yeah!" Nomie said. "And they'll bring the leftovers in the silver cup they used to blend it in!"

"And remember the seasoning salt on the fries?" Claire asked.

"Yum."

Claire's awful day felt magically redeemed: the four of them not only together, but happy. Nomie and her baby were healthy. Claire had told her parents about her face and agreed to call the neurologist Nomie's doctor had recommended. No one seemed overly worried about that, and their parents appeared to have forgiven Claire for forgetting about Nomie. Claire had shepherded her sister carefully from the mall to the restaurant, driving slowly with her precious cargo. In the car, she thanked Nomie for mentioning her ailment to the doctor, though, not wanting to dampen the mood, she didn't tell

Nomie what she and Dr. Dressner had in common. When they met up with their parents in the parking lot, they had all spontaneously hugged, as if they were the kind of family that hugged.

Think about the bad stuff later, Claire coached herself as everyone studied their menus. Live in the moment. Wasn't that what people always said?

A high school girl dressed in black wrote down their order, the old-time waitresses apparently having taken their white-and-mustard polyester dresses into retirement with them. It was long past lunchtime, and they had the place to themselves. Beyond the plate glass, snow had begun to fall, disappearing on the cleared sidewalk but covering the parkway's crusted ice like a lace tablecloth. Across the street, a brick-and-stone church set back on a long white lawn looked solid and serious, indifferent to would-be converts. Here in the midst of her family—in the *bosom* of her family, Claire thought—she felt sorry for the sad self she had been just half an hour before.

"So, Nomie," Nancy said, "what else did the doctor have to say?"

"Yeah, tell us," Claire said, winking across the table at her sister. In the car, Nomie had told Claire that she wasn't going to tell their parents the baby's gender until after she talked to Harry. Claire realized then what an honor it was that Nomie had wanted her at the appointment.

Smiling, Nomie shrugged. "I don't know. Just that everything looks good. I'm healthy, the baby's healthy, everybody's healthy."

"That's great, sweetie," their dad said.

"Have you come up with a plan for the birth?" Nancy asked.

"A plan?" Nomie said.

"You're going to try to push the baby out—right, Nomie?" Claire said. "After your water breaks?"

"Yeah, I think that sounds like a good plan."

The sisters grinned at each other. Humor always had been their one effective weapon against their sober mother, and it was usually Claire who mocked and Nomie who provided the laugh.

"Very funny," their mother said. "I *meant* whether you and Harry want all of us at the hospital right away, or if you want us to wait for a while, or if you just want Claire, that sort of thing."

"I don't know," Nomie said. "I hadn't really thought about it."

"That could also depend on where Claire's staying," Nancy said.

"She'll be at the coach house," Nomie said. She looked at Claire. "I mean, I assume you will be."

"Are Harry's parents coming to town after the baby's born?" Nancy asked. Harry's family lived in Columbus.

"Yeah, I think for a few days," Nomie said.

"So they may need the coach house," said Nancy. "Claire, have you thought about that?"

"That's four months away," Nomie said. "It's nothing to worry about."

"Harry's parents could stay at a hotel, I suppose," their father said. "Couldn't they?" He looked at his ex-wife rather than at Nomie.

Nancy frowned at him. "That wouldn't seem right, would it?"

The waitress arrived with their drinks, milk shakes for the two sisters and coffee for their parents.

"They did give us the extra!" Nomie exclaimed when the

waitress was gone. She and Claire clinked their silver cups together.

"I like the melted part around the edges," Claire said. "The flavor's stronger."

"Have you done any thinking about where you might live next, Claire?" Nancy said.

"I don't know." She knew Nomie was due in July. She should have memorized the date a long time ago, and now it was too late to ask. "I might move back into my studio." She had not been thinking about moving anywhere, but now that she was put on the spot, her studio seemed the only bearable choice. "I might move back to Short Long Street," she added, seeking out Nomie's gaze. Her sister smiled quickly at the old nickname.

"What about your house?" Nancy said, stirring Equal slowly into her coffee.

Claire would have sworn that everyone at the table held a collective breath at that moment. None of them met her eye.

"I don't think I'll live there again." As she said it, Claire realized this would have to be true. Earlier, in the garage, she had assumed she would visit the house when she felt ready, but no: she was done with it.

"What about all your things? They won't fit in the studio."

"I don't know, Mom."

"Do you want to put the house on the market?" her father asked.

She shook her head. "Not yet."

"I hate to think of you paying that mortgage if you're not going to live there," he said.

She felt, suddenly, as if she were going to burst out of her skin. "I thought money wasn't a problem. Isn't there life insurance?"

"There is," her father said. "You're fine."

"I need a little time," Claire said. "It's only been a month!"

"Never mind, sweetheart," Douglas said.

"You're right," Nancy said. "You don't want to rush into any major decisions." She shook her head. "It just makes me so mad to see you going through this."

"Well, that's the way it is," Claire said, irritated.

"What did Jay's therapist say, if you don't mind me asking?" Nancy said.

"Just, you know, that he could get depressed," said Claire.

"Have you read his note yet?" Nancy said.

"Yes." Claire fiddled with a straw wrapper while they all looked at her.

"I didn't know that," said Nomie.

"I'm up to speed," Claire said.

"I found it rather baffling, myself." Nancy leaned toward Claire. "Didn't you? The whole thing. It makes me feel like I didn't know him. He always seemed so . . . steady."

"You were his mother-in-law," Claire snapped. "What did you expect?"

"Claire," her father said, turning toward her.

Nomie was staring at the middle of the table, staying neutral.

"Oh, I know that." Nancy straightened her posture. "I just . . . I wish he had shown this side of himself before you got married. It doesn't seem fair."

He did show me, Claire thought, but of course they didn't know that. She had kept her family in the dark about Jay, not wanting them to judge him or, even more important, Claire herself. "I wish you wouldn't judge him, Mom," she said now.

Her remark hung in the air as the waitress approached with her tray. She doled out the dishes wordlessly and backed away.

"I wasn't judging," Nancy said in a small voice. "I'm just trying to understand."

"Well, maybe you can't. *You've* never had any trouble being happy." Claire took a big bite of her francheezie. The hot dog squirted its tangy chemical juice, the cheese oozed out, the bacon fat melted, and the buttery bun sopped everything up. Too late, she realized she should have let it cool off first. She let her mouth fall open and breathed in and out, circulating air around the steaming mess on her tongue, relishing her bad manners.

Her mother watched her, fork poised over her chopped salad. "If you see me that way, then I guess I did my job," she said. "Many a time I put on a brave face for you girls."

"Can we change the subject?" Claire said, and took another determined bite of her hot dog. Good God, if nothing else, she was glad she lived in the Midwest. She should have brought Jay here before he died, she thought, and snorted at her mistake. What *had* they done the night before he died? Watched a *Sopranos* rerun and gone to bed early?

"The food hasn't changed," Douglas said. He had gotten a turkey club.

"Nope," said Nomie. She was cutting into her francheezie with a fork and knife.

A cell phone rang, and Nomie scrambled for it in her purse. "It's Harry," she said. "Do you mind if I take it?"

"Of course not," Claire and her mother said in unison.

After Nancy let her out of the booth, Nomie made a beeline for the back room.

"I'm glad everything's all right," Douglas said. "The doctor said everything's fine with the baby, right, Claire?"

"Yeah."

"She was a big baby," Nancy said. "Nomie, I mean."

Douglas nodded. "Tall even when she was born."

"We just got a new camera." Nancy raked her fork over her salad. "We figure we'll be taking lots of pictures soon."

"Excellent," said Douglas. "Hope you'll share them with me."

"Of course."

This wasn't normal, Claire thought with a creeping sense of satisfaction. Her parents had been divorced for decades, yet they still went to the symphony together, attended each other's birthday dinners, and presented a united front when one of their daughters disappointed them. Claire thought of their heads close together in the doctor's office, their knees lightly touching.

"Why did you two get divorced?" Claire said.

Her mother set down her fork and dabbed at her mouth with her napkin. Her eyes darted at Douglas, and then she looked at Claire, her gaze level and unperturbed. "Why do you ask?" she said.

"It's just, you know, you're judging me for marrying Jay, but what about you two? You got divorced, what, twenty-five years ago? And Mom, you're married to another man, but you two still go on these . . . dates."

"Dates?" Again her mother looked at her father. "We go to the symphony together a few times a year, like we've always done."

"Your mother and I tried to keep things amicable, for your sake, and Nomie's," her father said. "We didn't hate each other after the divorce, and we still enjoy each other's company."

"Would you have preferred it if we fought all the time?" Nancy said.

"Were those the only two choices?" Claire asked. Whine, whine, whine, she thought, even as she spoke. This was the kind of thing Jay would do—blame his parents for his own mistakes—and she could see why: it felt good. "What kind of a message do you think that sent to us, to see you being so . . . *friendly* all the time?"

Nomie was edging toward them. She stopped a few feet from the booth, looking as if she might walk away, but their mother got up to let her back in, and Nomie had no choice but to join them.

"How's Harry?" her father asked.

"Good," Nomie said. "His meeting went well. He'll be back tonight."

"That's good," Nancy said. "Did you tell him we had a family reunion at the doctor's office?"

"I just told him we're all out at lunch." Nomie glanced at Claire, emphasizing the fact that she had not been disloyal.

"Your sister was just asking us about our divorce." Nancy turned back to Claire. "Tell us where you think we went wrong. I'd like to know." But nothing in her tone suggested to Claire that she wanted to hear the truth.

"I just wanted you to move on a little bit more, I think," said Claire. "Especially Dad. So that it didn't seem stupid that our family broke up."

"I never understood why you guys got divorced, either." Nomie spoke with her head down, as if she were addressing her baby, her curls falling around her face. Claire should have felt triumphant, having her sister back her up, but Nomie always took her side, she always would, and so her opinion did not count for much.

"Your mother fell out of love with me," Douglas said, and took a drink of water. "It was the most normal thing in the world."

They all stared at him.

"Why didn't you fight for her?" Claire said. She had started to cry.

"Claire," Nancy warned her.

"There's no sense in trying to persuade someone who wants to leave that they shouldn't," Douglas said calmly. He turned to look at his older daughter. "You might prolong things, but it never works out in the end."

Claire's tears plopped onto the tabletop. Nomie had started crying as well, for she had always cried when Claire cried, no matter the reason: there, in a nutshell, was the terrible power of being the oldest child.

"I didn't mean . . ." Douglas's gray eyes grew wide, and he reached for Claire's wrist. "I was talking about . . . ," he said, but he couldn't finish the sentence.

"It wasn't as simple as that," Nancy said. Her gaze, alighting on Claire, then Douglas, then Nomie, was beseeching. "We only wanted what was best for you. Right, Doug? That's all we've ever wanted."

"That's right. We did the best we could."

"Okay," Claire said. "That's enough platitudes for one day." She took a last swig of her milk shake, and the coldness burned her raw throat. She wiped her hand on her sleeve. "Nomie, are you ready?"

"Sure." Across the table, her sister's beautiful face was blotchy and glazed with tears.

"You're leaving?" Nancy said.

For a moment Claire expected her mother to say that they were not excused.

"Claire," their father said.

"What, Dad?" Claire turned to face him.

Sorrow, love, and anger flared up in his eyes, then dimmed. He shook his head and got up to let her out of the booth.

Their mother let Nomie out, too, and the girls put on their coats. "Can I leave some money?" Claire said, not that she had any cash on her.

"That won't be necessary," Douglas said. "I've got it."

"Thank you," Claire said. "And Dad, please don't follow me anymore. I've had enough of that."

"As you wish."

"I'm a grown woman," she added. "I'm not going to do anything stupid."

"I never thought you would," he said.

10

When they got to the Ridgeway's parking lot, Nomie took Claire's keys. "You're too upset to drive," she said, though she was crying harder.

"Shh, shh, it's okay, it's okay," Claire said, rubbing her sister's back when they were inside the car.

"I'm fine," Nomie wailed, her face a portrait of stoic misery as she gazed at the brick wall in front of them. "I'm fine, I'm fine, I'm fine."

"You don't have to be," Claire pleaded. "You can let it out. Let it out, sweetie." She realized she sounded just like Jay.

Nomie shook her head. She gasped once, then pulled her hair back into a ponytail. "I'm fine," she said.

Neither of them spoke again until Nomie had collected herself and was driving slowly south on Ridge. The snow was drifting down lazily, but Nomie had the wipers on high speed. Their hysterical whirring and thumping was reminding

Claire of the voice mail message and driving her a little crazy, but she resolved not to say anything after all the trouble she had caused her sister today.

"Why'd I have to start talking about the divorce?" she said instead. "Stupid. It's ancient history."

Nomie didn't say anything.

"I should move out. I should go to my studio or . . . something."

"You can stay with us as long as you like."

"You're having a baby . . ." Claire's voice trailed off; she couldn't follow that point any further.

"I'm fine," Nomie said. "I just want you to get the help you need. I feel like I never know what to say."

"I know I need help." They had reached a red light at a five-way intersection. "I know."

"What about that one therapist? The one downtown?"

"Yeah." Dr. Mercer. "He seemed pretty cool. He seemed . . . honest." But Claire hadn't been able to pick up the phone to call him. Not yet, she thought each time. It was as if he belonged to a different phase of grief, one she hadn't arrived at yet: a time when she was ready to let herself feel better.

"I could go downtown with you, if you want," Nomie said.

"Thanks."

They were quiet for a minute.

"I didn't know Jay was going to do that, Nomie," Claire said finally. "I didn't understand how bad it was for him."

Nomie glanced at her. "I know. None of us did."

"But he had these . . . spells. And I didn't tell anyone. I should have told someone. Instead I bought us gym membership. Stupid."

"I don't think I would have told anyone, either," Nomie said.

That made Claire feel better for a moment, but then she remembered that she and her sister shared the same legacy: tamping down the tough stuff, putting up a brave front. When their father moved out, Claire hadn't told any of her friends. She had simply let them figure it out for themselves.

"Was he mean to you?" Nomie said.

"Not really. He got frustrated. I wouldn't say he was mean."

"Jim used to be mean to me when he was depressed."

Jim was Nomie's boyfriend before she met Harry. "I didn't realize he got depressed," Claire said.

"Oh yeah."

"Huh." They were silent for a long moment. "But then you met Harry."

"Yeah. He gets depressed, too."

"Does he?"

"Well, maybe more anxious than depressed," Nomie said. "About work. It's not like he breaks down. But I can tell. He has trouble sleeping."

"Do you think he'll get help with that?"

"Oh no. He doesn't like talking about his feelings."

"Jay thought I didn't talk about my feelings enough," Claire said.

Nomie laughed. "Well, if that was your crime, the punishment doesn't really fit."

Bless you, Claire thought. "There's a support group," she said to reward her sister. "It meets tonight. I was thinking about going."

"That's awesome! I think that's great, Claire. I mean, if you decide to go."

"I think I'll go," she lied.

When they got back to the coach house, they collapsed without even flicking on the lights, Claire on the couch, Nomie in the easy chair.

Seconds later, it seemed, a woman was bending over her.

"Claire," the woman said.

There was something warm and heavy resting on Claire's belly. It must be Nomie's baby, she thought. I must have said I would look after it for a while.

"It's time to get up," the voice said, no-nonsense and sharp.

Mom, Claire thought, and opened her eyes. Fang stared back at her. The cat was lying on top of Claire, her front paws extended like Superman. So the cat could talk after all, and wouldn't you know it, she sounded just like Nancy.

"Claire," Nomie hissed. "You need to get up."

Claire looked up. Nomie's face was as round and white as a cut potato. "What do you want?"

"You've got to get ready for the support group."

"Already?"

"It's after six."

"Oh." Claire closed her eyes. "I think I'll go next time."

"Are you sure?" Nomie said. "I can take you if you like."

Claire opened her eyes again. She felt as if she were stumbling out of a dark cave. "That's okay."

"Claire. I want you to go." Now Nomie really did sound like their mother. "Will you do this for me?"

She had to keep her sister happy, Claire reminded herself, because where would she go if Nomie and Harry kicked her out? Not to the house. Not to her studio. She was done with those places. The model home, she thought. She could hide out in the model home she had just decorated. She could be a squatter. She could squat.

"All right," she said. "I'll go."

"Really? Are you sure?"

Claire sighed. "Yes, I'm sure."

She felt drunk. She wanted to be drunk.

You can get drunk, she told herself. You're an adult, and if you want to get drunk, no problem. Just go to the support group, or pretend you're going, and then you can get drunk.

"I'm making you a snack," Nomie called out from the kitchen area.

Claire got up and sat on one of the barstools at the counter. "Thanks," she said. But she was bloated from the francheezie and the milk shake.

Nomie dropped chocolate-chip cookies into a plastic bag. Wordlessly, she gave Claire one.

"Who brought these?" Claire said, examining the cookie. "These are the slice-and-bake kind. The ones where the dough comes in a tube. You can even get them perforated. Now, that's lazy. Pre-perforated cookies."

"I made them," Nomie said as she zipped the bag closed. "I didn't have time to bake from scratch, but I wanted to make some for you. They taste just as good."

Shit. "Oh, that's so nice! I just meant, you know, that it would have been funny if one of my friends brought these over and tried to play them off as homemade."

"People haven't been bringing things lately," Nomie said.

"Really?"

"Not in the past couple days."

"Huh." Maybe Claire's friends had deemed that her situation was no longer a crisis. They were still leaving messages, but they apparently thought she was now capable of feeding herself.

"Do you want me to take you?" Nomie said as she handed Claire a lunch bag.

"No. I'll be okay. You stay here. Or go to your house. Have a date night."

Nomie nodded. "Do you know where you're going?"

"To a church," Claire said. "I'm going to a church."

Because Nomie so clearly wanted her out, Claire left right away and got to the church early. She tried one of the front doors and was surprised to find it unlocked. When she crept inside, walking on tiptoes to keep her footsteps from echoing, she found she was not alone. A figure sat in a pew near the altar, rocking slightly, head bowed.

The church was Episcopal, and to Claire's surprise, there was a holy water font for her to dip her fingers in. She crossed herself swiftly and, by habit, genuflected before sliding into one of the rear pews. The church looked a lot like the Catholic churches she was used to—chilly, solid, and gray. Spiky wrought-iron lanterns spaced evenly above the pews shed a dim light, and the tall stained-glass windows behind the altar were framed in stone. In front of the altar, a pulpit rose slightly off the ground, like the basket of a hot-air balloon.

She opened her bag of food as quietly as possible to avoid disturbing the bobbing person at the front of the church, a good twenty pews away. She bit into a cookie and let the chocolate chips dissolve in her mouth. Nomie was right: they were just as good as homemade. Claire was fairly certain the bobbing person was a man, of slight build and wearing a knit cap (her mother would have disapproved of the cap, even if the church was Episcopal). He might be homeless, or crazy, or both—who else would show up to an empty church on a weeknight? Maybe he was a parishioner experiencing a Dark Night of the Soul—or a member of the suicide survivors' support group, just barely holding on, rocking out the minutes until he could let it all out.

She bargained with herself: If I spend the time usefully

with prayer, can I stay here instead of going to the meeting?

Yes, she decided. Yes, you can.

Dear God, she thought. Help me. Please help me.

She was rusty. When Jay was alive, she used to pray for him, and she had said a few swift prayers that they would have a baby, but she didn't think she had prayed at all this past month. Certainly she hadn't prayed at his funeral, which had been at a local Presbyterian church—the choice reeking of a negotiation between Jay's parents and Claire's mother. Don't make my daughter travel to Boston right now, Nancy might have said, and you can choose any church you like.

At least his parents hadn't had the funeral at the church where Claire and Jay were married, as they might have done out of misguided sentiment. For the wedding, Claire and Jay had chosen a conveniently located Unitarian church— a compromise, they told themselves, between Catholicism (her parents), Presbyterianism (his parents), atheism (Jay), and Claire's own spiritual muddle: her love of the Jesus stories and the sacraments, her distaste for the Catholic patriarchy, and her willful decision to stick with her childhood belief in a higher power for the sheer comfort it provided. The church had been vintage 1970s ugly, with severe, canted white walls. Its single stained-glass window, generically emblazoned with birds in flight, was placed high on one wall, as if the church were a prison cell. On their wedding day, the church was made starker by the monstrous gladioli the florist had propped up in vases on the riser that passed for an altar. ("I feel like we're in a Fellini film," Jay had whispered to her during the service, and she, the bride, had snorted with laughter right there in front of everyone.) Claire had decided it was the kind of church a home stager might have put together to promote a belief so vague and inclusive that really, what was the point?

She cringed, as always, remembering their exchange of

vows. They had written their own and kept them secret from each other until the wedding day. As Claire should have expected, Jay's were long and descriptive, referencing her favorite pizza, her quiet intensity, and even Orpheus Records. He had memorized his vows and pronounced them in a strong voice that broke at key moments. Reading from a note card, Claire had spoken her three meager sentences—something about laughter, something about forgiveness and forever—as slowly and softly as possible, so that no one would notice how short and boring they were. She had thrown the card away and deleted the "wedding_vows" file from her computer after the honeymoon.

If she ever got married again—the thought made her stomach flip—she would insist on doing Pre-Cana and having a full Mass. She might be wearing a taupe suit, there might be twenty people in the church, but by God, there would be a priest, a couples retreat, and personality tests to ferret out a poor choice or a bad match—the post–Vatican II Catholic Church: the original eHarmony.

But she was supposed to be praying.

How much of it was my fault? she thought. Ten percent? Twenty? Fifty?

It couldn't be more than fifty; Jay had a preexisting condition when she met him. But he had blamed her, in a way: *I think we are not compatible in certain ways, and it has been frustrating to both of us.* Dr. Hannah had alluded to his "deep need to communicate" and how she had tried to get Jay to accept people for who they were. When Claire asked if she and Jay were right for each other, Dr. Hannah would not answer.

Plenty of blame to go around, Veronica had said to Claire on the phone. What had Jay confided to his sister during their long, wine-fueled meals? That Claire didn't know how to deal with others' feelings or share her own? That sometimes she ran away to avoid their problems? She didn't think she and Jay had even had a conversation about suicide—whether they had ever thought about it, under what conditions they might do it. And wasn't that strange in itself, considering?

Even now, twisting her too-tight engagement ring, Claire felt panicky, and incriminated as a result.

She checked her watch again: five minutes.

I don't know if I should go to the meeting, she thought, continuing her prayer. I don't know if I'm ready. What if it's too intense? Maybe you could give me a sign or something.

Up by the altar, the man was still rocking—faster now, it seemed. Though actually, his right arm, the part that Claire could see above the pew, was rocking faster than the rest of him.

Oh, gross. No. He wasn't, was he? In a *church*?

She got up and moved as stealthily as she could toward the exit.

That was a good one, she thought to God. Very funny. I'm going, I'm going.

She had hoped, when she descended the stairs into the church basement, with its low ceilings lit by bare bulbs, that she would find a dark, empty room, the original members of the support group long dispersed, cured by the passage of time, the leader uninterested in drumming up fresh recruits. But the utility room cast a sickly fluorescence into the hallway, and when Claire walked in, she found six people, three women and three men, sitting quietly in a semicircle and looking straight at her.

"Hello," the youngest man said, rising and striding toward her. "I'm Michael." He looked startled, but he smiled as he shook her hand.

"Claire," she said. "This is the . . . support group?"

"That's right." In another life Claire would have found him attractive, with his curly brown hair, narrow frame, and pleasantly rumpled white button-down shirt. He looked younger than Claire, maybe thirty. "I'm the facilitator, and this is our group."

Another psychologist, she thought. Figures I would find him attractive.

"I'm sorry," she said, realizing she might have made a faux pas. "Maybe I should have told you I was coming. I got the information from . . . a friend."

"That's all right." But he ushered her into the hallway. "Normally," he said, voice lowered, "I do like to meet with people before they join us, to make sure it's a good fit."

"I'm sorry. I didn't realize that. I should have . . ." She shook her head. The idea that she might not be welcome here, of all places, made her want to cry.

"It's okay," he said softly. "I'm glad you're here."

"I could come back next time." And then she would never come back, not to this too-bright room with the odd assortment of silent strangers. But at least she could tell herself she had tried.

"No, please." Seeming to pick up on her distress, he smiled eagerly and then led her back into the room. "Join us. This is our group," he said, loud enough for everyone to hear. "Everyone, this is . . ." He flashed her a panicked look; he had already forgotten her name.

"Claire," she said. "I'm Claire." The new girl.

She half expected everyone to shout "Hi, Claire," in a booming communal voice, as AA groups did in the movies, but they only smiled vaguely, then looked down at their laps. Claire sat down on an empty folding chair near Michael.

"We'll start in another minute," he said.

"Lisa isn't coming tonight," said a chubby middle-aged woman with frizzy carrot-colored hair. "She asked me to tell you. Her daughter had a basketball game."

"Oh, okay," Michael said. "Thanks, Philippa. We'll still give it another minute, just in case anyone else joins us."

Because the group members were keeping their heads down, Claire was free to study them and guess which loved ones of theirs were dead. Philippa, the helpful woman seated across the circle, might have lost a teenage son, or maybe a husband. Claire wondered about Lisa, the absentee with the basketball-playing daughter. Probably it was Lisa's husband who had died.

At least we didn't have a child, Claire thought. I would never forgive him then.

But in the days leading up to the wake, she had hoped she was pregnant. Which was worse—abandoning your child or not having that child at all?

She would consider that question later. For now it was more pleasant to wonder about Philippa and the absent Lisa. Had they become friends through this group? Maybe they met for lunch to talk about their pain and make gentle fun of the quirks of the other group members. Claire wondered if they would like her enough to include her in their private circle, their support-group subgroup. They could have a name, the Suicidal Spouses Club—something wicked and subversive that they could hide from outsiders with an acronym: the SSC. They would meet at wine bars, where they would drink flights and order the entire dessert platter, and Philippa and Lisa would tease Claire about having a crush on Michael. They would take turns breaking down in tears, and the waiter would back away from the table as they consoled each other. *Damn him,* one of them—which, it didn't matter— would say, speaking of a dead husband or son. *I could kill him.*

That line, first uttered unthinkingly, would become their catchphrase; each time someone uttered it, they would laugh so hard that other diners would smile at them, baffled. The SSC would close the place down, and then, out on the street, they would share long hugs and call out as they parted, *I love you! See you next week!*

So maybe it was true that God, in his all-knowing wisdom, had sent his messenger, the Masturbator, to guide Claire from the church and into this dingy basement room where the walls were decorated crazily with torn, mismatched wallpaper scraps and the ancient linoleum was worn away in black patches, as if people had survived a war down here.

After a few minutes, when no one else had shown up, Michael cleared his throat and thanked everyone for coming. "As most of you know," he said, leaning forward with a half smile on his face, "we come together here in the spirit of support and community. Our common bond is depression and the pain it can bring. Now, can I ask you to introduce yourselves to Claire?"

"I'm Larry," began the large, bearded black man to Michael's left. He was wearing an unzipped parka with a fuzzy collar, and there was a puddle around his galoshes. He looked to be about forty-five, and he pushed up the bridge of his glasses and looked right at Claire when he said his name.

Next came Philippa, who smiled widely as she introduced herself, displaying small, rounded teeth, then started fanning herself with a notebook—hot flashes, Claire thought.

The young Asian American woman next to Philippa, Sarah, gave a little wave as she introduced herself; she looked cool, with her biker boots and long black cardigan. Maybe, with a little coaxing, Claire could get Philippa and Lisa to let Sarah join the SSC, even if she was young and even if, as seemed likely, she had lost a sibling or a boyfriend rather than a spouse or a child.

The two members closest to Claire completed the circle: Meg and Paul, who both appeared to be in their seventies, about the same age as Claire's father. They had been speaking to each other in low voices before the meeting; rather, Meg had been speaking to Paul, who looked down at his shoes, which led Claire to speculate that they were married. They might have lost a child to suicide, and really, Claire had to admit, wasn't that the worst loss of all? Meg's silver hair curled girlishly above her shoulders. Paul, when he turned briefly toward Claire during his introduction, had a weathered, weary face. He was tall, his knees jutting up from the chair, and had excellent posture.

Michael turned to Claire. "We like to give our visitors and new members a chance to speak first, though if you're not comfortable with that, you don't have to. We're not big on rules here," he added, which drew a knowing chuckle from the group.

Claire was not comfortable speaking first, but she wanted to be brave.

"I've never been to a group like this before," she said. "I'm not exactly sure where to start or what to say."

"Just tell your story. Wherever you'd like to start."

"Okay," Claire said. "Just—if I start rambling, cut me off." She smiled to show that she was joking, and their kindly smiles were as warm as sunbeams in the basement room.

"So, here goes," she said, glancing furtively from one group member to another. "I'm here because my husband killed himself. He jumped off a balcony. On Valentine's Day. We were at a party."

The room had gone still. No one moved; no one seemed to breathe.

"Take all the time you need, Claire," said Michael. "Just say whatever's on your mind. Don't worry too much about trying to get it right."

She nodded.

"I wasn't expecting it," she continued. "He—his name was Jay." She looked around the room for a flash of recognition, for Jay was known in certain circles, and how had Alan heard about this group in the first place? Possibly from Michael, who might know Jay or know of him, this group being close to campus. But Michael didn't flinch.

You're safe here, she told herself.

"He would have these . . . spells. That's what he called them. Depressive . . . episodes, I guess. I talked to his therapist today—he was in therapy—but she wasn't able to tell me much. She said she couldn't."

Focus, she told herself. Her gaze landed on Philippa, who nodded encouragingly.

Until now, Claire realized, other people had been telling her story for her. She wasn't even sure what they had been saying, since they told it when she was out of earshot. She had told Dr. Mercer what happened, but not in detail.

"I didn't know he had this problem until we were almost engaged, but I decided I could deal with it. Once we got married, his spells—his depressive episodes, I mean—started coming every few months or so. They'd come on real strong, he'd be laid up in bed and would barely speak, but after a week or so, he'd be better. He didn't want to go on meds—he was convinced they wouldn't help."

Larry was nodding.

"I'm sorry. Is this taking too long?"

"Not at all. That's what we're here for," said Michael. Nods around the room.

"We were married for less than two years when he did

it. I didn't have any indication. He left a note, though, so it was all planned out. I wasn't going to go to this party with him, the party where he did it, but then at the last minute I decided to surprise him. But that didn't matter—he jumped anyway."

Sarah was looking at the floor, and Meg was, too. She should hurry it up.

"There were tough times, but we also had a lot of fun. We enjoyed each other's company. We were talking about starting a family. So I'm just really . . . angry at him. For leaving me. It just seems so selfish." She thought she was done, but then she added, her voice trailing off, "I don't understand how he could have been so selfish."

All of them were looking at her now. Meg's milky blue eyes, in particular, were staring straight at Claire.

Michael cleared his throat. "Have you experienced depression, Claire?"

"No. Not really. I mean . . . not until recently, I guess."

"Have you ever been suicidal?"

"Um . . . no."

"So, you know that a number of the people in this room have attempted suicide," he said.

"Oh." *What?* "You mean . . . after."

"After . . ." He shook his head. "Sorry."

"After someone else did it," she clarified. "After someone close to them did it."

"Not necessarily. In fact . . ." He glanced around the room. "I don't think we have any cases like that." He leaned toward her, elbows on his knees. The Asian girl—Sarah, was it?—was staring daggers at Claire.

Bewildered, she considered simply running out of the room. "I was told this was a group for people who've survived the suicide of a loved one." She realized how she sounded:

like a woman from Lake Forest trying to get a refund at Marshalls without a receipt.

Michael shook his head. "There must have been a mistake. This is a group of people who have personally grappled with depression and, often, thoughts of suicide."

She glanced around the room. She pictured Philippa belly-up and bloated, an empty pill bottle at her side. Sarah bleeding into the bathtub. Larry dangling in his closet with his head in a noose. She was in a room full of zombies, the living dead.

"I never tried to kill myself," Meg said in a high, pinched voice. The old woman was looking past her husband, straight at Claire, her black pupils piercing through her rheumy blue eyes.

Paul sat rigid beside her, his hands balled into fists on his knees.

"Not everyone here has attempted suicide," Michael said, "but everyone here has battled depression." He turned back to Claire. "Which is not to say you're not welcome here, Claire. Sometimes misunderstandings like this turn out to be worthwhile. Maybe there's something you can teach us about the pain of being left behind. And there may be something the group can teach you."

"I don't think so." She got up and yanked her coat off the back of the chair. Her purse flew onto the floor. "I don't think there's anything you people could teach me. I could probably teach you a thing or two, though." She shrugged into her coat and stooped to grab her purse from Michael, who had risen to collect it. "I could tell you about the pain you've caused." She looked directly at them, one by one. "You should be ashamed of yourselves," she said, her voice choked with fury.

She moved swiftly for the door, Michael following behind her. "Claire!" he shouted.

He caught up to her in the hallway, and she paused because that was how she was raised: to stop and listen when someone was calling her. Not like some people, who ran and ran and ran and ran and ran.

"What?" she snapped.

"I'm sorry," Michael said. Close-up, she saw the fine crow's-feet around his eyes. He was older than she had thought, just another aging boy.

"What about you?" she said. "Are you one of them, too?"

His eyes fluttered shut, then opened. "It was a long time ago."

"I thought so." She turned and ran toward the stairs. "You fucking need to improve your advertising," she shouted over her shoulder.

Claire drove south on Lake Shore Drive, the windows cracked. Her seat belt flapped wildly in the freezing wind.

Join a support group, join a support group, wasn't that what all the doctors had told Claire to do? Dr. Hannah, Dr. Alan, Dr. What's-her-name—the obstetrician. Even Fang's fucking vet had encouraged Claire to join a support group.

Well, now she had been to one. She hoped they would all be happy, and if they weren't, they could jump out a fucking window.

She had found a punk show on the local university station—"Old-timer's punk," the nerdy young announcer called it—and had turned it up loud to cover the sound of her own screams.

Fang was waiting for her at the door of the coach house. Claire pushed the door closed and fell back against it. The cat did figure eights around her ankles, letting out kittenish squeaks.

"It's all right," Claire said gruffly, scooping the little white cloud into her arms. The cat purred and nuzzled her chin. Claire felt her muscles unclench, her heart slow its crazy beating. She had stopped screaming and turned off the radio once she got off the Drive, but she cried with frustration as she drove around in circles, trying to find a parking space in the Triangle District at this time of night. When she finally did, in a questionable spot by a crosswalk, she'd had to trudge four blocks through the cold. She was drained. But for the first time, maybe, she understood Fang's appeal. "You're okay. I'm here."

She set down the cat, who trotted away, glancing expectantly back at Claire. Beyond the long hallway, the television illuminated the coach house's pale green walls, making it look as watery as a fishbowl. The TV was emitting a tinny buzz that changed in pitch with the flashing light on the walls. Nomie must have fallen asleep with it on mute, maybe in the middle of her yoga DVD.

But Claire found Harry sitting on the couch, alone, leaning back with the remote pointed at the TV. He clicked it off, and the large room turned as dark as the bottom of the ocean. Nomie was nowhere to be seen.

"Hey," Claire said.

"Hey." He was still wearing a suit, though he had taken off his tie, which lay next to him on the couch like a noose.

Claire took off her coat, kicked off her boots, and sank into the armchair. She reached and turned on a lamp, but when she saw Harry's face, dull and weary as he squinted against the light, she snapped it off.

"Too bright," she said.

A beer bottle sat on the coffee table. So did the binder,

Claire saw—at the edge of the table, no longer buried under magazines and mail. Its blue cover looked black in the dark room.

"How was your trip?" she said.

"Fine." He leaned back and rubbed his eyes, then ran his hand over his bald spot. "How was your meeting?"

"Fine." She shook her head. "Actually, not so much. I went to the wrong group."

"What do you mean?"

"It was a support group for suicide attempters, not suicide survivors."

He reached for his beer and took a swig. "That sucks."

"Yeah. Is Nomie in bed?"

"Yeah."

"Here or . . . at your house?"

"At our house."

Claire nodded.

Harry raised his foot and kicked the edge of the binder. "I heard you read the note."

"Yeah."

"What'd you think?"

She shrugged. "It could have been worse, I guess. He could have blamed me for everything."

"I thought it was a little vague, myself."

"Yeah."

"I've been so *pissed* at him." Harry sat forward and laced his fingers.

"Depression is a disease," Claire said flatly. The suicide disease, she thought, and rubbed the numb spot by her ear. "Apparently he couldn't help himself." She didn't know why she was defending Jay to Harry, when just an hour ago she had been ready to trash him to a roomful of strangers.

"Okay, fine," Harry said. "But you know, some mornings when I wake up, I think I'd rather slit my wrists than go to the office. But I get up and I put on the coffee, and that's what I'll do every morning for the next thirty years, and I know that, and Nomie knows that. Because I live for her, our weekends together, and our retirement, and our kids' birthday parties and college and weddings and all of that crap my stupid job is going to pay for."

"Jay loved me," Claire said, taken off-balance by the speech. She couldn't remember the two of them ever having a serious conversation before. "In case you're implying something."

"I'm not implying anything. I just think he should have tried harder for you."

She didn't want to cry any more today. "I was late for Nomie's appointment," she said to change the subject and because she sensed he had stayed up to scold her. Might as well get it over with. "I screwed up."

"It's not that you were late, really, though." Harry stood up and took his beer bottle into the kitchen. He came back with a fresh one and set it down too hard on the coffee table; foam spilled over the edge. Claire watched the beer run away from the binder, off the edge of the table and onto the rug. Fang, who had been watching them from beneath the glass table, sniffed at the drippings, then backed away. "You forgot, didn't you? You never picked her up."

"Yeah. That's right." Claire's heart was pounding again.

"I had a feeling. I called Nomie to see if you had picked her up. She wasn't even going to call you—she said she didn't want to bother you—but I told her I'd call you myself if she didn't."

"I'm really sorry. That's not how I usually am. You know that." Nomie had thought that her own wedding started at two-thirty, when it was actually at two. She would have been late if it wasn't for Claire.

"I know, Claire." He scooted forward on the couch and smiled at her sadly. "But I have to ask you something."

"Name it," she said.

"I need you to give Nomie back to me."

She stared at him. "What do you mean?"

"I don't want her staying here anymore."

"I never asked Nomie to stay here. She offered, that first night. And then she just kept doing it."

"I know. She's been worried about you."

"I told her that I'd move out. I can go to my studio."

"You don't have to leave, Claire. You can stay here as long as you like. But Nomie's pregnant. It's not right for her to be here at night. I want her near me." He smiled slightly. "We've got a daughter coming."

"Yeah." Claire took a used tissue out of her coat pocket and twisted it around her fingers. "Congrats on that. A girl!" She laughed hollowly. "That's pretty great."

"Yeah. So I'm just asking you to remember that you have a lot of power over your sister." That was true: Claire had even given Nomie her name. Claire couldn't say "Naomi" when she was little, and Nomie had stuck.

Claire nodded. "You're a good husband." Hearing resentment in her voice, she tried again. "You're a *great* husband, Harry."

"Thank you." He looked bemused.

"I'll do better," she said. "I promise."

"I know." He picked up his tie and stuffed it into his jacket pocket, then stood up and stooped to kiss her on the top of her head. "I love you, Claire. I'll see you tomorrow."

"G'night," she said. "I love you, too, Harry."

11

White light filtered through the loft's high window. Outside, a shovel scraped against the sidewalk. Claire rolled onto her side. Fang, who had been sleeping against her legs, moved and settled on the other side of the bed, where Nomie usually slept.

Claire looked at her watch: almost nine.

Standing at the window, she saw that the world had turned white. Parked cars were draped with thick blankets of snow. The sidewalk had been cleared, but the streets hadn't been plowed yet, and a ridge of snow snaked down the middle of the street between the tire tracks. The sound of shoveling echoed through the air. Above the snow-laden branches, the sun pulsed dully. Claire could tell from the stillness, and from the thin wisps of heat fluttering from the stovepipe of the building across the street, just how bitter cold it had become.

Her father wasn't out there.

She got back into the bed and hugged the pillow as the cat settled beside her again.

Later she heard the front door unlock, then the thud of a boot, then a second boot, hitting the mat. Plastic bags rustled; the refrigerator door smacked open and closed.

The smell of Nomie's strawberry perfume wafted up as she climbed the stairs to the loft. Claire lay still. When she knew Nomie was watching her, she shifted and let out a little groan, just to let her sister know she was alive.

Claire's whole body was stiff, as if a weight had been pressing down on her back for hours.

The coach house was dark. She held up her wrist and caught the streetlight's glow on her watch face: it was 7:25. She had slept through the day.

She sat up. The cat had gone off somewhere.

Downstairs, she found a note on the kitchen counter:

Dear Claire,
I put some food out for Fang. There's some soup in the fridge for your lunch. Come to our house for dinner at 7?

Love,
Nomie

p.s. I hope you are feeling OK.

She heated the soup in the microwave and made herself eat it, sitting at the counter, with cheese and crackers and a glass of milk.

A half hour later Claire left her own note on the kitchen counter:

Dear Nomie,

I'm sorry I missed dinner. Thank you for the soup. I am going out to do some things. I won't be back until late. I will be safe. You can call me on my cell if you need to, but I would prefer not to be disturbed.

Love,
Claire

p.s. In case I forgot to tell you, I am really happy that you are having a girl.

Claire walked north through the campus from the double-decker parking lot, following the winding paths along the lake, passing others similarly bundled and huddled against the cold. The paths, lit by security lamps, had already been plowed, and a thin layer of packed snow squeaked like Styrofoam underfoot. Claire's bag, heavy and awkward, rattled under her arm. To her right, beyond the piles of boulders at the edge of the landfill, waves bubbled, frozen in mid crest. A craggy, lunar sheet of ice extended far into the lake, then dropped off into darkness. *When I moved to Chicago,* Jay had told her, *I expected to be able to see Michigan on the other side of the lake. I didn't realize it would look like the ocean. I'd like to take a boat all the way up to the Upper Peninsula sometime. Wouldn't that be cool?*

Her eyes were tearing and her nose hairs were frozen, but Claire wasn't cold. She had lived her whole life in Chicago, and she knew how to dress for this weather. She had put on long underwear, two wool sweaters, and a down coat that brushed her ankles and covered her mittened hands. She had wrapped her mohair scarf around her head so that only her eyes peeked out, then added a knit hat and pulled up the hood. She had found the coat in the closet of the coach house, one of Nomie's, along with a tote bag that read EVERYTHING

I TOUCH TURNS TO SOLD! on one side. She had put the binder in the bag, and on her way to campus she stopped at Jewel and added four more items to it: a bottle of water, a bottle of vodka, a bottle of cranberry juice, and a bag of Goldfish crackers. She skirted the student union, where overhead televisions flashed to an almost empty dining room. The psychology building stood ahead on a rise, a perfectly square box with pillars and a dome, like an oversize mausoleum, strings of smoke shivering from its roof vents.

She had Jay's keys, but the building's front door was unlocked. Inside, a group of college girls, underdressed for the weather in peacoats and clogs, were flying down the marble steps, their voices echoing in boisterous confusion. Claire clung to the railing, tote bag tucked against her side, head down in case any of them happened to work at the Baby Lab.

Not that they would say anything. At the wake, the research assistants had avoided the receiving line and the casket, instead standing in a clump at the other end of the room, weeping and hogging the tissue boxes. The girls had been there most of the evening, but they never said a word to Claire. Only girls signed up to work in the lab, Jay had admitted, but he didn't like it when Claire teased him about running off with one of them. She hadn't taken seriously the idea that one or more of them might have a crush on him, but that night she felt they resented her, the Grieving Widow, and her privileged position in front of the coffin. Or maybe they scorned her, a woman past her prime—middle-aged, even— newly alone and childless, a cautionary tale.

On the second floor, Claire moved swiftly past the departmental office, her tote bag brushing the far wall. The office door was propped open, and inside, an unfamiliar male voice was saying, "They wanted to send it to *OBHDP*, but I said, hey, this is *JPSP* work." Once past, she felt she was home free. Most of the professors' offices were on the third floor, so anyone working late on a Friday night was likely to be up there.

At the end of the hallway she peered around the blind corner, then moved down the short hall to the door at the end of it. The mottled pane of glass set into the top half of the door was dark. INFANT COGNITION LABORATORY was stenciled on the glass, gold letters outlined in black, like a private investigator's office. She set down her bag, took off her mittens, and fished Jay's keys out of her pocket. She tried one key, then a second. The third key turned.

Claire let herself into the Baby Lab's darkened waiting room and closed the door softly. The computer on the reception desk was buzzing, but otherwise the room was still. There were four other doors in the room. She stooped and saw darkness beneath all of them.

Reassured that she was alone, she switched on the light. Two nubby institutional beige couches stood perpendicular to each other, a bin full of plastic toys between them. Two chairs that matched the couches sat in front of the reception desk, and on the far wall between the two office doors was a low bookcase filled with board books and blocks. A long, framed poster of ten or twelve babies of different races, propped up next to one another in diapers, hung over one of the couches. Claire noticed, as she had in the past, that the waiting room smelled like babies—like spit-up, and the sugary, slightly sour smell of a baby's scalp, a smell she still remembered from her years of teenage babysitting.

One of the doors on the right led to a workroom filled with TV monitors and computers. The adjoining room was the Baby Lab, with its puppet stage and two-way mirror. The two doors on the far wall led to the office of Jay's colleague

Arielle and his own office. Jay's nameplate, PROFESSOR JAY MONROE, was still tucked into the slot next to the door, Claire saw to her relief. She had been afraid she would walk into Jay's office and find nothing: a bare desk, empty bookshelves, white walls, all of his clutter gone—or, worse, someone else's in its place. Nomie or her mother might have warned her that this was coming, that the department had contacted them, but it was the kind of news Claire would have dismissed in the early weeks, saying she would deal with it later, and then never thought of again.

She found the right key and opened his office door slowly, struck by fear, as if she might find Jay's corpse sitting upright at his desk. Through the window at the far end of the narrow room, the night sky, bright from the reflected snow, splashed a grainy light onto the floor. Claire's eyes identified dark shapes one by one as harmless furniture—a couch, a bookcase, an empty chair.

Even before she turned on the floor lamp, Claire knew the room was still Jay's. It had his smell, that familiar musk, but with a sour undertone, like old books and sweat. The door would have been shut all this time, no one coming and going, no need even for the Haitian janitor Jay had spoken of to vacuum and empty the wastebasket.

Claire went back into the waiting room and turned off the light, then returned to Jay's office. The window faced the steel-gray, empty lake, so no one outside would see the meager light from the floor lamp. Inside, the darkened waiting room served as a buffer; she would hear anyone coming before they were aware of her, and she could snap off the light.

She closed the door and looked around the room. She hadn't been here in a while, but nothing much had changed. Jay's desk still faced south, so that he could see the lake to his left. Framed movie posters hung on the wall behind his desk chair, above the credenza: *Ordinary People*, one of his favorites, and *Look Who's Talking*, a joke Ph.D. graduation gift from his sister. Bookshelves covered the south wall, almost filled from floor to ceiling; rows of journals marched in even lines. A milk crate served as a step stool to help Jay—whose height had been average—reach the highest shelves. A blue dress shirt, sleeves rolled, hung on a hook on the door. Next to the door was a nail where Claire's painting had hung.

Vents were softly forcing heat into the room. Claire hung her coat over Jay's shirt, then sat down in his desk chair—one of those ugly, comfortable ergonomic ones—and turned on his computer. This is where Jay would have typed the note and everything else in the binder—at night, Claire guessed, when the Baby Lab was quiet and she was working across town at her studio.

The desk was neater than he usually kept it; the piles of papers, folders, and books were gone. The new, sleek flat-screen monitor he had mentioned was positioned on the right side so as not to block the lake view. In the left corner of the desk, next to the phone, she and Jay smiled on their wedding day from a silver frame. A pencil cup, a box of tissues, a stapler, a tape dispenser, a pad of Post-its, and a paper clip dispenser—that was all. She stroked her finger over the desktop and came away with a fine film of dust. She opened the shallow top drawer: business cards, paper clips, and pencils.

She took the binder out of the tote bag and placed it next to the computer keyboard, right where he must have left it on Valentine's Day to be discovered. Beside the binder she set her bottles of vodka, water, and cranberry juice, and the bag of crackers. Opening one of the deep desk drawers, she found plastic tumblers. She poured water into one of them and ate a few crackers. How much she drank tonight would depend on what she found, if anything; just in case, the water and the crackers would ward off a hangover.

She spotted a red goblet standing upright in the drawer, and her eyes welled. It was from their set of Depression glass at home. She lifted the glass to the light, admiring the ruby color. The glass was dimpled all over with raised dots, and its footed base was scalloped like a mermaid's tail.

Claire's mother had inherited the Depression glass from her mother, and she passed it down to Claire and Jay when they bought their house, telling them the cheery red dishes would look cuter in their place—"It's never really been my style," she said. When Claire and Nomie were growing up, Nancy had kept the glassware in a hutch. There were stacks of plates, serving dishes of all sizes, glasses and goblets, dessert cups, a gravy boat, and even ashtrays, all of it a deep, clear red decorated with round bumps that Claire had liked to run her fingers over. Her mother had told her that movie theaters and department stores had given away the glassware during the Great Depression. Claire had heard her mother use the word "depression" once before, to describe her father, who in the years before the divorce sometimes went to bed right after dinner, even before Claire and Nomie did. And so Claire had come to her own conclusion about the Depression glass: that the theaters and stores had hired depressed people to make the brightly colored glass in a kindly attempt to distract them from their sadness.

Her mother had used the Depression glass only twice a year: at Fourth of July barbecues, paired with blue napkins, and on Valentine's Day, for the girls' breakfast. Claire and Nomie would come downstairs in the morning to find the dining table set with a pink cloth and napkins, a vase of carnations and baby's breath, heart candies in a little red dimpled bowl, and cards in red envelopes at their places. Their mother, who usually let them eat cold cereal, would serve them orange juice in the red goblets and waffles and bacon on the red plates. Later, looking back, Claire and Nomie had agreed that having their mother serve them like ladies before they went to school had been even better than Christmas morning.

The goblet looked clean, so Claire mixed herself a vodka and cranberry juice and took a long swig.

She looked through the files in the credenza first, but everything seemed to be work-related. Then she started looking through his computer files. There was a folder for research, another labeled "Baby Lab admin," one for teaching, and so on. She couldn't find anything that had to do with her or the binder. To her surprise, she was able to open his e-mail without entering a password. Dozens of new messages popped up from the weeks after his death, but the last one was dated a week ago, when his account must have been shut off. The most recent messages were irrelevant: spam, bill alerts, calls for papers, requests for recommendations from former students. She went through the messages he had received on Valentine's Day and the days before it, but she found only random notes from students and colleagues. He had sent a few brief work e-mails on Valentine's Day, nothing to family or friends. She opened up his Web browser and looked through the sites he had visited recently: the New England Patriots home page, iTunes, *The New York Times*, some university sites. There was nothing incriminating, frightening, or even embarrassing—no suicide sites, nothing to suggest he was in any kind of trouble, not that she knew what kind of trouble that would be—not even porn.

When she was about to give up, she stared at the desktop icons and saw that one was labeled "for Claire."

Heart thudding, she clicked on it. Inside was a series of

files, each one corresponding to a tab in the binder: "insurance," "house," "my car," "Fang," "finances," and "benefits." She opened the files and, scanning through them, saw that they matched the pages in the binder. The note wasn't there, but she found it in his recycle bin, named "for Claire." He had last saved it on February 13 at 7:20 p.m. and deleted it six minutes later. When she read through it, she saw that it matched the version in the binder exactly, except for the lack of his handwritten signature. He must have deleted it after printing it out for her. He could be old-fashioned, at times— she thought of his search for record stores, and the old vinyl he collected—and probably would not have liked the idea of his suicide note leaving an electronic trail.

Wondering if he had any voice mail messages, she picked up the phone to see if there was a stutter tone, but it was dead.

She scratched the numb spot by her ear, feeling nothing, as she tried to think of where else to look for clues.

Nothing, she thought. There's nothing here.

She took a long drink from the red cup. Warm and slightly dizzy, she took off her cardigan and hung it on the door.

She opened the binder to the note and read it through again, pausing on certain phrases: *a wall of glass between us . . . not compatible in certain ways . . . Please forgive me . . . the gift of contentment . . .*

"*Valentine's* Day, Jay?" she said out loud. "How could I not take that personally? What the hell?"

She looked wildly around the room and remembered his shirt, hidden beneath her coat on the hook. She got up and put it on over her sweater. Change jingled in the breast pocket. The shirt smelled like him.

Back at the computer, she opened Word. She closed her eyes and breathed deeply. Then, looking down at the note, she began to retype it:

Dear Clairey,

I'm so sorry. I have let you down, just as I have let myself down, and everyone else. I have you, I have an interesting job, we have a nice home and a good life. And yet I feel myself going down deep again and it feels like I will keep on sinking forever.

She stopped, thinking there should be music. Jay listened to music all the time. He would fall in love with a song and listen to it over and over for an entire night, an entire week even, obscure songs by Billie Holiday or Jonathan Richman, or something hard-driving by the Clash or the Pogues.

There was a CD player on the credenza behind her with one of Jay's mixes inside, marked "January '08." She turned it on. Someone picked out notes in a minor key on an acoustic guitar, and then a man began singing gently in a high voice, his words hard to make out. Sad, she thought: perfect. And, of course, not surprising.

She put the song on repeat play and turned back to the computer. "I . . . know . . . that . . . each . . . time . . ." Never having worked for very long in an office, she typed slowly, but that was just as well. Jay himself was a two-finger typist.

I know that each time I have come up for air again, but the next time I go down even lower and I know that it would only get worse. I don't know why I can't just be happy, like a normal person, but I can't.

In college, one of Claire's art teachers used to take the class to the local museum, where they would set up their easels and try to re-create on their own canvases one of the paintings hanging on the wall. By breaking a painting down into brushstrokes, they started to learn how it had been made, and in the process they glimpsed the inspiration and purpose behind it. "Imagine yourself in the artist's body," the teacher told them. Only after doing so would they be ready to break free and explore their own vision, he said.

She mixed a new drink for herself, took a gulp, ate some crackers. She typed:

The only thing that brings me relief is the thought that soon this will be over.

She cried out and cupped her hand over her mouth. But she forced herself to keep going.

She and Jay had closed on their house two weeks before their wedding. The movers weren't coming until the next day, so they spent the afternoon cleaning, then plugged in their air mattress in the dining room and made a picnic on a blanket by the decorative fireplace in the living room: *cava*, Lou Malnati's pizza, pillows, and candlelight. Her mother and Robin had stopped by that afternoon with two big plastic tubs filled with the Depression glass, and Claire had unwrapped plates and goblets for their dinner.

"I like eating on red plates," she said.

"Red plates make life festive," Jay agreed. "And the plastic silverware is a nice touch." He lifted his goblet. "To my beautiful fiancée and our lovely new home."

"To us." They clinked.

"Two more weeks," he said. "Did you know that in France, if your fiancé dies, you can legally marry them anyway?"

"No way," Claire said mildly. She found it cute that Jay had a quirky research study or news report for every occasion.

"Way." He had read a newspaper article about a Frenchwoman whose fiancé had been killed by a drunk driver while riding his motorcycle. Thanks to an obscure law from World War II, the woman had received permission from her fiancé's family, and then from the president of France, to marry the dead man at the town hall. She had recited vows and celebrated afterward at a restaurant with family and friends, including the dead groom's mother. "She seemed really happy in the article," Jay said. "She called it the perfect wedding."

"Only in France." Claire put down her fork. Her wedding dress was tight, and she was allowing herself only one piece of pizza.

"You don't think that's romantic?" he said with his mouth full.

"Well, I guess in a cuckoo sort of way. But maybe she has the right idea. Didn't you tell me that most married women are unhappy?"

"No, it's like this: Married men are happier than single men, but married women are generally less happy than single women. Married women are the least happy of all four groups, but that doesn't mean *most* married women are unhappy."

"Hmm." She fiddled with her ring, which she kept forgetting to get adjusted; it was still uncomfortably tight. "Why are you telling me this right before our wedding, exactly?"

"You'll be happy," he said. He looked happy himself, cross-legged and barefoot, in his dirty T-shirt and jeans.

"I think so," she agreed.

"So you wouldn't marry me if I died tomorrow?" he said.

She took a sip of *cava*. "We're not French."

"But if we were."

She saw that he was serious, so she mulled the question over for a few seconds. "Mmm . . . no. Sorry, sweetie. Too weird. And too showy."

"Really?" He looked crestfallen.

"Don't tell me you'd marry *me*."

"I would." He smiled. "I'd do it."

"Liar."

"No, I would," he said dreamily as he pushed his plate away and reclined on the blanket.

"Hmm. Well, I'd want you to move on. After a respectable mourning period, of course."

"What if I didn't want to?" he said.

"Of course you would. Why should you have to be alone?" She padded over to the air mattress and lay down. "I'm just saying that if I get leukemia or I'm impaled by an icicle, I want you to know that it's okay for you to move on."

"Leukemia or icicle. Hmm, which would you prefer, if you could choose?"

"Don't change the subject," she said.

"Fine. Have it your way. If you suffer a freak icicle tragedy, I'll move on."

"And I think you should say the same thing to me."

He shook his head. "Uh-uh."

"C'mon."

"You think I'm being selfish," he said.

"Yup. Very."

"I think it's romantic."

She shook her head.

"Okay, fine," he said. "If I die one day, icicle, leukemia, or otherwise, you have my permission—"

"Permission?"

"You have my *blessing* to eventually move on," he said, "after a respectable mourning period, as long as you always remember that I was your great love and that no one will ever take my place in your heart."

"Deal," she said, and held out her hand. He got up to shake it, then lay down next to her on the mattress.

"You're weird," she said, staring up at the chandelier that had come with the house, an ornate gilt-gold monstrosity with lights shaped like candles.

"You're weirder," he said.

That week, Claire had put the Depression glass in the kitchen cupboards, declaring it too pretty not to use every day. But they had quickly broken several of the dessert plates while doing dishes, and Jay started using the salad bowls for Fang's food and water—and, for some reason she might have known about and forgotten, he had brought one of the goblets to work. It would all have been gone, she thought, chipped and smashed, by the time they grew old together.

Try to get over me as fast as you can so you can start a family and forget about me.

Love,
Jay

Claire turned off the CD player, then curled up on the couch by the window, where Jay used to sit and read. A thin line of frigid air whistled in under the window frame. She pulled up the collar of Jay's shirt and inhaled.

"Sweetie," she whispered. "I miss you."

Tears ran down her cheeks. "I'm sorry you were hurting," she said softly. "I'm sorry I couldn't help you. I'm sorry if you chose the wrong person, if you thought I would be different. I'm sorry I ran away sometimes, that I worked too much and didn't know what to say. I'm sorry I couldn't understand how bad it was for you."

She wiped her eyes with his shirt, then shifted on the couch so that she could see the lake, steely gray beneath the oddly bright night sky.

"I'm so mad you sent the painting to your therapist. I can't believe you did that. Why did you do that?"

She stretched on her side and covered herself with an afghan that had been draped over the back of the couch.

"And after I got to the party, why did you go through with it? Why didn't you spare me? Why wasn't I enough for you?"

On a chest in front of the couch sat a small framed photograph of Claire from the previous summer. She was grinning across the table from Jay at a Thai restaurant near their house, her hair pulled back, her face flushed from the sun. They'd been to a street fair that day, and she had felt pretty in her flouncy white skirt, lustful and alive in the heat. Jay had brought along a camera and snapped pictures of her. She remembered goofing around, sticking out her tongue. She didn't remember this shot, though.

She held the photograph close to her face. Her eyes were lit up, and there was a softness in them. God, she had loved him. He must have seen that in this picture, too.

You have the gift of contentment, something I have always admired about you.

It was true: she would not say she was a happy person, if happy meant being cheerful and outgoing, which it seemed to in America, but she knew how to be content. Before and after her marriage she had taken pleasure in her routine and her good friends, and though she had ignored them the past month, she would go back to them. She would always have a warm home and enough food to eat. Her parents were healthy, and so was her sister, and soon they would all fall in love with a baby. And even during this time she had found moments of comfort: her sister softly snoring beside her, the cat greeting her at the door, Harry forgiving her with a kiss on the head.

"I miss you, sweetheart," she said. "I miss the way you pursed your lips when you were thinking hard about something. I miss the way you'd glance at me when you told a joke, to see if I caught it.

"I know you loved me. I *know* you did. Don't think I doubt that."

She sighed and wiped her eyes on the blanket. "I'm taking care of Fang," she said. "She poisoned herself, but I guess I saved her, and now she likes me." She told him she had picked a fight with her parents and she felt guilty about it.

"This spot by my ear went numb, but Nomie's obstetrician thinks it's psychosomatic—don't ask." She told him she needed to be more respectful of Harry and Nomie's marriage, and that they were going to have a girl.

"I went to a support group, but it was the wrong one. I saw a therapist who I liked, though. I think I'll go back and see him."

She paused. "I don't know where you put the photograph of the first layer of my painting—the photo of me in Orpheus Records. Maybe I shouldn't have bothered painting the top layer. Maybe I ruined it by covering it over with all those flowers."

She fell silent and lay there looking out at the small, cozy room.

After some time had passed, half an hour or more, she buttoned up Jay's shirt and gathered her belongings in the tote bag, including the goblet, which she wrapped in printer paper. Leaving her cardigan hanging on the door, she bundled up, then looked around the room. She imagined Jay sitting at his desk, typing, head bobbing to the music. She saw him stand up and go to the shelf for a book. She watched him sit down on the couch and glance at her photo, smile for a second, and then look out the window at the vast lake, peering in vain to see the other side.

"Goodbye," she whispered, and turned to leave.

12

The morning after her visit to Jay's office, Claire slept in, waiting out a mild headache from the vodka, then bundled up again and ran some errands in the neighborhood. When she got back to the coach house, she found a cleaning lady vacuuming and all of Nomie's things gone; it was as if she had checked out of a hotel and the maid was now clearing all traces of her. But Nomie stopped by that afternoon to invite Claire over for dinner—"Harry was asking if you'd come," she made a point of saying—and when Claire told her she had scheduled an appointment with the neurologist the obstetrician had recommended, Nomie offered to go with her.

Claire turned down the invitation to dinner, wanting to keep a low profile and not minding the idea of being alone. She lit some candles and, with the radio playing low, tossed a salad and cooked the salmon and squash she had picked up at Treasure Island. She found she enjoyed bustling around the kitchen amid the savory smells and the oven's warmth. It was pleasant to be doing something so ordinary; too often these days, she and Nomie had eaten leftover casseroles straight out of the fridge. She found a cloth napkin for herself and filled the red goblet with water. Sitting down at the counter, she gave herself permission to try to prolong her good mood by pretending, while she ate, that Jay was away on a trip and would be back soon.

Claire's neurology appointment was on the second floor of the same building where Nomie's obstetrician had her office, in the middle of the mall. Dr. Fridell appeared to be in his eighties, a short man with comb marks in his sparse white hair; he wore a bow tie with his lab coat. In the exam room, he asked Claire the same sorts of questions the obstetrician had asked, about pain, loss of vision, loss of hearing, family history of strokes. "No, no, no, no," she answered. He peered into her mouth and ears with a scope and hit her knee with a mallet; her leg swung obligingly. Finally he ushered her into the hallway. As if he were a cop and she an erratic motorist, he had her walk a straight line and touch her nose with her fingertip.

"How'd I do?" she asked when they were sitting in his office.

"Aced it," he said as he wrote a referral to an MRI facility. "It's probably nothing. But better safe than sorry."

"MRI . . . that's the thing where they slide you into a machine, right?"

The doctor looked up and cocked his head. "Claustrophobic?"

"Kinda." Claire hated crowds; she had avoided the Taste of Chicago since she was little. And whenever she wanted to give herself a scare, she remembered Jay telling her once, God knows why, that when the grave of a Russian writer—

she thought it was Gogol—was exhumed, scratch marks were found on the inside of the coffin's lid.

"This place has an open MRI," said the doctor. "They only slide your head in. The rest of you sticks out. Most people find it a lot less scary."

"Okay."

"You'll be fine. Healthy girl like you."

"Okay." Her eyes welled with gratitude that this old man saw her as a girl. She was glad he had not asked her about recent life stress or trauma; he seemed to be from a more genteel era, and she would have been ashamed to tell him her sordid tale.

Back in the small, empty waiting room, the receptionist was telling Nomie about her grandchildren. "Break a leg!" the woman called as they left, and it took Claire a minute to realize she was talking about Nomie's baby.

Outside, Claire and Nomie crossed the mall; the sun was out, and it was incrementally less frigid than the day before. Nomie told Claire that she and Harry had signed up for a Lamaze class and that they were starting to decorate the baby's room. "For the walls, I'm thinking pink, but very pale," Nomie said as they shopped for curtains at Pottery Barn Kids. "Not bubblegum pink."

"You could do, like, a sunrise pink with a hint of orange, like a pale salmon. I can help you pick it out if you want." Claire thought of the green paint swatches hanging in her and Jay's second bedroom—green because they had agreed they wouldn't want to know their baby's gender in advance. Maybe Jay had known at the time that the conversation was purely hypothetical.

"That sounds great. It's hard to get Harry interested in stuff like that." Nomie glanced at Claire. "I hope you'll stay next door for a while."

"I'll stay for a little while," Claire said carefully. "We'll see."

The young woman who answered the phone at Dempster Open MRI scheduled Claire's appointment for the following Wednesday night, then asked if she had a pacemaker or any metal plates in her body. "We recommend that you leave any jewelry at home," she added in a mechanical-sounding voice, "including any rings of significant financial or sentimental value."

Claire extended her left hand and studied her rings. She wasn't sure of the etiquette. Was she not supposed to be wearing them anymore? A normal widow—say, someone who had been married for forty years before losing her husband to a heart attack—would wear them until she went on a cruise and was swept off her feet by some nice white-haired widower in a tux at the captain's dinner. But Claire was not a normal widow. She was some sort of divorcée-widow hybrid—a divow, maybe, as exotic as some odd endangered bird.

Since visiting Jay's office, Claire had felt drained and shaky, as if she were recovering from a bad case of the flu. She treated herself gingerly, trying to live on the surface of life for the time being, fearful of a relapse. Her mother called every day with a scrap of random news: she had picked up a cashmere sweater for Claire on sale at Neiman Marcus; she had run into an old friend from high school who was fighting cancer; a family Nancy had been representing had defaulted on the mortgage on their lakefront estate. Neither of them spoke of Claire's flare-up at the diner. As for her father, he came by every other morning with coffee for Claire, but he didn't come inside, and he drove away after his delivery.

She didn't force herself to return to her studio or take on any new staging projects, but she did start returning her friends' phone calls, which felt like a job in itself. She had not seen or talked to some of her friends since the wake; others she had admitted only briefly into the coach house with their casseroles and brownies. On the phone, she deflected their questions of concern by asking them about their own lives, but it was good to hear their voices and to see how sensitively they filled the silences, how patient they were with her, their missing friend.

Tidying up the coffee table one morning, she found the unopened card from Sally. Instead of opening it, on an impulse she called Sally at her office.

"Oh, Claire!" the older woman exclaimed. Within a minute Claire had agreed to meet Sally at a pub near Nomie and Harry's house later that day.

Claire arrived early and got a table by the window of the basement bar. It was a little before four o'clock, and the staff was eating a communal dinner at a table near the back of the room. No music was playing, which made Claire feel like a nuisance.

She straightened when she saw Sally walk by the window above, wearing a down coat and a fur hat. She descended the steps slowly, clutching the railing, then hurried over. Claire leaned into the puffy coldness and felt fur tickle her cheek. They rocked back and forth for a long moment.

"Now tell me how you've been doing," Sally said when they were settled with mugs of tea. The older woman's cheeks were rosy, either from blush or the cold, but she had dark circles under her eyes. "I've left messages, but . . . I didn't want to call too often."

"I'm sorry. I've been staying under the radar." Feeling

shy, Claire was reminded of the fact that she did not know this woman very well. They had chatted about food at Sally's party and had shared a couple of similarly benign conversations at other social events, but the two of them had never spoken intimately, and why would they have? Sally had been Jay's seventy-something colleague. Claire thought of a bit of conversation she had overheard at the wake out of the corner of her ear as she was heading to the bathroom to find out if she indeed would never carry Jay's child. "We were all having such a good time," a doctoral student named Francine—who had been at the party—said in a hushed voice, and the clutch of people around her fell silent, their eyes on Claire as she passed.

"Have you been able to talk about it with"—Sally threw her hands up in the air—"people?"

"Um . . . not too much, yet. That's next on the list, I guess."

"It'll take time, I'm sure."

"I'm so sorry, Sally," Claire said. "It must have been awful for you and Bart."

"Well, I haven't been sleeping too well, I admit."

Claire nodded. "I'm really sorry."

Sally reached to pat her hand. "You have *nothing* to apologize for," she pronounced, sitting up straight in her seat. "Let's agree on that."

Claire stirred her tea slowly. "But people must think he hated me. I would think that if I were them." Because she didn't want Sally to think that, she added, "According to his note, though, it was just an . . . opportunity."

"The balcony."

Claire shrugged.

"Bart beats himself up for not locking it," Sally said.

"There was a key, you know. But people smoke at parties, and it didn't occur to us . . ."

"Of course not." They sat for a moment in silence. "Why do *you* think he did it, Sally?" Claire said finally.

Sally shook her head. "I don't know. If you're asking about work, he was doing very well. He was on track for tenure; everyone liked him . . ." She sighed. "I feel I should have noticed something, though. I'm supposed to be an expert, of sorts."

Claire nodded. "I feel guilty. Embarrassed. It's hard to think of going out in the world again. I feel like I'm not *me* anymore. I'm a . . . tragic suicide widow."

"You'll always be Claire to those who really matter, though."

"I guess." She imagined going back to online dating, checking the box marked "Widowed." No matter how glib and flirty she tried to make it, the profile would have a stench of tragedy that would repel everyone but nut jobs. "You're happy," she said. "You and Bart. What's your secret?" Sally studied married couples all day long in her lab, and she had been married for more than forty years. "I'm not saying I'm ready, but I'm thirty-seven, and I want a family. How can I keep this from happening all over again?"

"Well . . ." Sally frowned, thinking. "I guess you keep your eyes open. You see how someone handles stress. And you pay attention to how you fight. Couples need to be compatible in how they argue. It's a problem if one person likes to hash things out and the other clams up."

Claire nodded. *I think we are not compatible in certain ways, and it has been frustrating to both of us.* But Jay wasn't always open with her, either. *My only secret, maybe, is that I often feel worse than you might think.*

"And—well, frankly," Sally continued, "you shouldn't put up with anyone's shit. Life's too short, you know?"

Not wanting to bother Nomie again, Claire had planned to go to the MRI appointment by herself. But on Wednesday, when she awoke to the sound of wet snow spattering the loft window, she found herself dreading it.

She spent the day on the couch with Fang, thinking she would allow herself to sleep through the appointment. But she couldn't sleep, and instead she simply wasted the day watching TV, so there was no excuse. In the early evening she showered and dressed, leaving her rings in a dish on the kitchen counter. She could decide when she got home whether or not to put them back on.

Driving north on Western Avenue, Claire found herself whimpering. The open MRI would not be open enough for her, she was sure. She imagined the machine trapping her head like a vise. It was still sleeting, and she started to worry that there would be a power outage while she was inside the machine and she would be stuck there.

While stopped at a red light, she called her father at home. He answered on the first ring.

"Dad, I'm sorry to bother you, but if you're not too busy, do you think you could come help me with something?" she asked.

"Sure, sweetie. You name it."

Dempster Open MRI was located in a strip mall near the expressway, tucked between a gourmet ice cream shop and a mattress store. After parking in front, Claire turned off the wipers and the lights but left the engine running. Beyond the sleet-streaked windshield she had a full view of the empty waiting room, which at this time of night was surely waiting just for her. A wide-screen TV was presenting a crime show to three couches and a giant fish tank.

She kept an eye on her watch, fretting that her father would not arrive in time, but he pulled in a few minutes before her appointment. They got out of their cars and met under the awning.

"Thanks for coming, Dad," she said.

"No problem, sweetie." He looked from right to left, avoiding her gaze. She had told her parents that the exam was strictly routine, but that wouldn't have stopped him from worrying.

Inside, the receptionist, a sleepy-eyed young Hispanic woman, sat behind a glass partition. As Claire approached, she pointed the remote control at the TV, hushing a round of gunshots. "Claire Kessler?" she said. "Brain MRI?"

"Brain," Claire confirmed.

I'll be happy if I never see another waiting room again, Claire found herself thinking just as a red-haired technician wearing green scrubs appeared from behind the reception desk. "Claire Kessler?" he called out, though Claire and her father were the only people waiting.

"Be right back," Claire said to her father, who had been staring into the fish tank, which contained very few fish but an abundance of miniature castles and plants. He nodded and turned back to the tank.

The technician introduced himself as Georgii. As they passed into a locker room, he complimented Claire for not wearing any jewelry or "any other metal objects on your head," whatever that meant. She left her coat and the rest of her outerwear in a locker, but she did not have to change her clothes.

An enormous arched gray contraption, like something out of a sci-fi movie, dominated the next room. A padded board, covered by a sheet, stuck out of the front of the machine like a tongue.

Claire and Georgii approached the machine and stood there for a moment, studying it.

"I'm a little claustrophobic," she said when he didn't say anything. "How open is open?"

"Very open. Just your head goes in. How does that sound?"

"That sounds okay."

"Some find it rather loud," he said, and handed her some earplugs.

After she had stuffed them into her ears, he had her lie down on the board and lower her head into a rounded cradle. He tucked some foam padding around her head, then turned a lever that lowered something like a hockey mask, but bigger, over her face. "After I slide you in, try to lie as still as possible, okay?"

"Okay."

Georgii retreated, and Claire was flooded with the urge to run.

"Wait!" she shouted.

Immediately Georgii was hovering above her again. He turned the lever and lifted the mask. "I can bring you out anytime," he said. "Just start yelling. Nobody but me will hear you. Deal?"

"Deal," she said, though it made her nervous that no one else, not even her dad, would hear if she yelled.

He lowered the face mask again.

The machinery whirred. Claire started whimpering, as she had in the car, and then she let out a sound that was something short of a scream, more like a yelp, the sound a puppy would make when someone stepped on its tail.

The machine quieted, and Georgii was at her side again. "Having trouble?"

"I was just wondering," she said, trying to sound like a sane person. "Would it be possible for my dad to be in here with me?"

His lips scrunched to one side as he considered. "I think that would be okay."

"That would be great. Thank you so much!" She sounded frantic rather than perky, she realized.

"Wait here," he said.

Soon Georgii and her father were standing above her. She felt ridiculous, splayed out on the board.

"Hi, sweetie. Feeling a little nervous?" her father said.

"Yeah." Tears spilled out of her eyes and dripped into her ears. She thought of her father's visit to the morgue to identify Jay. She wondered if the body had been pulled out of the wall on a board like the one she was on.

Georgii wheeled over a desk chair for her father. "Here you go."

"Thanks." Douglas sat down and reached for Claire's hand. "You take all the time you need, honey."

Her father's hand was cool and broad. "Thanks," she said. "I think I'm ready."

"Okay, then."

"All right," Georgii said. He lowered the hockey mask over Claire's face again and moved out of sight. "Now, Claire, you're going to start to slide in, but you won't go very far. The test will last for about half an hour. You'll be able to hold your dad's hand the whole time, but I need you both to be as still as possible, okay?"

"Okay," they both said.

The board began to slide into the machine. Claire closed her eyes. Scooting along with her on his chair, her father kept hold of her hand.

Given the earplugs and Georgii's warning, she should have expected the clanging and buzzing, but Claire could not have predicted the odd, off-kilter rhythms that filled the room, like an avant-garde composition performed by a child armed with a hammer and pots. She kept her eyes shut. She squeezed her father's hand and tried very hard not to move.

Jay's parents had picked out the casket. It was tasteful, made of ash, like something Pottery Barn would sell if Pottery Barn ever decided to sell caskets. The handles were wooden, small and discreet, like drawer pulls, rather than the usual long, brassy bars that made Claire think of a Bennigan's.

If it had been up to her, she would have had Jay cremated, but his mother had not wanted that—so Claire had heard through her own mother. Claire had not protested. What did it matter, really?

His parents bought a plot in a cemetery by the lake, just past Chicago's northern border, alongside the same curve of road where Claire had her treacherous drive with Jay on New Year's Eve. It was freezing the day of the funeral, and the graveside service had been quick.

"You should probably know, my folks bought a single plot," Veronica said afterward to Claire in the dim back room of the Italian restaurant where the families had converged for lunch. "I think they figured, you're young, and someday there'll be somebody else you'll want to be buried next to."

"I can't imagine who that would be," Claire said, and it was the truth.

———

"These are photos of your brain," Georgii said, handing Claire a large, thick manila envelope with KESSLER, CLAIRE written in the top corner. She had survived the MRI, and the three of them—Georgii, Claire, and her father—were standing next to the machine. Feeling disoriented, Claire touched her father's arm for support.

"What should I do with them?" she asked.

"Your doctor might want them. Probably not, though. He'll get an electronic copy and a report tomorrow from the analyst. The machine spits them out, so we give them to people." He shrugged. "Some people find them interesting."

He ushered Claire and her father into the waiting room. Standing by the door in her coat, the receptionist turned a key to let them out.

"Good night!" they all called to one another, like old friends. "Thank you!"

Outside, a breeze was blowing bits of ice and snow from the spindly trees at the edges of the parking lot. The sleet had stopped, and the weather was turning balmy. Douglas looked out at the parking lot, his jaw set tight.

"Do you want to get some ice cream?" Claire said. "My treat. To thank you for coming out on the spur of the moment."

"Sure," he said. "Sounds good."

The ice cream store was empty except for the man behind the counter, who sized them up as they approached, his eyes darting to the envelope tucked under Claire's arm, then back and forth between them. He might have been in his early fifties, with shaggy grayish blond hair, and he wore a turquoise Hawaiian shirt covered in white starbursts. "What can I get ya?" he said without smiling.

Claire's father ordered plain chocolate in a cup; Claire got vanilla with Oreos. They waited in silence while the man chopped the ice cream and cookies on a board and folded them together. "That's seven sixty-nine," he said as he pushed the two cups of ice cream toward them.

"I got it, Dad," Claire said, but as she pulled her wallet out of her purse, she realized there was a good chance it would be empty. Still, she made a show of opening the wallet and riffling through the compartments. She felt her face flush as she grimaced apologetically at the counterman. "Do you take credit cards? Or checks?"

The man tapped a little sign by the register: CASH ONLY.

"I got it," her father said, pulling out his wallet. "No problem."

"Thanks, Dad. Sorry."

As Claire turned to pick up her ice cream, the envelope Georgii had given her slipped from under her arm and fell to the ground. The MRI films, huge sheets of dark plastic, slithered out of the open top of the envelope and separated as they hit the floor. Six or seven films covered with pictures of the inside of Claire's head, taken from all angles, splayed out on the white tile, glowing under the store's fluorescent lights.

"Damn," Claire said, stooping to gather up the films. Her father knelt down to help, and the counterman was suddenly there, too, on his knees.

"We've got it," her dad said. The counterman stood up and hovered uncertainly as they started to collect the films. Douglas thrust a ten-dollar bill at the man. "Keep the change," he said. "We'll take it from here."

"Thanks," the man said, and retreated behind the counter.

Unable to stop herself, Claire held one of the films up to the light. It was covered with twenty different cross sections of her head, seen from the top, each one cut slightly deeper into her brain. Her eyeballs had a frightened look, perfectly round and black within triangular sockets. As for her skull, it looked delicate, no thicker than a seashell and scarcely equipped for the task of restraining the two tight bunches of cauliflower inside.

"I don't see anything," her father murmured.

Claire turned, surprised to find that he had been staring at the film along with her. Up close her father looked haggard, his jowls sagging as if pulled down by invisible fishhooks. His eyes were bloodshot.

"Me, neither," Claire agreed. Absently, she stroked the side of her face. She felt the scratch of her fingernail against her skin and realized the numbness was gone. Just as Nomie's doctor had predicted, the problem seemed to have disappeared as mysteriously as it had arrived.

Not wanting to disturb the moment, Claire decided she would tell her father later, if the numbness didn't return.

They finished tucking the films into the envelope and picked up their ice cream cups from the counter. "Thanks, folks," the counterman said, shifting on his feet. "Have a good night. I hope everything turns out okay."

"Thanks," Claire said.

Her father said nothing.

Out on the sidewalk, they stood in front of their cars. The envelope flapped beneath Claire's arm in the wind.

"Dad?" She looked up at her father, forcing herself to be brave. "I just want you to know, this wasn't the life I expected for myself."

"I know that, sweetheart." A smile played on his face. "It never is."

He helped her with her car door.

"Want to come in and eat that?" she asked, nodding at his ice cream.

"Sure," he said.

She let him in and tossed the envelope onto the back-seat. She turned on the engine, and they sat in silence, looking straight ahead as they ate. The lights were already out at Dempster Open MRI, and then the ice cream shop went dark as well. Outside, the wind picked up and began to howl. But Claire had turned on the overhead lamp and the heater as well, and in their little bubble there was warmth and safety, and a dim, shadowy light that would last for as long as it was required.

ACKNOWLEDGMENTS

My dear family and friends made the process of writing my first novel much easier: I love you, and I thank you. I am indebted to those who offered comments that helped shape the book, especially my amazing writing group. I thank Amy Williams, my agent, for her steadfast support and encouragement. Finally, I'm deeply grateful to Gena Hamshaw, my editor, whose wise insights brought me closer to Claire and her story.